ROYALLY REBELLIOUS

RESPLENDENT ROYALS

BOOK ONE

MAUDE WINTERS

EDITED BY

DANIEL FLASPOHLER

ISBN: 979-8-9892609-3-5

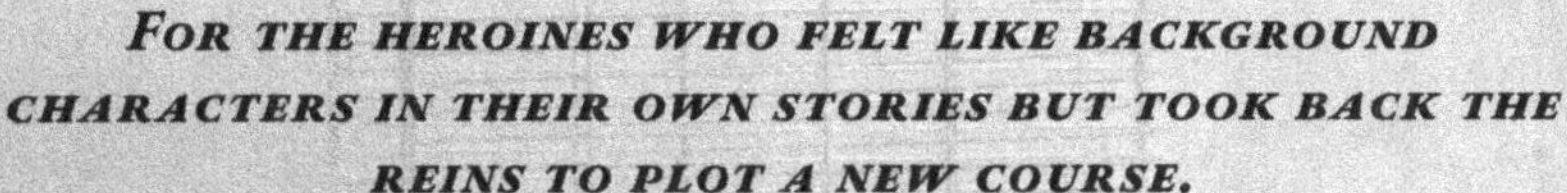

For the heroines who felt like background characters in their own stories but took back the reins to plot a new course.

Author's Note

General Notes

You can expect all of the following:

- Swearing
- Dirty talk
- On-page spice
- A virgin heroine taking charge of her sexuality
- British English (no those aren't typos)

Content

This story leans heavily into fairytales. There are dark elements of control by the evil Dowager Queen Celeste used to keep her granddaughters locked in a tower. Such means of control include restricting their diets, emotional abuse, and isolating them from peers. There is mention of physical abuse, but none on the page. The Deschamps sisters lost both parents. Suicide and mental illness of a parent as well as the loss of a parent to childbirth are mentioned but not shown on the page.

PART ONE

THE DUBIOUS PRINCE

One

ALEXANDRA

It took twenty-one years, but I finally attended my first royal occasion outside the walls of the palace where I was born. Serving as Queen for almost seven years, I came to "power" at the tender age of fourteen. Until now, I attended limited royal engagements. Fooled by palace accounts, my subjects believed I attended few events because I focused on my studies or just getting my feet wet.

The reality? My freedom was still tempered by a regency that put my grandmother, Dowager Queen Celeste, in charge of nearly every aspect of my life. From diet to schedule, I did nothing without prior approval. I didn't attend a module at university without her saying so. I never exercised without her agreement. Since my grandfather passed, it was all the same. Without him as a buffer to shield me from my grandmother's wrath, I became the target of her interest and anger.

My attendance at a party celebrating the entrance into society for the Belgian heir-to-the-throne surprised everyone. People expected Neandia would send a representative to attend the event in neighbouring Belgium, but my appearance raised eyebrows. I hadn't been formally brought "out" into society. I never travelled. Grandmother forbid such things. However, as she was ill and no one else suitable was available to do the honours, I earned my freedom for a few days.

On my first day at the Belgian court, the Queen welcomed me with open arms. She understood. She became monarch unexpectedly at a young age, married quickly, and swiftly produced children. She and her American husband were accommodating. Their sons were beyond lovely. It was a nice break.

I was free! I planned to fill these few blissful days with simple pleasures forbidden to me. I inhaled food. I adored pastries, but they were usually prohibited. Celeste feared me gaining weight more than anything. She insisted I avoid anything with carbs. I consumed all the lovely chocolate I could, free from prying eyes.

I luxuriated in adult conversation. The only time I conversed with adults was the short time I spent on campus at my university in Neandia's eponymous capitol or with my new staff members. Celeste recently allocated me a lady's maid, a dresser, and a private secretary— all tasked with teaching me how to be a proper royal. I was rough. I longed to be treated like an adult but wasn't permitted. I took meals with my younger sisters. I loved them, of course, but they weren't fit for adult conversation any more than a wall.

I began to appreciate my appearance, too. There was the magic of putting on jewellery for the first time and sporting an evening gown. Kitted out in a proper dress—assembled last minute by my staff—I passed for the average ball attendee. Compared to my royal peers, my ensemble was conservative but sufficiently womanly. Everything was terrifying and new.

The ball was spectacular. No expense was spared. A famous photographer—so I was told—took photos of the royal attendees. I was the youngest monarch in the photo of attending kings and queens. It pained me to be iced out of the heir apparent photo. I never had the benefit of being a young, hot princess who got to have a good time. I was plopped at the grownup table—doomed to stay there far from my hot young peers.

Queen Margaux was protective and helpful—almost like an older sister. She sensed my confusion. I appreciated her thoughtfulness. I imagined how I could come back to Belgium to see her more frequently but came up at a loss. I knew Celeste would never let me visit my Belgian friends willingly. It would "give me ideas" as she always said. She ruled with an iron fist.

"You're enjoying yourself?" Queen Margaux asked.

"Very much, thank you." I beamed.

"And you won't dance, won't drink?"

"I don't know how to... dance I mean. I have never learned. And I had wine with dinner."

Margaux pitied me. "Never learned to dance? Darling, that is essential. I will speak to your grandmother—"

"No, please don't," I pleaded. "Look, it will make it worse."

Margaux took a long breath. "I won't intervene if it will make things worse for you, Alexandra, but I worry."

"She is protecting me."

"From what, darling? At your age, I was in the UK with my British cousins. I was going out and living. Do you ever go out? Do you have any mates?"

I shook my head. "I have my sisters."

"I have five sisters, sweetheart. It's not the same."

It wasn't. She was right.

"You look beautiful," Margaux said.

She knew I needed to hear it.

"It is a shame you cannot dance. However, at least go get a glass of champagne and walk about."

It was another painful reminder I was under house arrest until twenty-five. People expected Celeste would dissolve the regency by now, but that was unlikely. She longed to control and wear me down as long as she could. My sisters and I all understood. We were at her mercy. Do not poke the bear! Doing so led to serious consequences and even more controlling behaviour. My actions affected everyone.

My detail reported everything back to my grandmother. They were spies. My life was never my own and hadn't been since Grand-Papa died. He made sure I got out to the stables and played tennis. He ensured we could go to the zoo and cinema—even rented places out so we could enjoy ourselves without prying eyes. He allowed us to attend school with other children. When he died, life became a surveillance state. Celeste said it was for my protection, but it was so Celeste could maintain her grip over the court. She finally had what she longed for—absolute power.

I thumbed my nose and rebelled by taking the Queen's advice. I bellied up to a bar next to a tall blonde man in a tuxedo. By all rights, he was handsome. I rarely noticed such things. Well, I had no opportunity to notice them. I was cloistered away from almost any man. I marvelled at how tall he was and how broad his shoulders appeared. I didn't understand why he appealed to me. Then any thoughts of interest faded. The bartender refused him, and he was unhappy about it.

He asked in broken French. "Do you enjoy this? Telling people no?"

The bartender explained, polite but curt. "I cannot serve you two shots of whiskey because you are already drunk, sir. I can lose my job."

The blonde man's brow furrowed; his fists balled. I assumed he didn't understand the bartender. I tried English, assuming we all knew it.

"He says he cannot serve you two shot glasses of whiskey," I said.

The man glared at me. "Do you think I am stupid? I understand that!"

Annoyed, I said, "I was trying to help. Take one shot and come back. What does it matter?"

"No one wants your help. I want to drown my sorrows and this fucker won't listen."

I tried to be calm. "Sir, there is no need to be upset at him. He's just—"

"You think I'm a prick, don't you? Well, I don't need your ire!"

He took the shot and stormed off. I set my jaw, annoyed.

I thought many uncharitable things but approached the bar. "I am so sorry for that."

"Do you know him, miss?"

"No. Thankfully," I chuckled. "But he's out of line. If I can get a glass of champagne, I'd be grateful."

I assumed the man was a rude American out of place based on his accent and poor French. He was probably a normie—what we called commoners. I ignored the man and went to enjoy my champagne in peace. Tomorrow, I would travel an hour across the border to the gilded cage that consumed my life. It was nice while it lasted.

TWO

RICK

Ow dare the bartender cut me off! I wanted to get drunk and forget my troubles. This was one more middle finger preventing me from zoning out. I would survive the weekend and move on. Tasked as the official attendee for the Lundhavn court, this was no vacation. It was no holiday for fun times. It was punishment.

My indiscretions finally caught up with me. After months of running around with a woman I loved but could not possess, I got caught. I was too bold. Her husband filed for divorce, but he wasn't done there. It was a mess! My father paid off her ex to keep things under wraps, but he swore he'd never do it again. Moreover, if I didn't follow the rules and shape up, he would toss me out and cut me off.

It was fucked, but it was life now. I slogged through the last couple of months holed up in the palace. My father finally released me on official duty. I was here being a good boy, trying to run from what haunted me. My brother and sister-in-law were on their honeymoon aboard the royal yacht in the Caribbean while my parents skied in the Alps. I cursed them all.

I pushed things too far, but I was heartbroken. No one cared.

What I had did was despicable, yes. Still, I loved her. I loved her even now! And after all this, she was finally free, but it could not be. Her ex threatened to go public with the details of their divorce if I so much as looked at his ex-wife. It was a risk I couldn't take.

I was sent to impress women in hopes that one of these royals might marry me. As the spare, I existed to look attractive and to maybe produce children. My socially awkward brother and his wife weren't a sure thing on that front. Both loathed children. I might have to shoulder that burden.

Any woman of good reputation in attendance was warned by their mothers or older sisters to avoid me. Hell, I may have already dated their older sisters! Marrying me off was difficult. The best I could hope for was a woman who turned a blind eye to my little liaisons and settled for having babies. It would live—an otherwise charmed life. I could muster that if there was such a woman.

To this point, I'd had little luck. So, I drowned my sorrows. The only woman I'd had an actual conversation with was Queen Alexandra who treated me like a stupid child. She was a child herself! How would she know better?

I viewed Alexandra as young, boring, a waste of time, and on my list of potential wives! She was saintly. Her grandmother was a family friend—my godmother— but -I didn't know her. It wasn't unusual to be born into royalty and have ten godparents you never met beyond your christening.

Neandia was a conservative, religious hellhole where dreams went to die. My dear Lundhavn was pleasant and beautiful. There was nothing but low country and sadness in Neandia. If anything, I pitied Queen Alexandra. She was a figurehead in a pointless tax haven.

A blonde with impressive tits sat down by me at my assigned table assigned—a singles table. I hated this. It was forced and typical for any royal occasion where you arrived alone. She was pretty enough.

She asked, "You here alone, too?"

"Yes.-" I slammed my pitiful shot.

"Boring."

"Absolutely. The Belgians are ridiculous. I blame their British connections for them being snoozefests."

The woman scoffed. "And what would you say if I was one of them?"

I groaned. "I thought... you have an American accent."

"Raised off and on in the States. Apologies, but don't shit on my cousins."

"Your cousins are also mostly raised outside—"

"Well, fuck off if that bothers you!"

"It's a fucking compliment, okay?"

I knew who she was now, but it didn't matter. She didn't care who I was. I didn't care who she was. She was gorgeous with legs up to her neck. I wanted to fuck her with abandon. And, if she'd have me, I would.

"You're Rick the Prick, right?"

Ouch. Well, I could tell word had spread about that—even to those who didn't speak our language. I'd gotten a reputation among anyone who spoke English. I'd gone by Rick in college. It was a lot easier than explaining to Americans how to pronounce my given name. A college nickname was now an annoying artefact.

"Most people around here call me Prince Rikard, but sure. You can call me whatever you want when you're screaming my name."

She bit her lip. The blonde of the evening was thinking about it.

"You want to disappear?" I asked. "I'm bored. We could get up to trouble."

She stood and held out her hand. "Why don't we? You know this place at all?"

I shrugged. "You've seen one palace, you've seen 'em all. C'mon."

Three

ALEXANDRA

The morning after the event at the palace, I woke for breakfast. To my surprise, Queen Margaux invited me for an informal breakfast in her sitting room. I found myself on a couch eating tiny tea cakes. I was important. Who was I to enjoy an audience alone with Her Majesty? I still felt out of place among my peers. Until the regency was gone, I was unworthy.

"Do you know why I brought you here, Alexandra?" Margaux asked.

"To have breakfast?" I wondered, unsure.

"Well, state the obvious, Alexandra. Yes. But I wanted to check in with you. You came alive last night—as alive as I've seen you, darling."

"I very much enjoyed myself." I smoothed my skirt nervously. "Thank you for having me."

"Alexandra, you *can* be honest with me. I am on your side. I grew up the oldest of six girls. I was kept out of public scrutiny. I became Queen in my twenties and understand. I want to hear from you—the real you deep down. We are friends. Or, at least, I would like us to be."

"We cannot be friends."

"Why not?"

"You're a proper grown-up!" I shook my head.

"And you're a clever little thing but you're holding back. We're peers, Alexandra. And I've taken a liking to you. I want you to be honest and happy. I am only now seeing the light in your eyes as you tuck those cakes away."

I snickered. "Well, but they're delicious. I cannot—"

I stopped myself. I worried about what she might tell Celeste.

"Can I trust you to keep this in confidence?" I asked.

"Of course. From everyone. I gather you fear someone?"

"My grandmother restricts all I do—everything the girls do, too. I cannot even eat sweets. It's forbidden. Celeste worries I will put on too much weight. I cannot exercise in excess because I will be too fit. I cannot ride horses because it is too dangerous. I cannot have friends because they will put ideas in my head. I cannot speak to boys because it is a risk to my most valuable commodity."

"And that is?" Margaux sat her cup and saucer on the table.

The look on Margaux's face suggested she knew what I was about to explain but I didn't want to say it.

"My virginity, which is prized most of all." I rolled my eyes.

Margaux chuckled. "No one cares about your virginity! They will care much more that you are a clever, kind person. And since you have arrived, I know both are true."

"I cannot change my fate," I said. "So, I must trade in what I can. Unfortunately, I worry she is right. If I can be a good prospect, perhaps I can marry well. And at least then I would have children and be happy. She wants me to marry—badly. And I must have children lest we have a succession crisis. So, I must avoid all allegations of impropriety."

"Any man who would be worthy of marriage would not care," Margaux said. "Oh, darling, I wish you were mine. I wish you could stay. I would love to scandalise the people back home by letting you out to enjoy life. It kills me you can't even dance."

"I'm not out properly—"

"This isn't Regency England. Would you like to marry, Alexandra?"

I shrugged. "Not particularly. However, if I could find a man who would let me be me and would mostly keep to himself, I could tolerate it. A kind enough sort of man. Not cleverer than me. And I would like to have children eventually."

The Queen furrowed her brow. "Would you like some advice?"

I shrugged.

"Learn to dance. Meet someone who makes you do wild things. Go mad for him and enjoy your life. Be free. Live for yourself. Make friends. And, yes, your impulse is correct. Marry someone you outsmart. As a woman leading the charge, you need someone to delegate to, not someone to argue with you every step."

"But she owns me. She owns everything. The idea of even learning to dance—"

"You are a brilliant little thing. You can strike a bargain with her."

"How?"

"Play into something that makes her think it is her idea. Use what leverage you have. Or wait it out another few years. I'd love to see you happy, Alexandra. You're clever. You will figure it out."

I left breakfast, going round and round. What was my leverage? What would she want? It dawned on me. She wanted to marry me off. I couldn't be married without setting the regency aside. She worried about protecting me, but an engagement would soften that. If I chose the right man, I could find someone good enough I could be satisfied with. If I could find a man to take me seriously, she settle for securing the line of succession. Most of all, she'd be flattered if I asked her for advice.

Four

RICK

I woke the next morning unable to function until I popped an aspirin and drank water. I wished to return to bed and prayed my liver would not fail me now. The night before was dreadful. Yes, I'd managed to do something dirty in a staff office with an unbelievably hot blonde. I should have been happy but I wasn't.

"Sir?" There was a knock.

"Yes?" I groaned.

"May I come in?"

It was Martin, my favourite protection officer. He'd been dispatched to me.

I choked out a yes and sat out, having more water. My whole head throbbed. It was awful.

"Sir, Queen Margaux and the Prince Consort would like to host you for lunch."

"Motherfucker," I groaned.

That was non-negotiable. I must attend. If a hosting monarch invited you to luncheon, you sucked it up and went.

"Did she say *why*?" I asked, nervous that my indiscretions from the night before had come to light.

"Her private secretary intimated she would like to catch up. A kind invitation. She hopes you enjoyed your evening. Perhaps, a bit too much, sir?"

I grimaced. "Yes, indeed."

"It could be good for you."

I knew what Martin meant. He was like an older brother to me—in a way my strange and awkward older brother was not. He sometimes offered his opinions too freely but knew I needed and valued that. He'd told me to stay away from my ex. He'd tried to stop me from getting involved with her but ignored him.

"Martin, I will go. But... I need something."

"I can bring you a sports drink?"

"Great, thanks."

He turned to leave but I had to say something.

"Did she find out, Martin?"

"What sir?"

"Don't lie. You know what I got up to last night."

Martin shrugged at me with pity. "Sir, I think you are in the clear. However, it would behove you to not do that again."

I hated myself. There was to be no redemption arc. I embarrassed myself at the bar. I'd used a woman because she was convenient. She probably used me, too. She mentioned something of a breakup. That still didn't make my view of her as replaceable any *less* reprehensible in the morning.

Martin had the staff bring me a sports drink. I sucked it down, knowing in about ninety minutes, I would need to act like all was well. The deafening pounding in my head served as a reminder it was not. Regardless of what I told myself, I was heartbroken. I attached myself to a woman I couldn't have and was reaping the rewards of that "choice". I miss her even now. I knew better than to try and reach out, but it killed me to think I may never speak with her again.

She swore she'd leave him. She did, but only after she blew up my entire life. I was dumb enough to believe we'd get away with it—that she'd leave him, that we'd be able to run off, and that we could make a life together. I don't know why I thought I deserved that much. People like me didn't live happy lives with their forever person.

Licking my wounds and feeling sorry for myself, I attended my scheduled lunch with Queen Margaux and Prince Consort Alex. People called him Al. He was American and I liked him. She frightened me.

"You slept well?" the Queen asked.

Her tone suggested she knew what I got up to with her distant cousin—maybe generally what I got up to. She and my father spoke regularly. I was certain he'd told her how much of a fuck up I was.

"I did, thanks." I lied. "Is anyone else attending?"

"No. Your father said you might be interested in chatting. He thought it would be good if we spoke."

I cursed my father internally. "Oh, did he?"

"Yes. I usually entertain your parents. I adore your mother."

"Who doesn't?" I asked.

My mother was the one person in my life who never deserted me.

The Queen smiled. "Well, we missed her, but we were happy to host you. How is your brother doing after the wedding?"

"Haven't heard from him. Didn't expect to on his honeymoon."

Everyone heralded my brother's wedding as a triumph. It took a vast media circus to keep up that appearance. He had the charisma of burnt toast. While his wife was rather affable, they had no sexual chemistry. He provided a life for her that she enjoyed, and she tolerated him. It was no fairytale. The press just billed it that way.

"Weddings are always nice," Prince Al said. "Might be a while until we see another one."

I shrugged. "They are expensive and a lot of work."

"People adore them," Queen Margaux insisted. "It's good for morale. Do you have anyone you're holding a candle for, Rick? Might you follow close behind?"

"No," I replied.

She gave me a sad look. I hated pity. It was better than ire, but it was still judgement.

"There was someone. It didn't work out," I said. "My father has probably described me as hopeless, but I am not."

I loved to lie to myself. If I said it enough, I'd be right. Rick the Prick was the public persona that both haunted me and felt most comfortable in defensive moments. Yes, I was a prick, but I was free to be me. I wasn't beholden to anyone else.

"Sorry to hear that," the Queen said. "Well, maybe there is someone out there. Did you meet anyone or see anyone I could make a nice introduction to?"

"She thinks of herself as a matchmaker." Al rolled his eyes. "Sweetheart, not everyone wants to be set up. What is it with every queen being a matchmaker?"

"I love seeing a happily-ever-after, so shoot me! I am only *asking* him."

"No," I answered, "but thank you. The only person I spoke to of a similar station—the only one my parents would consider remotely interesting—was Queen Alexandra. And she chided me for my poor French. Made fun of me, honestly."

"Oh, I couldn't see Queen Alexandra taking the piss," Queen Margaux chuckled. "That darling thing would never hurt a fly. What was it?"

"She insinuated my French was poor while trying to translate for me."

"Your French *is* poor. She's an angel. I wouldn't read anything into it," Queen Margaux said.

"I try not to," I said. "Neandia is bad enough. A nursing home for billionaires. It's not as though she is so worldly."

I realised I'd spoken poorly of a Belgian ally. I cringed.

"It may be conservative and a tax haven," the Queen allowed. "However, she's dealing with a regency and trying to find her footing. Don't attribute to malice what might be awkwardness. Becoming queen in your teens isn't simple. I became queen in my mid-twenties, and it was bad enough."

I nodded. "Apologies. I spoke out of turn. I will grant her some grace. That's all I meant by that."

The Queen nodded. "So, really, *no one* piqued your interest?"

"Apologies, ma'am, but no."

"Well, damn. Your mother had high hopes I could at least make an introduction," Queen Margaux sighed.

Ah, yes. Every queen in Europe was conspiring to wed me and get me settled. It was as if my parents were sure a prospective spouse would end all my nasty habits and mend me. I hated to tell them that was tomfoolery. I wasn't to be mended. This was who I was. No woman deserved to get roped up with me. I wanted love and happiness, but the girls capturing my attention were unavailable, unsuitable, or saw me as a fling. The girls who wanted to settle down bored me to tears.

FIVE

ALEXANDRA

I returned to Neandia wanting to shed everything. I was back to my prison—locked down and depressed. Yet, I had hope. I wanted my freedom now more than ever. I had tasted it, now I wanted to bathe in it. Was this what a power trip was like? Or was it me advocating for myself?

Every Monday, I was forced to attend a tea with Celeste. It was mostly her complaining about how I was getting fat and telling me I couldn't do things.

"You know you put on weight in the time you were there."`

Even recovering from pneumonia, she was relentless. I hate to admit it, but I often wanted her to just die already. She was in her eighties but fit as a fiddle. It was a pipe dream. My younger sister, Astrid, was more vengeful. She read about poisons and contemplated killing our grandmother years ago. Of course, she wasn't serious, but it seemed a good creative outlet for the darkest among us.

I said, "I cannot have gained weight."

"They weighed you this morning?"

I nodded. I was weighed on Monday, Wednesday, and Friday. I feared the Monday weigh-ins most. If I even put on a bit of water weight, she would come after me as if I had let myself go over the week-end. I was grateful I hadn't gained a pound. I attributed that to the panic attack and lack of appetite I'd had upon returning home yesterday and realising the dream was nothing more than that.

"Hmmm…"

"I promise you I was on my best behaviour, Grand-Mama!" I insisted.

"Well, Margaux's review of your behaviour was promising. She said you were a perfect guest and complimented all your manners. She asked when you would officially have your coming out. I am tempted to wait another year."

"Another year?" I choked, spilling my coffee all over the skirt of my dress.

"Calm yourself. This is why you aren't fit for public consumption!"

Tears welled. "I cannot do this anymore."

"Do what? Drink coffee? I didn't want you to if you remember. You said it would be good for you to drink coffee—to feel more adult."

"I… I cannot be both chastised about my public persona and forced to attend engagements. I am ready to be out and about. I am ready to attend parties. This proves I am. Please, believe me."

"You do not have a choice, young lady."

Your Majesty. I was the Queen. She didn't care I was a queen in my own right, not some sort of consort-turned-tyrant.

"Grand-Mama, I met many people there—lovely people. And Queen Margaux was keen to introduce me, but without your blessing could not in good conscience do so. I am ready to be out in society. I know my duty to marry and have children is pressing. I want to take the next step."

The words rolled out of my mouth, my stomach turning. I was in no way excited at the prospect of having children. I wasn't ready. Yet, if my choices were to have children and freedom or no freedom for the next few years, I knew which I would choose. Lord, to be able to ride a horse and eat pastries would make the sacrifice worth it. And, sad as it was, I knew Celeste fancied the idea of some man telling me what to do. The joke was on her because I'd never settle for that type of man.

This was my only card and playing it was difficult. I stood firm and put my neck out. I had only this domestic card to play. I was not powerless because I held all the cards. I was empowered. She didn't expect it. I blindsided her. I worried Celeste might take it out on my sisters. I could take her wrath. She could hurt me, but not them. It killed me to see my baby sister, Ingrid, tortured at her hands. Ingrid was the same age I was when I became queen. I wanted her to have a better, happier childhood.

My grandmother thought for a moment. She crossed her arms and set her jaw. I knew my defiance perturbed her but I must play this hand. Emboldened by the sheer joy I experienced in my three-day-stint as a free girl, it was now or never.

"Well, if you think you are old enough, then it is time to get serious about it."

Worry crossed my face.

"I cannot let you be out in society—not officially—until we can end the regency."

"But you *won't* end it. I've begged for years, grandmother, and—"

"And it was imprudent. I will end it under one condition."

"Yes?" I was on the edge of my seat. I suspected a bait and switch, but what else did I have?

"You marry. Well, you get engaged with the intent to marry. I will end the regency right before your marriage—no funny business—after there is a point of no return where I am assured you will be properly invested and cared for. Should you become engaged, I will allow you to be out in society and grant you more freedom."

I beamed. "Alright, if you feel it is best."

"I would like to marry you off before you have time to fall for the tricks of men, end up sullied, and disappoint us all. I only want the best for you."

I nodded, trying not to look too excited. I hated that she saw my virginity as such a selling point. Part of me loathed having to carry it around as if it meant something.

"Take it or leave it. I will find a suitable—"

"You will find?"

"I arranged your father's marriage. Did you not love your mother? Was she not good enough for you?"

Of course I loved Mamma! She was everything to us. She was the one who took care of us until her dying day. Unfortunately, when delivering baby Ingrid, she was taken from us. My father left us shortly after that—first mentally and then physically. It was too much for him. Celeste's words cut like a knife.

"Mamma and Papa met through friends."

"Untrue. Mamma and Papa met when I introduced them. They met at a royal wedding, but who do you think engineered your mother's appearance? She was visiting from Denmark. She was young, beautiful, and a perfect choice for your father."

She was. They loved one another endlessly.

"Mamma and Papa... they had a choice?"

"Royals don't get the benefit of a love match. I didn't, either. Your grandfather and I learned to live together. That was the point—partnership. Love may come later. It did for your parents. They fell in love soon after they wed. The same could happen for you, my dear. It is easier this way."

It wasn't. I worried about the choice she would make. When I decided to engineer this, I did so under the assumption I would choose my match—not her. Celeste again held the cards. I refused to let her win. I needed to get my freedom. I would figure it out. I had to fight her.

"So you could choose some controlling brute of a man?"

"I would never!" Celeste was scandalised by the mere mention. "No. I would choose someone suitable for you."

"Someone old?"

"Certainly not. You must have children! He would be young, handsome, and never rough. I would pick someone who I knew would take care of you."

I sat with that for a moment. It would never be so easy.

"You are precious, but you need someone to guide you. And right now, you will never be worth more to a respectable family than you are. You're a virgin, you are of good breeding, and you haven't had time to develop bad habits or a negative view in the eyes of the press.

You've never been seen out doing something dreadful. This is for the best."

But was it? She never had my best interest in mind.

"As a queen, your prospects are limited. No man will prefer you to a princess born lower in the line of succession. Your appearance is rather unremarkable, you are small, have the hips of a broodmare, and lack the beauty your mother possessed. She didn't come laden with the responsibility of being a monarch out of the gate. You not only have that, but you have an immediate need to produce heirs."

My grandmother was right. No man would want to sign up for this mission. I was in charge and he would always be secondary. A husband's job was to like me enough to bed me and produce children quickly. I had little desire for perfunctory sex for the sake of popping out babies. It frightened me. We'd lost my mother that way. Maybe we could agree to hold off on that bit for a while? Once the regency ended, Celeste had no say in my affairs.

"I don't think you are ready for this," Celeste sighed. "But, if you do change your mind, I know of one possibility that would fit the bill. Even Queen Margaux is sure he might benefit from such a match. I am glad to invite him here. Let you get to know one another. Give you some time to see if it would work. You may decide it is a favourable choice?"

I sighed. What could I do? And if Margaux approved, maybe he wasn't the worst choice in the world? Given how kind and sensitive her boys were, I assumed she'd never stand for an abusive, controlling sort of man. Her husband was a sweetheart. She knew what it took to be a queen and what to look for in a consort.

"Sure," I said quietly. "I can try."

I wanted to end my regency at any cost. I returned to my room and flopped on the bed. Astrid came up.

"Did the bitch release you?"

"Astrid, don't use such language!"

"Oh, come on. You could. You just won't."

Astrid was only a year younger, but we were so different. She was feisty. She watched American crime dramas and liked to swear. She was rough-and-tumble and down for a fight. Astrid protected me by causing unrest and provoking Celeste. There was no one in this world I loved more than my dear sister. I envied her. She would never know this burden, but I couldn't free her until I was free myself. The guilt weighed heavy on me.

She lay down next to me. We both stared at the canopy on my bed.

Astrid asked, "What's up, buttercup?"

"The most ridiculous thing I've ever heard."

"What?"

"Celeste agreed to end the regency if I married a man of her choosing. She has someone in mind. She is bringing him here."

"What!? That's madness!"

I sighed. "I know. And yet, it could make us all much happier, right?"

"What do you mean?"

"If I wed, I am free. You all are free."

"If you wed, you are tied to some dickhead who could ruin your life, Alex. That's no better. I don't want that for you."

"You don't understand, Asti. I saw freedom. I saw it and it made me happy. I am circling the drain. I will end up like Papa if I stay like this. Four more years? I will be mad by then!"

Our father was a complicated man. He struggled to maintain normalcy and keep himself together. He had always been eccentric, but my grandmother's controlling behaviour and constant shaming of his differences made him spiral out of control. Then, when he needed help grieving the loss of our mother, she stowed him away in a country house. He wasn't seen for two years. And then, we lost him. We never got a chance to say goodbye. It was heartbreaking. I knew she would relish doing the same to me.

"What can you do then?"

"I can meet him."

"What if she changes the rules?"

"I will only become engaged if she makes a formal proclamation about the regency ending? I don't know. I didn't get into it because it sounds ridiculous. In our world, who does this?"

"Royals. Just royals. It's backwards and fucked up."

I looked at Astrid. Her pretty face was twisted. All Astrid wanted in this world was to be free. She was a wild spirit. She could be an unbridled force for good left to her own devices.

"I admire you so much," I said, tears welling. "You remind me every day of Mamma. It is heartbreaking to think how much she would have adored you, too. But... I know it. And... I only want for you and the girls to be happy."

"You shouldn't sacrifice your happiness, Alex!"

"It's my lot. I was born first, Asti. It's the way it was always meant to go. I can do some good or I can hurt you all. What would you have me do? Besides, Mamma and Papa began this way. Celeste said so. They eventually fell in love. Mamma loved Papa like the moon and stars, and he didn't want to live without her. Maybe it is for the best after all?"

"Do you really believe that?"

"If you were able to go to school abroad and study whatever you wanted, wouldn't you?" I asked. "If I could give you that..."

"I could never ask you to! God, I couldn't—"

"Stop!" I shook my head. "Just stop. I must make this choice for myself."

"I'm not going to say anymore, but I think it's stupid!" Astrid popped up. "Do you want to watch a movie?"

"No, I think I'm going to go take a walk."

I stood up and walked down a long hallway, opposite our TV room. I stopped before the door to Celeste's sitting room. She had the best quarters in the house, while I remained in my childhood bedroom. I was announced. I entered and remained standing.

"Yes, have you thought better about our conversation?" Celeste asked.

"Possibly. If I do this, I expect you to proclaim an end to the regency before my engagement. Then, you can ask parliament to dissolve it just before the wedding. I need that assurance."

She shrugged. "Let's cross that bridge when we come to it."

"I also want you to assure me the girls will be free. They will report to me."

"I cannot guarantee—"

"I will only do this if you comply. I will marry a man of your choosing—quietly and meekly do so if you promise me this."

"I will promise you this," she said. "But really, you won't need that. You will be queen in your own right. It will be up to you and your husband to make those calls."

She was right. If I could make this work, everyone would get what they wanted. If I could tolerate being married to a man for a few years, having a baby or two, and existing with my freedom, my sisters could have much better lives. Celeste was still running a grift. When wasn't she? This time, it might benefit all of us for me to play along.

Six

My father summoned me to dinner at the palace. I had a swanky condo overlooking the sea and rarely came by unless my presence was requested. Attendance was never optional, of course. When my father rang, we came. My brother was still on his honeymoon—lucky bastard—and got out of it.

"How are you?" Mamma asked.

"I'm well, Mamma," I replied. "You?"

Father said, "I was told you stayed out of trouble while in Belgium."

"Yes." I lied.

Of course, I had gotten up to something. I had only gotten away with it.

"Good. For once, you followed orders."

"You're welcome. Now, can we cut the shit, Dad? Why did you call me here?"

"Rikard, please!"

My father set his jaw. "I would like you to go to Neandia on Thursday. You can have dinner with the royals there, attend a trade summit, and be a good boy. If you can do that, I will allow you to spend some time on the yacht this summer. I need to believe you won't cause the family too much disgrace."

"Really?" My ears perked. "Well, that's great! I mean, there are things I'd rather do but... if that's all I must—"

"There will be more, of course. But I would like you to go."

"What is the catch then?" I groaned.

"You will meet with Queen Alexandra and get to know her."

"I saw her this weekend—we barely spoke. She's awful."

"She is a nice girl," Mamma said. "Her mother was a dear friend, and her grandmother remains your godmother—"

"I know that. She seems prickly. We did not hit it off. She implied my French was poor—"

"And it is compared to a native speaker's. Which she is."

"Well, then what is the hope for us?"

"She speaks perfect English. Stop putting up walls, Rick."

Father bellowed. "It would be good for you to settle down and stay out of trouble. She is a perfectly nice girl, not ugly, and young. She is well-behaved—unimpeachable—and would make a good wife."

"No, no, no, no. You handpicked Marie for Mikkel. That isn't going to happen here."

"It worked out!"

"Mikkel is awkward and complicated. Marie puts up with him because she likes to be spoiled. She tolerates him. They aren't in love. I have been in love," I insisted. "Even if you won't hear it. If I marry—and that is if—I want it to be about love, not because I am forced."

"You loved someone who—"

"Loved me?" I asked vein in my neck bulging. "I still love her. I'd run off with her and leave all of this behind if it wouldn't cost you everything. I do care about this family, believe it or not!"

"Show it, then."

"August," Mamma said. "He's allowed to love her. He is not with her. We don't need to rehash this again."

Mamma loved us. She was always good to us. She was a mother before anything else in this world. Without her, I would have been toast ages ago. My father had it up to his neck with me more times than I could count. I knew he wanted the family to live on. That's why he cared so much, but he took a sledgehammer to me and my self-esteem more than he knew. I had a heart. My mother cared for us, and she knew I was sensitive.

My father dropped it.

"I hit bottom," I said. "I will give anything a shot. However, I am unconvinced that I could ever love a woman like that."

"And why? Because she is a kind, sweet person?"

"No, Pappa, because she is an uninitiated baby who struggles to relate to people. She's practically a nun! If I marry her, I will be obligated to have children with her. If I'm not attracted to her, that isn't going to happen."

"You haven't even given her a chance," Mamma said. "Queen Margaux spoke highly of her. She and I both believe you deserve someone kind and would benefit from someone like Alexandra."

"This is a ridiculous arranged marriage!" I shook my head.

"It works for many. We live in a bubble—"

"Pappa, you, and Mamma fell in love! You cannot talk—"

"And my parents didn't have the benefit, son. Get over yourself!"

I sighed, rolling my eyes.

"They fell for one another eventually," Mamma continued. "And you could, too. No one is forcing you into this. She's not perfect—nor are you—but she is open to meeting you. You certainly don't have to marry her. Just think about it as a blind date."

"Exactly," Pappa added.

"Pappa, it's nothing like that when the stakes are this high."

"How is it different from any other date, son?"

I couldn't give the actual answer to that question as I planned on bedding any woman I went out with. I didn't find Alexandra remotely attractive at our first meeting. She was nothing to write home about. I bet she was a cold fish in bed. I liked my women enthusiastic, willing, and adventurous. I didn't want to have to teach her everything.

She'd probably never been properly fucked—if at all—but I wasn't in the business of playing daddy and raising her. No, she either had to come to me a fully formed woman or I would back right out. I could go to get my father off my back. Maybe she was the sweetest girl, but that alone would not hold me. I'd bore of her and hurt her. I may have been a prick, but I was done with hurting other people like that. I was making amends. She deserved better.

"She's a nice girl," Mamma said again. "She's young, yes, but maybe that is what you need—someone young and sweet who can see all of you as a person rather than prejudge you."

"You want me to pull the wool over her eyes."

"Not quite," my father said. "But you are much more saleable if you are a good boy. She doesn't know much about you. Hopefully, you didn't anger her on your first meeting."

"I didn't, no."

I may have, but how would I know? It certainly wasn't a good first impression, but also not the worst.

"I will give it an honest try," I promised. "I will only say I find her unremarkable."

"You may change your mind after you give her a chance," Mamma said kindly. "Instant attraction is rare. Pappa and I loved one another, but we also grew much more as a married couple. It wasn't lightning in a bottle at first sight."

"Yes, possibly, but also unlikely. Best I can do is try, Pappa. What advantage is this to us? There must be something else?"

"The advantage would be I would be able to sleep at night knowing you are in a place where you cannot get into much trouble. Celeste runs that palace with an iron fist, and you'd get away with nothing."

"Gee, you're making this sound better and better, father!" I dripped with sarcasm.

I did not know my godmother well, but rumour had it she kept the princesses under lock and key for years before Alexandra came of age. She was a hardass. Of course, if I had little Alexandra wrapped around my fingers, I would have an easier go of it. Alexandra might give me the best chance yet.

"You can decide for yourself, but make a choice, son. And think about what you are doing with your life. Now, you can leave."

I looked at my mother. She looked down, pained to be there. I wanted her so badly to say something. She was the only one left who saw the good in me. Pappa thought I was a big fuck up.

I left, unable to say more. I stormed out, past Martin, who caught up. We took the car back to my place. He was silent and sensed my seething disdain.

"They want me to go to Neandia to marry me off to this boring young girl," I scoffed. "Martin, what the fuck do I do?"

"What if you don't?" Martin asked.

"My father will cut me off. He all but said it."

Martin let out a rare wince. "Well, it could be worse. Neandia has some beautiful countryside."

"She is a child. I've seen her. It could *not* be worse," I groaned.

"Is she hideous?" Martin asked.

"No. She's not hideous. She's not ugly. She's... judgemental and stuck up. And far too young for me. She didn't seem to like me at the ball. I didn't make a good impression. I don't blame her, but we are no love match."

"Neither were Mikkel and Marie at first but I would say they've done well."

"They've barely been married. It's not how I wanted this to go."

"How so?"

"Me in contrived royal matrimony with a woman ten years younger than me? A woman who is square and boring? It sounds stupid but I want to fall in love—mad love. I did before but it was all wrong."

"I didn't like my wife when I met her," Martin chuckled. "But she's been the best thing that ever happened to me."

"What was wrong with her?"

"She was always right."

"Hate women like that," I groaned. "How did you fix it?"

"She fixed me. She is usually right," Martin said. "Her foibles became things I didn't only endure but adored. You will never know what is possible until you try. You can fall in love again."

I stared out the window.

"Martin?"

"Yes, sir?"

"Thanks for saying 'again'. Thanks for acknowledging it."

He had been the first to do so. It was sad that the *one* person who saw me was my paid bodyguard.

SEVEN

ALEXANDRA

I was told nothing about the man I was supposed to spend the rest of my life with until the morning I met him. Celeste informed me he was Prince Rikard of Lundhavn—a small nation much like my own sandwiched in Northern Europe which spoke a dialect like my mother's native Danish. I hoped his English was good because my Danish was poor with limited practice.

I assumed nothing honest would come of this but practiced my pitch for two days. I would come in guns blazing. This wasn't about love. It was about winning. I would beat the old crone at her own game and win my freedom. Maybe I was the sacrificial lamb that allowed my sisters to live a normal life, but I would take my chances.

Celeste met with my presumed future husband first. I was announced by a footman when I joined. A blonde head popped up from a seated position catching me off guard, but his height pleased me.

As I tried to assess the situation, our eyes met. I realised I had met him before. He was the drunk arguing with the bartender in Brussels. I shook my head and stepped back. He stared at me, confused by my reaction. Why? Did he not even remember when I tried to help him?

He was a total ass! But Queen Margaux approved of him? How? We made eye contact and he decided to go first.

"Your Majesty." the man bowed.

He knew who I was already.

"This is Prince Rikard of Lundhavn," my grandmother said.

"Yes, obviously," I stammered. "Um... hello, Your Royal Highness."

I was angry, deep down. He was not what I wanted, but if I ran out of the room in anger, Celeste would win. No matter what, Celeste could not win.

"We've met before," I said. "But I did not know who he was."

"Briefly," the Prince's voice sounded forced or pinched.

He was nervous I would tell on him, I gathered. He worried I would mention his inebriated and awful state during our last meeting.

"I wasn't introduced properly. I didn't know who he was," I said. "Nice to make your acquaintance, Your Royal Highness."

As I needed this to go well, I was unable to embarrass him. It wouldn't help things. Again, anything that threatened the peace of this potential union was bad for me. Even if I wanted him to be embarrassed, it didn't matter. I was now stuck with him. For better or worse, this was my future. I would have freedom!

Despite my kind remark, he pulled a face. I'd hit a nerve.

"I had no idea who you were, either," Rikard said. "You are... new."

I glared at him. New? That was the best he could come up with.

"Well, now I am, but aren't we all new in this situation?" I tried to turn things to the purpose of this strange meeting.

"Rikard was telling me about his interest in sailing," Celeste said as if I had ever even *been* sailing.

"Well, I'd like to go sailing," I said.

Away from here right this instant!

"You have never been?"

I shook my head. "No, Your Royal Highness. I have never been sailing."

He perked up. "It's a shame, Your Majesty. You're missing out."

"I try not to let the girls do anything that might injure them," Celeste said as if we were so beloved she could not part with us.

"Well, sailing is safe if they can swim. You can swim?"

"Yes, Prince Rikard, I can swim."

Who did he take me for? I tried to hide my sarcasm, but my voice was flat as could be. Rikard took everything as a slight. He set his jaw, angrily. It made me want to grumble at him about being an idiot—in French since he really couldn't understand it. Anger made him *more* attractive than before. Maybe that was the thing with assholes like the Prince? Women found them attractive only because they pulled angry faces and threw their weight around. It didn't do it for me. One can only be so outwardly attractive to make up for all the ugly inside.

"Good, good," the Prince grew even more sarcastic. "I wasn't sure since you seem so..."

I used his word. "New?"

Celeste looked satisfied. Was she enjoying us sniping at one another? Maybe her whole pursuit was to dangle freedom but to make it as painful as possible. Was he a plant? I wanted to crawl out of my skin both in confusion and anger. No matter what I did, I was damned to ruin.

"What do you think of Neandia?" I changed the topic.

"It's... nice," he answered in a way that implied he did not think that. "It's... calm."

I nodded.

"And your... trees... they are... nice."

I held back laughter. *Our trees were nice?* That was all he could do to make conversation? God, he was simple, wasn't he? Trees, sailing, liquor. This man would be an easy mark. Celeste could do her worst, but this man would be no match for me. I was far more intelligent than Rikard. He may be older and more experienced, but I could outsmart him. However, hatching this plan and deciding the rules of engagement required a one-on-one chat. I needed my grandmother to leave. I figured I might have better luck if he suggested it. I decided to turn up the charm.

"Perhaps, if I am ever in Lundhavn, you could show me your boat?" I said.

That failed. I'd insulted him.

"It's a sailing yacht. Not just some boat."

"Oh, well, your *yacht* then. I'm sure it is... beautiful?"

"Are you now a yacht aficionado?" He leaned back, his body posture spreading out over the couch with his arm looping over its back.

"No, but I am sure I could learn a thing or two from you," I said, realising suddenly that I had leaned *too* hard into being charming.

He gave me a cheeky grin. "Yes, I am sure I could teach you a thing or two. As you are... new."

His gaze was unwavering. My palms sweated. I suddenly wanted to flee. It wasn't worth the risk of a one-on-one. He was reading this wrong. I had no interest in pursuing him in a genuine sense. This was about an agreement—a business transaction of sorts.

"I think it was nice to meet you," I said. "I look forward to speaking to you again at dinner."

"Alexandra, that is all you wish to ask the Prince. To speak to him about?"

"Yes, Your Majesty, I wish to get to know you more."

He still had this expansive posture as if he were looming there. He *leered*. I was sure that was the word to describe it.

"I think perhaps we can best chat at dinner."

"Well, why wait?" Celeste asked.

I glared at them both. "I think this is about all we have to say right now. We do not know one another yet. And having people right here... is awkward if we are to speak on a personal level. I would prefer to have a conversation with the prince in *private* rather than with you here, no offence Grand-Mama."

"No offence taken. But it is... improper." She shook her head.

"I promise to be on my best behaviour as will His Royal Highness. Won't you, Prince Rikard?"

"Yes, yes, of course. I wouldn't *dream* of getting into trouble," the Prince said.

He had the same smarmy look on his face.

Celeste looked at us both. "Alexandra, you may take Prince Rikard on a tour of the palace followed by your detail. Be on your best behaviour!"

I nodded, grateful for her to leave. We started our tour, going by each of the staterooms. He stared at me as if expecting me to fall into his arms and... well, I wasn't sure what. I suspected he thought I would throw myself at him. I was no fool.

"And this is where the ballroom is!" I declared loudly.

We stopped in front of the ballroom. Rikard broke the silence.

"Yes, I see that. I am interested in a quieter room," Rikard said.

"And that would be... inappropriate."

His tone changed. I'd again annoyed him.

"I am sorry I wasn't the one you expected, clearly, but I gather neither of us planned for this. Can we just.. wrap the tour up and say we did our best?"

"No, that is... what were you told about this?"

"That you were someone my parents wanted me to meet and try to get to know, but this was a mistake."

"Indeed. It was a joke. I am confused. You're supposed to be a prince!"

He joked. "My father said the same."

"What?"

"It was a joke, Your Majesty. Call me Rick."

"Oh." I was unamused. I crossed my arms.

"It was a good joke."

I didn't argue with him. I didn't care to.

"I thought you were American... your accent."

"I was educated in American schools and by American tutors, as I am sure you were educated in British schools by British tutors. Most women love the accent."

I was not *most women*. And I was educated by British tutors. He was correct. However, there was no time to give him my life's most mundane details.

"Look, we haven't much time. My grandmother has butted out for now, but no doubt will be scheming by dinner," I said.

I was determined. I could tolerate his grip better than Celeste's stranglehold. Rick annoyed me, but he was easily plied with drink. I was cleverer. I channelled my most zen Queenliness and began walking again towards the state dining room.

"Where are you going?" Rikard asked.

"I am taking you to the dining room, then the throne room."

He caught up.

I kept my voice low. "And I'd like to propose an arrangement."

He sputtered, "Oh... really... we probably should... like... talk?"

"Oh, you don't think we're... going to have sex?" I burst out laughing.

He looked deer-in-the-headlights. "Well, yes. Why not?"

I flushed hot. "I wouldn't... I don't even *like* you—"

"You don't even know me, Your Majesty. How can you judge?"

He confused me with the way he said it. It wasn't as flat or angry as he had been before. Was he flirting? If so, I wouldn't know. There was no time to waste. I trudged on.

"Look, I'm not making an indecent proposal, but a decent one. If we marry, we can end the regency. I get the feeling you're in a rough place. Your parents want you to settle down, right? I'm not a terrible choice. I'm not much of a choice, I'll grant you, as I don't much know myself and—"

He cut me off. "What are you talking about? And don't sell yourself short. You're at the top of a short list of women my parents wish I would marry. And I'd say you're in the lead by a mile."

Was that a compliment? I blushed. I hated that his words could *make* me blush. Or was it the way his eyes focused on me? Or was it the stupid cleft in his chin?

"Don't act surprised," Rick said. "Now what is this about a regency and going straight to marriage? That seems an... escalation, Your Majesty."

"I am trapped in an abusive regency. My Grand-Mama controls everything from what I eat to who I see to what activities I do. I am a prisoner here. I know it sounds quite mad but... it's true. My choices are to wait until I'm twenty-five or wed someone of my grandmother's choosing. For some ungodly reason, it's you."

"She's a tyrant. She promised me this if I wed you. Moreover, it's not just me. It's my sisters as well. The three of them are all at the mercy of whatever happens to me. I can free us if I just do the thing. I know, like I said, you probably think I'm mental—"

"You do not know me!" He feigned offence.

"I do not but let's just say our last meeting gives me little confidence I'm about to fall for you hook, line, and sinker in the next twenty minutes."

He laughed. "You underestimate my charm, Your Majesty. Vastly. And despite this, you want to get married? You don't know me, don't find me attractive, but let's run down the aisle? I'm so confused."

"I don't care. You may be a supreme wanker, but you are still better than bloody Celeste. The point is, I don't think you are cruel. Queen Margaux approves of you. I trust her. She's the one person who has tried to get me out of this and help me. Please consider it. I know it sounds mad, but you are better than the alternative."

"Wow! That's a vote of confidence! What is wrong with your grandmother?"

I took a deep breath and led on towards the throne room. He wasn't saying no. He wasn't being *rude*. We walked down the hall and stepped in. The guards stayed outside.

"She's a tyrant. She promised me this if I wed you. It's not just me, either. My sisters are at the mercy of whatever happens to me. I can free us if I do the thing. I know, like I said, you probably think I'm mental—"

I sat on the larger of two thrones and shook my head.

He snickered, sitting on the other. Letting out a long sigh, Rikard played with the curls in his hair. He was nervous. I should have been annoyed by him laughing, but damn if I wasn't struggling to loathe him. He was downright handsome in this light. And the gall of him to *sit down* in the consort's throne! I doubted it was symbolism as much as it was his own self-obsessed belief he should be able to sit next to me without a question asked. I met his glance. He didn't turn. I didn't expect to feel anything for this match, but his jaw alone had me going.

"I'm not sure I follow completely. Let me lay my stuff on the table here, Your Majesty. My father thinks it would be good for us to see one another—you might have a good effect on me. I dunno. Problem is... I'm not marriage material. And, no offence, you seem like a nice girl, but... you're not my type."

"That's fine. Let's stay married long enough to get everyone free and put the old bag in the sod. Then, I will set you free."

"But you're Catholic!"

"As if I care if I give the Pope a heart attack! My life has been someone else's since I was born. You don't get it. At all. I am a prisoner here. I would do almost anything to get out of this mess—including marrying someone who insults bartenders and speaks poor French."

"Excuse me! My French is—"

"Dreadful."

"You cannot help but be judgemental, can you?"

"And you cannot help but be quick to judge."

He glared at me and popped back up.

"What is it that has your father upset?"

He took a long breath, pacing now. "I dated someone unsuitable, and it bit me in the ass. I should have known better."

I was sympathetic. He'd been in love.

"I know, I know. We were friends for ages. I fell in love with her. She fell in love with me. Someone tipped my father off. And... he was unhappy about it."

I softened further. Forbidden love sounded an awful torture.

"It's a whole thing. She wasn't going to work out and I should have avoided her. I know, but I love her still. I don't want to end up stuck with someone—even someone like you—because I'm hoping to find love. But the love I find is either unrequited or out-of-bounds. I know this is only common anymore among royals and that you all seem to almost expect it."

"Well, we're a bit backwards, I'll grant you, Rikard."

"Rick, please. Or, if you're everyone else, just call me Rick the Prick."

I burst out laughing uncontrollably.

"Yuck it up, Your Majesty."

"I'm sorry." I tried to rein it in. "But... you're... oh, that's awful, Rick!"

"I told you. I have my issues. No need to inflict them on a young thing like you. You're practically an infant."

"I very much am not but I haven't been allowed to go anywhere or do anything! Don't call me an infant."

He sighed. "Yes. Okay, that's fine. You're not an infant. You're also not my future wife."

"Maybe not, but... what? You can't ride out a fake, arranged marriage for a year? And, if you're quiet about it, I don't care if you... you know."

He understood my meaning. I couldn't bear to say I was fine with him sleeping with someone else. The idea of sharing him was unattractive, but I could endure.

"What about you?"

"What about me?"

"Should you not get the same?"

I pulled a face.

"Oh, okay. I don't get to bring that up?"

"I'm a monarch! It's impolite."

He sighed and shook his head. "Fucking hell. Alright, Your Majesty. You're not hideous and you're too young to deny yourself pleasure. I wouldn't tell you no if you'd give me the same levity."

"Alexandra, please. Just... Alexandra."

I didn't want to respond to his prior comment. The word *pleasure* flustered me. I tried not to think about it.

"I will stick around for a bit. I must. Pappa is... well, he'll skin me alive if I go back there without making it look like I'm trying."

"Cool, cool. Brilliant." I was nervous.

Why did I expect him to jump at the chance to enter a sham marriage? We stared at one another awkwardly. If it was true that my parents were in an arranged marriage gone well, I must believe it started better than this. It wasn't that Rick was hideous. He was objectively handsome. I loathed the way he could make me blush. He was fit. It was his attitude. He was cocky. He *knew* he was hot and acted above the law. Furthermore, he didn't seem the type to physically hurt me or control me.

"She really keeps you locked up?"

I nodded.

"Why?"

"Because as soon as I can free myself of her control, I will do whatever I please, and she can't imagine that. She spent her life torturing my father and mother. She never broke my mother the way she did my poor father, but things were not good. And when Grand-Papa died, it broke something inside her. It made her even worse. She went on a power-hungry campaign to ease her grief and she hasn't given up. Without me under her control, she thinks she will lose everything when I take over. And if she can break me before then—break my spirit —I will always let her exercise undue influence."

"Don't you... worry... she will—"

"She has spies everywhere. But there is little she could do to me at this point that would surprise me."

There would be retribution when any of my reasoning made it back to my grandmother, but I was to be paraded around like a horse for sale as an engaged young woman, she couldn't smack me around. She was slowly losing control. I didn't understand why she gave me this much power to begin with. I guessed she hoped to tie me to someone and pop out babies who would dominate my life. I needed to make it her idea so we could be free.

"Okay, so, a princess in a tower—a relatively brave one at that— needs saving."

"Don't flatter yourself, Rikard," I said, flatly. "I engineered this plan. I will save us. You will assist."

He rolled his eyes. "Let's not debate semantics. Look, I'm considering it if only to throw a big middle finger at both sets of families, but I think the reaction to a divorce will be worse for you than it will be for me."

"I can handle anything as long as I can eat an unlimited number of pastries, Rick."

He chuckled. "Okay, okay. Let me think about it. I'm not saying no. I will give you a chance if you do the same for me. Let's put our first meeting behind us. Can you grant me that? Give me a clean slate?"

I nodded. "You have yourself a deal."

EIGHT

RICK

I didn't expect Alexandra to proposition me. I thought the call was coming from my parents. No, it was *inside the house!* Marry her? Was she insane? I left the meeting reeling, pacing until I decided to take a walk. Martin followed but I walked to walk.

"Martin, what do you know about the girl's mental state?" I asked. "She just propositioned me in a ridiculous marriage plot!"

"Mental state, sir?"

"Alexandra. Crazy Crown Prince Christophe *was* her father. They locked him up—that's the story. She's told me that everything is a mess here. As in she is held captive by her grandmother—a little old lady! Come on!"

"I don't know much, sir. These people keep everything buttoned up. They are known for their eccentricities. I know little about Her Majesty, but her father was... disturbed."

"Yes. I cannot imagine a sane girl would propose something out of a regency costume drama."

"I have heard things. Yes, I am sure he had... issues... but it was my understanding that the girls have been very sheltered. To this point, they are protected from prying eyes. Clearly. I haven't heard anything about the princesses. And until she passed me this morning, I did not see Her Majesty. We've been here a day. It is odd. I agree it is strange, sir."

"I'm not angry with her. What good does it do to be mad at her? She's just a girl. But my parents? They brought me to this creepy fucking place and put me up to this. Am I simply expendable? I thought Mamma would at least care about me. This girl has a poor grip on reality, don't you think?"

"I know nothing, sir," Martin said. "I apologise."

"Maybe she is just immature? Is this her damsel fantasy?"

Martin shrugged.

"I don't like damsels. I like my women feisty and loud. She's basically a walking doormat."

"Sir, if she was a doormat, would she have engineered a marriage plot?"

"Maybe she is less doormat and more immature child?"

Martin looked off as a man approached with an envelope.

"Your Royal Highness." The footman bowed. "An invitation."

I popped the letter open. This was all high and mighty. Did they do this to impress everyone here?

I read the letter. It was an invite to dine with the Queen and Dowager Queen. I wanted to run but didn't have a choice. That would be rude. If it got back to Pappa, I'd be toast. I nodded in agreement.

"Yes, I will attend."

The footman bowed again.

As he left, Martin looked at me for a sign.

"Dinner. I've been invited. Let's... take a walk in the garden. I need some air."

We walked through a grove of trees when we heard voices. A girl was shrieking, sounding like she was fighting off a slasher. I was sure I was about to avenge someone. I rushed towards the sound, Martin following. There, I found a stream flowing through the gardens. One girl stood in the middle of the stream glaring at another who laughed on its banks. *N-o murderer in sight.*

My heart's racing beat slowed. Martin stood down and stepped back, fading into the grove of trees upon seeing the girls.

The one in the stream asked in French, "Who are you?"

"Me?" I pointed at myself like an idiot. "I'm... Rick."

"Who? How did you get here?"

"Ingrid, calm down," the girl on the shore said.

"I'm visiting from Lundhavn. A guest of your sister's... I'm assuming?" I asked.

"Which sister?" They said in unison.

The girl in the stream, hands on her hips, said, "Yes, there are *four* of us. You should specify."

"Alexandra. The Queen."

The other asked, "And how do you know her then?"

"I don't... not well anyway," I answered. I wondered if everyone in this place was mad.

I heard a third voice calling out before another girl appeared. This one looked like Alexandra in the way the other two didn't.

"Who the fuck are you?"

This third one had a mouth on her. I admired that.

"Uh, this is Rick. He's not Alexandra's friend. He's not sure what he is," the one I knew as Ingrid said.

"Oh, I know about him," the girl said. "I'm Astrid. Call me Asti. And that's Ingrid, the baby. And the typical middle child, Odette, right here."

"Nice to meet you all," I said.

"You shouldn't be out here. The bitch will get after you. She'll assume you're up to something," Astrid said.

"What? Who?"

"Our grandmother. She's always got eyes and ears out. She'll know. Does Alex know you're out here?"

"Can a guest not walk in the gardens?" I asked, confused. "And who is Alex?"

"Told you he's not her friend!" Ingrid shrieked in French, slapping water in Odette's face.

They were delightfully childlike. Silly. It had been ages since I was so playful and carefree. And, yet they were very aware of the evil Queen supposedly hiding around the corner. It was as if I wandered into a Grimm's fairytale. Who the hell were these girls?

"Back off, Ingy!" Astrid said. "Chill, okay? I've got this. You don't need to be so openly hostile. I'm that enough for all of us."

I snickered. "At least you're honest."

"Walk with me." Astrid gestured for me to follow.

"Oh... okay, yeah," I trotted to keep up.

For someone short, she had impressively long strides.

"Just... I don't want to involve the girls," Astrid said. "They are big and tough, but they're children, okay? I am my sister's primary confidante and I know everything, even if she tells you otherwise. The two of them... they don't know much. We'd prefer it stay that way. Makes it easier on them mentally."

"What?"

"Alexandra and I shoulder the burden for them. Has she told you what is happening?"

"Are you all crazy? All of you sound—"

"I'm not crazy! This is our life—or has been. She controls everything that we do. The little ones haven't been in normal school since they learned to read. They have a tutor. Alex and I break them out in the afternoon like this. Meanwhile, Alex says you think she's nuts, and she's sequestered herself in her bloody room now."

"Oh. Well..." I wasn't sure what to say. I *did* think she was mad, but he also wondered how they could all have lost reality this much.

"She's not mad. Celeste is—the mean bitch that runs this place."

I could tell that Astrid was the spicier of the two. She was feisty. Alexandra was the well-behaved oldest daughter, another reason we'd not get on. The last thing I needed was a well-behaved woman. I judged Alexandra too harshly. I began to believe what the girls said.

"She said the regency has kept her locked up," I said.

As I spoke, a man approached.

"Well, whatever you do," Astrid said, "you must check out the zoo. It's so brilliant."

"What?" I asked.

Then, I realised she was covering for us.

"Sir, the Queen would like to see you inside," he said.

"The Queen or the Dowager Queen?" Astrid clarified.

"The Dowager Queen."

"Well, let's not confuse those two, Lord William."

I assumed this was one of the Dowager Queen's henchmen if the girls' story was to be believed. I admitted that the timing was suspect if they were delusional.

"Sure," I said.

I followed the man into the house, arriving in a large drawing room filled with too many cats. I loathed cats. They were never to be trusted. In my opinion, women who had more than two cats were immediately suspect. The dear Dowager Queen was one of those women. She sat in a high back chair with a cat on her lap purring, as if a supervillain.

"Prince Rikard, I wanted to check in. Ignore me. Octavia will never leave my lap and I loathe to disturb her."

"No, wouldn't want to do that, would you?" I chuckled nervously, dodging cats.

"How was the tour?"

"Her Majesty showed me the sights. We spoke. I enjoyed it."

"What were your thoughts of her? I warn that she might not look like much at present, but if she is like her mother, she can be buffed into quite a diamond with a bit of work."

It was an unkind statement—below the belt. She may not have been my type, but Alexandra was far from hideous. "She's a perfectly nice young woman. She was very kind. I ran into the other princesses in the garden. You have four interesting granddaughters."

"Interesting is putting it kindly, Rikard."

"They are. Cannot be easy growing up without your parents in a word like this."

"That is why I shelter them so much. To hear our Alexandra or—God forbid—Astrid tell it, you'd think I kept them under lock and key and tortured them! The truth is that young women are wilful if not properly controlled. And I am looking out for their best interest, Rikard. That is it. I hope they haven't told you otherwise?"

"They have said you are very much looking after their health and well-being, Your Majesty," I smiled. "Yes. They say you're strict, but I can understand why."

It was uncomfortable. At this point, I was lying. If the girls weren't crazy, I was saving them from her admonishment. If they were lying, then what was another lie? Why would she bring it up? Alexandra and Astrid were both grown. Why did she need to keep them under lock and key? Maybe Alexandra was right, Celeste was the madwoman.

Either way, I was called to defend these girls. An hour ago, I thought they were nuts. Now, I wanted to help—at least as much as I could without stepping too much into the fray.

"Good. So you met before?"

"We met at the ball in Belgium for the Duke."

"Oh yes, she was all aglow I am sure. She can clean up nicely. I dressed her myself."

Of course you did!

"She tried to help me speak to someone in French. I didn't… I didn't think much of it."

Alexandra couldn't win. She was dressed like a pensioner anywhere she went. It dawned on me that in another set of clothes, I might feel differently about her. I doubted it, but a wardrobe refresh wouldn't hurt.

"I am glad the two of you spoke and took a walk. Dinner will be divine. Please let me know if I can help with anything else."

"Sure." I nodded at the old woman.

I stood because she wouldn't and left.

This whole place was odd if not slightly cursed. Perhaps all the rumours about it were true? Maybe Neandia was a backward hell hole? At best, the Dowager Queen was strange and the place too conservative. At worst, the woman *was* a tyrant. Alexandra and her sisters were in danger.

NINE

ALEXANDRA

"I am jealous you get to go," Ingrid whinged. "And not me? And you get to eat dinner with the grown-ups?"

All three of my sisters sat on the bed while Marta, my dresser, worked on pinning my hair up for tonight's dinner. I had on a full face of makeup and a proper dress in hopes that I wouldn't completely frighten Rick off. He left our meeting a bit odd. I didn't blame him.

"It is as if she is on offer for dinner," Astrid said. "You don't want that."

"What do you mean?" Odette asked.

"Oh, run along will you?" Astrid swatted at them. "Shoo! Find something to do."

The little girls left, annoyed they were being left out. Astrid was, as usual, glad to be left out of whatever this society nonsense was. She wanted to be free but not free to attend dinners solely for the interest of eligible men. I wasn't much for this, either. I knew in some backward sort of way that this was a last-ditch effort—my lone shot. I was born into this hell, and I would have to dig myself out on my own, too.

"He's not hard on the eyes," Astrid said. "You could do far worse."

"Do you know what his nickname is? Per him?" I asked.

I watched her shrug in the mirror.

"Rick the Prick."

She burst out laughing. "Oh my God! That's brilliant. Can we call him Prickard?"

I snickered. "He's been up to some trouble. I dunno. I can suffer through it—"

"Why not wear her down?" Astrid asked. "You find another man—"

"Because she wants a man she thinks will control me as best as he can. The thing is, that man doesn't have his life together. I am more organised than he is. And for that, I am grateful. Because I will be fine."

"Don't you want to fall in love, though?"

"I want to eat, swim, ride my horses, make friends, and play tennis. I don't want to be sequestered here for the rest of my life! I can give up falling in love if I can make the rest of it work. We can coexist. We can make it work. If it was good enough for Mamma—"

"I am not telling you not to do it, Alex. I am just telling you that you don't need to settle on our behalf. We will all be okay. You being miserable isn't the takeaway the little girls need."

"I don't know how much longer I can do this."

"And you think some random man is going to be a better person to answer to?"

"You assume I would answer to any man?" I scoffed. "No. He's not the brightest bulb, I can assure you. I've got this. I might puff up his ego a bit, but really, I will be in control."

My sister quieted.

"Fine," Astrid said. "Know that I love and support you, but that I also think a woman should stand on her own."

"I agree with that. However, right now, we're all stuck in this place. I will have my day but I would never be able to live with myself if I didn't ensure you all were happy. The little girls still have a chance to have a few normal years before adulthood. I could give them that."

I was frightened of what might be next. Without my sisters, I would be much more alone. When I looked at them, the choice was easy. I had been on the other side. I wanted them to be there, too. Of us four, I'd had the most time outside these walls.

"You look lovely, ma'am," Marta said.

I did. Marta gleefully altered my dress, pulling it in at the waist and slightly bringing down the neckline. I finally looked youthful. She promised to continue making nips and tucks here and there to ensure I looked more age-appropriate. Her assessment of my wardrobe was not positive. She was also the nicest person, so she wasn't about to say it was all rubbish even if she felt it.

"Thank you." I stood, giving myself one last look in the mirror. "And I'm off."

I teetered in heels down to the main dining room where I found my grandmother and Rick. Rick stood to greet me, bowing deeply, and waiting for me to sit. Grand-Mama didn't bother to acknowledge me beyond a simple hello.

I took a seat and we all stared awkwardly at the first course as it arrived.

"Do you like Neandia, then?" I tried my hardest to make conversation.

"Oh, well, it is different than I recalled," Rick replied. "The gardens here are lovely. I ran into your sisters."

His voice was nervous. I wasn't sure what to make of that.

"They said, yes. Ingrid thinks you are rather handsome."

Rick snickered. "Tell her I appreciate the confidence boost. She's the littlest one? She was playing in the stream?"

I nodded. "Yes. She rarely can be tied down."

"She has few manners. Is part dog," Celeste snarled.

Rick defended Ingrid. "She's just a child. The girls were nice and full of questions. I can tell you have four bright granddaughters, Your Majesty."

"Bright is relative. Ask anyone about Alexandra's maths scores."

I flushed bright red.

"Oh, I'm so bad at math. I am sure she could smoke me."

Celeste glared. I shot an encouraging look Rick's way.

"Alexandra, I was wondering. Do you ride horses at all?"

"I do," I beamed.

There was nothing I loved more.

"She doesn't ride anymore," Celeste said.

"Oh? Why not?"

"It's not necessary. Risky. There are more suitable sports."

"Do you miss it?" Rick asked, ignoring Celeste.

"Very much," I replied. "I love riding. Grand-Mama says it is a bad idea for me given that I am... well, I'm the queen and I shouldn't ride."

"Kings rode into battle. I think you could manage a lazy stroll," Rick chuckled. "I do not mean to overstep but I, myself, ride."

"What do you do?" I asked.

"Polo."

"Predictable," I snickered.

"Guilty as charged. Is it possible we could go out? For a hack?"

I looked at Celeste. She scowled.

"It would be a good way to get to know one another," I pointed out.

"Yes, if you take protection officers with you." Her tone was less-than-enthusiastic.

"I will remain on my best behaviour and not encourage her to do anything silly," Rick said. "Promise."

"Well, that's good. Your father would not like to hear otherwise," Celeste muttered.

I was overjoyed and excited. Rick was *trying*.

Throughout dinner, I sat quietly and played with my food. I had little interest in talking about anything and eating like I was hungry would provoke anger. Rick held the conversation almost on his own. I knew anything I said would upset Celeste at this point. I didn't want to make matters worse. I had made my point. I had won my argument. That is all there was.

"Are you not a fan of sea bass?" Rick asked.

"Oh, just not very hungry." I lowered my fork gently.

"Is there something else you would rather eat?"

"No, honestly, Your Royal Highness, I'm quite well."

"She doesn't need to pack on the pounds, Rikard. Look at her!" Celeste laughed.

"I think she has a lovely figure," Rick said. "I don't know what you mean. People shouldn't starve themselves. I'd rather see her happy than picking at things. Alexandra, is there something you'd rather have."

He looked at me differently. Was this his genuine interest showing through?

"Dessert?" I asked. "We will have dessert?"

Celeste glared. The answer was yes. There would be dessert, but I would be required to pick at that as well. A good girl and prospective wife has a poor appetite. She makes herself smaller to appear more attractive. That was all Celeste had taught us.

"Chocolate soufflé. But if you don't eat your dinner—"

"Is she not a grown woman, Your Majesty?" Rick cut her off.

I fought a snicker.

"Can she not choose?" He doubled down. "I say bring her two."

Rick was overstepping but I liked this side of him. He was wilful and we were both about to get in trouble.

I was brought two chocolate soufflés, of which I ate both. They were heavenly. I loved chocolate more than life, something he now knew. My grandmother watched in dismay. If she said anything, she'd frighten the plant she'd brought me. If she said nothing, I would hear about it after cake.

After dinner, we took a walk around the garden, followed closely by a guard.

"You're really never alone, are you?"

I shook my head no.

"I'm sorry, Alexandra. That's shitty. You're grown up and she treats you like a child."

"She's dreadful."

"I'm sorry," Rick said. "Look, I don't want to lead you on. I don't know what I will do. I'll get back to you, alright?"

"Okay. I know I'm not what you'd choose. You shouldn't feel obligated—"

"Let me figure out how I can help."

"You don't have to—"

He placed his hands on my shoulders and met my gaze. "You don't deserve this. You girls have grown on me. I know you are responsible for them. I love my family, too. I get what it is like to make sacrifices to save the ones you love. I can only admire you for it."

I wanted him to stay—like this—giving me this look. I wanted him to pull me closer— unsure where that impulse came from. Rick pulled away.

"Now, let me figure out on my end what I can do." He began to walk off.

"Thanks," I said. "Rick?"

"Yes?" Rick turned, running his fingers through his blonde curls.

"I promise you that if you choose to do it, I will treat you with respect and give you space."

He nodded. "I appreciate that, Alexandra."

He disappeared into the darkness, heading back to the palace. I wanted him to say yes unequivocally. I hoped he would, anyway. I wanted to know if I would be free soon. I longed to tell my sisters the good news, but it would have to wait. I had to trust that Rick wasn't the big asshole I assumed he was in the beginning.

TEN

RICK

I went to bed thinking Alexandra lost her marbles, but she made more sense with time and context. Her grandmother was vile, yes. But was she as bad as Alexandra made me believe? Alexandra wanted freedom, but why tie herself to me? If she made things up, what did she gain? I gathered she did not want me in a romantic sense —at least not yet—so she wasn't here to trap me. She didn't seem like that kind of girl. I mulled it over. The more I laced the threads, the more I believed her.

My father called me at half past six.

"Rikard, we need to talk."

Never a good sign.

I sat up, cradling my phone against my ear. "What?"

"That bastard who blackmailed me wasn't supposed to go to the press. Now, he's gone to the press."

"Who? What?"

"The woman's husband."

I snapped out of my stupor. "He went to the press?"

"He did. They want a comment. Rick, it is only a matter of time before this blows up. I cannot hold them off forever. No more pay-outs —I told you."

"Give me a few hours," I said.

"A few hours for what?"

"I have an idea."

I did not have an idea. I had no idea. However, I needed to buy time.

"I will call you back at noon and we will... well, I don't know what we will do."

His voice wasn't angry. It was frightening. My blood ran cold. A scandal of this magnitude could permanently end the institution. My father wasn't perfect, but he was a good man who cared about the future of Lundhavn and its people. I still loved her. I probably always would, but this was my family. Even I could admit that I loved them. And, even if I did not care for my father—I did—my poor mother deserved better than what I dealt her.

Panicked, I pulled on enough clothes to go out and walk in the garden. I went back to the stream and sat. I thought about the way that Alexandra's baby sister had been playing in the stream the day before, I took my shoes off, rolled up my trousers and sat there with my feet in the cold water. I needed something to wake me up.

I dialled her. She answered.

"You cannot call me."

"Bridget... please do not hang up."

"This... we cannot... my settlement is at risk—"

"I know. This is not personal. Or, rather, it's not an attempt to get back together."

"Oh," she said. "Alright. What do you need?"

"Anders went to the press. And he's telling everyone about it."

"I cannot control what Anders does."

"Bridget, it's my family. I need your help. Please, if not for me just know that this will hurt my mother—"

"When you and I got lazy and got caught, that was because you swore you would marry me. And now you won't—"

"I can't."

"He promised not to talk and now he has," Bridget said. "So what difference does it make?"

"A lot of difference."

"You were never going to marry me, Rick. You were never all that serious."

"I was. I love you, Bridget. I do. And it was *you* who wouldn't leave him completely."

"Men like you don't marry girls like me. Staying afforded me security until I could dump him."

"Bridge, please," I begged.

"Goodbye, Rick."

She hung up.

I slammed my phone into the bank of the creek in frustration, kicking my feet. What could I do? I thought I had leverage—assuming she cared enough to pity me. She didn't and I had no pull. I wondered if I could pay them off but came up short.

Hearing her voice pained me. I wanted to see her. All the desire to be near her rushed back but I had no hope. She was no longer in the cards. Never again would I hold her or wake up next to her. The finality hit me like a wall. We'd never had the conversation to end it. I'd been radio silent because of my father's threat to cut me off.

I looked at the grove of trees shading a bench and focused on the sound of leaves flapping. The breeze distracted me momentarily before it dawned on me. A distraction was what I needed. If it could be done, I would pivot. The press wanted to line their pockets with a scandal but maybe they could print money instead with a juicy feel-good story.

Martin stood behind me. I knew he'd heard everything. He was very much aware of the situation.

"What would you do?" I asked. "If the press knew and you needed to spare your entire family the shame, what would you do, Martin?"

"The press work where the money is. If his story is most compelling and they have already paid, it will be imperative they run it. They have families to feed, too. He's in the wrong. He's horrible, but the press are just trying to pay their employees. Unless they have a better offer, I know they will run the story. It's sad. I am sorry."

"We need to give them a better story, then," I said.

"Yes, that could work. But what?"

"Well, I am not about to cure cancer, Martin. However, I do have a girl proposing a marriage scheme and what do the press like more than royal weddings?"

"Sir, your brother was just married."

"And he dated Marie in total secret. There was no lead-up. They barely allowed the press to do anything until the big day. They would be salivating for a royal-marrying-royal set-up, yeah?"

"I suppose that could work, sir." Martin fought a smile, but I suspected he agreed.

"It will only work if it is the one outlet. We can't let everyone have an exclusive. It's an eye for an eye. We give them an even juicier exclusive, right?"

"That makes sense, sir."

I was elated. I dialled my father.

"I have a proposition," I said. "For the press. Whichever outlet has the proof. Is it only the one?"

"Yes. It is an exclusive. They paid him handsomely."

"Then we need to guarantee we have something that can bring in more money."

"We just had a royal wedding. While I'd like to believe that your brother was going to produce an heir shortly, it could... be awhile. I wouldn't bank on that."

"Could we not sell them another royal wedding and let them break the scandal of an engagement?"

"Plant it?"

"More—offer them an exclusive look into a love story-turned-wedding. My affair is well done and over with. But, if I was falling for another woman and about to marry into another royal family—fairytale and all that—it could be juicy."

"Are you about to marry into another family?"

"I could be?"

"Do you get on with Alexandra? Because you swore up and down the girl was unappetising."

"I enjoy her company. We have plans to go out riding shortly."

"Really? That is good."

"I can make it work if it will spare you and Mamma the humiliation, Pappa."

"And you haven't angered her?"

"No," I lied.

I had but she was willing to put it away and accept me if I otherwise left her alone.

"I will float the idea. Is Alexandra comfortable with this?"

"She will be, yes," I answered.

"I will see if it works." Father sounded suspicious, but there were no easy answers.

I sat, wondering where I went wrong with my life and if this was what I had to look forward to—a sham marriage, press coverage to cover my affair with a married woman, and a move to another country. It was terrible. I could only blame myself, though. My poor decisions landed me here.

I pulled my shoes on and disappeared to my room, hearing no more from my father. Soon, Martin appeared.

"Sir, breakfast is being prepared in the kitchen. Will you take your meal here or in the dining room?"

I wanted to have breakfast here, but that would appear antisocial. Now, more than ever, I needed to impress Alexandra with how wonderful I was. I had no room for error. I needed her to marry me *and* go along with the press scheme.

"In the dining room," I answered.

"Follow me, sir," a footman said.

I walked to the family dining room and was introduced, but Alexandra was nowhere to be found. I encountered Celeste and several men she introduced as her courtiers.

"Will Her Majesty be joining us?" I asked.

"The girl will not be joining us," Celeste answered.

The way she flippantly referred to Alexandra as "the girl" annoyed me. Like it or not, Alexandra was a queen. Despite this regency and through no fault of her own, she was the monarch. She deserved the respect. I didn't understand how Celeste squared an arranged marriage to a man of nearly thirty by referring to her granddaughter as "the girl".

"Oh. Well, that's a shame. I was hoping to make plans with her for later," I said.

"Plans? I must remind you, Your Royal Highness, that her reputation is sterling," a male courtier said.

"Lord William, it's alright," the Dowager Queen said. "Well, depending on his intent."

"I wanted to take her out on a hack, as I indicated. If we are to be serious about this, I would like to get to know her better. She wants the same. We discussed it on our short walk yesterday," I explained. "She's a sweet woman."

That wasn't a lie. I might not have been attracted to her, but Alexandra was sweet and clever. She may have also been slightly mad, but you took the good with the bad. Celeste almost recoiled at my compliment.

"It is good for them," Lord William said. "Majesty, they must acquaint themselves if they are to pursue this. Is that your intent then?"

Everyone stared at me. I swallowed hard.

"I would like to, yes. I think it will be good for us both. She is a wonderful person, a kind one, and we are connected in some sort of way. It sounds crazy, but... I do enjoy her company very much."

Celeste smiled. I couldn't tell if this was good or not, but I hoped it meant Alexandra and I would be let off the leash a bit.

"I'd like a moment to get to know her still," I said. "And to propose properly, of course."

That would buy me time.

"But it would be good for your country and mine. There is great media interest in covering such an event in Lundhavn. It's my understanding, that since the great King's death years ago, the country has been looking for a bit of happiness. Alexandra and I believe that anything which raises morale is the right thing to do. We are committed to securing the institution—for us both."

Celeste beamed. "That sounds lovely."

"A marriage would be popular," Lord William said. "Especially a royal groom. That would be a fairytale. They'd make a happy, handsome couple. But we need to be careful how we approach—"

"I think we might use the media to build the narrative and invite them in." I hoped I wasn't getting in over my head.

"We do not do that."

"Yes, I know. It is a risk—all things are—but this would be so very curated. You see, one of the big problems with my brother's wedding was that the costs were obscene, and he and his wife never spoke to the press. People felt out of it and wondered if it was all just something on the take. I'd hate for anyone to think that about Alexandra. I don't mean to be critical, but people don't feel they know her. She's a wonderful person. If people got to know her, it would be a bonus for your country and the institution. Because what you need is a succession plan—one that secures it for years, right? The world is changing, ma'am. I am saying what I saw happened with my brother's wedding."

Celeste groaned.

Another courtier added, "Ma'am he may have a point. The biggest criticism of Alexandra is that no one knows anything about her. People think she is only a sterile figurehead. A royal engagement with a bit of press coverage couldn't hurt. And it could defray some of the costs of a grand celebration."

Lord William nodded. He was Celeste's henchman. I knew it now.

"Get her to articulate this to me, Rikard, and we will discuss the particulars," Celeste said.

I tried not to grin too wide. We were on our way. Now, I only hoped my father was able to get it together with our press nightmare. If he couldn't, there was no way Alexandra would marry me. She was too good to put up with such a scandal and I wouldn't drag her down with me.

Eleven

Alexandra

Rick invited me out on a hack the day following dinner with Celeste. I was not invited to breakfast, which made me uncomfortable. Frightened about what she told him in my absence, I focused instead on the barn. My sisters were jealous. It had been years since any of us had been allowed to climb onto a horse. It was "too risky" but so was Rick getting away. So, Celeste stayed quiet.

I spent an hour planning what to wear—unlike me. I wasn't interested in Rick in a genuine sense, but impressions mattered. I didn't want him to see me as an ogre if he was still on the fence. He'd have to look at me every day for at least a couple of years. Maybe he'd have to look at me long enough for us to struggle through having children. That idea did *not* appeal to me at this time, but I'd cross that bridge when I got there.

We rode over to the stables together, spending time sitting close to one another. I wanted it to work. I wanted a connection with him that went beyond a business relationship. I'd felt something the night before, but now it vanished. We had little in common until we picked our mounts at the barn.

There, we immediately bonded over horses. Rick wasn't just a polo player. Unlike many of the men in our social strata who would show up, ride a few horses at a match, and then leave, he was tender with herd. He *doted*. They weren't solely a means to an end with his sport. I respected that about him. The common bond broke us out of our shells.

We headed out to the trails.

"We have the nicest trails to have a hack on," I said. "I know you do not find Neandia exciting, Rick, but... we have some areas of natural beauty. This place is a little hideaway. You'll grow to love it if you spend time here."

"It's very nice—like your garden. Do you not come here? It is beautiful."

"I used to stay here for hours! Before his health declined, I would come out here every day with my grandfather. Asti and I hacked out with him most days. Then, when he couldn't manage that, he would sit in the stands of the indoor ring and watch our lessons. We kept up with it until Celeste put a stop to it a couple of years ago. I had a fall—not even a bad one—on a green horse and she refused to let any of us return."

Rick grimaced as we trotted down the lane. "Well, that would make me go crazy. It's my favourite place to escape to. I can think. No one bothers me. I've taken refuge at the barn as of late. Shame you cannot do the same."

"I agree."

"If I stay on for a bit, do you think she will ease up and let you come with me?"

I perked up. "I'd assume yes. Would you consider it?"

"I have," Rick said.

"So, you changed your mind?"

"I softened to the idea, Alexandra. I enjoy your company enough to enter into some sort of agreement. It might be the best thing for us both. Celeste is oppressive. I would like to help you. I am obligated to help."

"But would you be able to manage it? I mean, we're... in an agreement?"

"I am alright with that for now. It's not forever, right? We do this to get you your freedom, give everyone a fairytale, and then reassess."

I smiled. "And should you... well, I am not encouraging things... but it's not unusual that a man in your position might..."

He shook his head. "I appreciate that, Alexandra. We do not need to address it now. I don't need to discuss this."

"I don't know what I can promise you, Rick. I'd hate to see you miserable. I know I don't know you, but it isn't my intent—"

"I know. Don't apologise, Alexandra."

I blushed, not sure what to say. He was dutiful. Maybe we could do this after all? I wasn't sure what it would completely require, but I was excited to try. I could taste freedom. His intent to break me out of the palace walls to go riding alone spoke volumes. I trusted him more than I should, but it was a better chance to be happy than being locked in the palace walls with a tyrant. So far, he did not seem a control freak.

"Race me?" I asked, knowing full well my mount was faster.

I gave Rick no time to react, kicking my horse into a rolling canter. I gave him a moment to catch up before flicking my gelding's shoulder with a crop and picking up a gallop. The horse roared forward. It was heaven to have the wind in my face. Seeing the world through a horse's ears was the greatest blessing. I relished it until I pulled up at a large paddock gate. Inside, broodmares and foals grazed.

Rick soon caught up.

"Unfair!" He laughed. "Damn, you are fast!"

I beamed. "I can be, yes."

"Having fun at my expense?"

"Oh, come on. It's not that bad, Rick."

He chuckled as I opened the gate and let him through. We walked out for a bit, finally finding the herd grazing. Foals ran up, curious about the new arrivals. We let our horses munch momentarily. As they grazed, we played with the foals.

"New babies are my favourite thing," I said. "Who doesn't love foals?"

"Pesky things," Rick said as a liver chestnut nibbled his bootlace.

I giggled. "That one is Rickie. I got to come out here for a PR stunt on the day he was born."

"No wonder he likes me."

"Clearly."

"You have such stunning land, Alexandra. It's heaven out here."

"You don't have anything like this?"

"We have pastures, but our country is mountainous. It doesn't afford vast spaces like this. It's beautiful in a different way. Have you never been to Lundhavn?"

I shook my head. "Embarrassed to tell you I have not, but I will be honest. I have been few places outside of here, Belgium, and Denmark. My mother was Danish—"

"That I know. Well, we will be expected to have a stop in Lundhavn, of course. If we are to do this thing, then that will be expected."

I was unsure of how to react. Was he on board now? Was this a confirmation? Was I getting married? It was all confusing. I needed a final determination—something clear to go on. If so, we needed to make plans. But how?

"How do we do it? And is this your final decision?"

Rick nodded. "I would like to try. And I think I have some ideas about how to make this a bit better for us both. Let's cause a media firestorm."

I cocked my head. "How? Why?"

"Tip off the press. Sell it. Make it the greatest love story of all time. I'm not the best actor, but I can be convincing. And you are surprisingly good at getting your point across. We could be a dynamic duo, Alexandra."

I blushed. "Well, I'm shy."

"I'm not. We're good."

"How do we do that?"

"Hire a real publicist to manage it. Work with the press through back channels. They will make your grandmother and my parents *very* happy with lovely, fluffy stories that make us seem the Couple of the Century."

I smiled. "And it will make the people happy."

"Exactly! Celeste may have the upper hand now, but when people fall in love with you, they will want more and more of you—and us—than boring old Celeste. She's old news."

"People loved her."

"Nah. We're much more attractive, I think."

I snickered.

"Do you want to do it? Leave breadcrumbs for a couple of weeks and blow it up? Then, announce it. Make a big deal out of it. We gotta play it up. We're a couple now. We will get caught because we're so in love that we cannot hide it anymore."

"How will we do that?"

"Plant stories. Get caught. Finally admit we're getting married. And then do the thing. By that point, we will already have the date held and throw ourselves into full planning mode. I leave that up to you, of course."

I smiled. "Fairytale wedding even if it's a farce?"

"It's a farce but the ends will justify the means. You will be free, Alexandra. Your sisters can do their own things. We will make the people happy. We are the heroes in this timeline."

"The heroes," I echoed, thinking it through. "I've never thought of myself as a hero."

"You will be the wonderful heroine who falls for the handsome prince," Rick said. "I will be taken aback by the cunning queen. And together, we will rule the world, right?"

"We will rule the world. Let's do it!"

I locked eyes with him, unable to escape his boyish grin. This must do for now.

We returned to the stables having decided on a plan. I was golden, beaming ear-to-ear over our agreement. However, my happiness was short-lived. Rick and I took the horses back to their paddocks, chatting all the while. As far as horses were concerned, we were a united front. We both loved them. Talking about this was easy. Everyone was in good spirits until we ended up back in the stable aisle.

There, several grooms assembled.

"What is going on?" I asked in French.

I saw a horse down in a stall. It was my beloved Barney. My heart raced.

"Barney," I said, pushing the grooms aside.

I sat in the stall, pleading with him to get up.

He was colicking. Feeling helpless I stood and pulled, begging him to stand. I sobbed, demanding he comply in three languages. I felt terrible. Losing a horse was awful but losing one to colic was even worse. It wasn't the first time we'd lost an animal like this, but it might be the hardest loss yet. Barney was everything! If we didn't get him up he would be a goner.

Tears in my eyes, I turned to Rick.

"Can you help me get him up?"

Rick nodded and moved closer. He knew as well as I how bad this was.

He took charge. "Can someone bring me a lunge line?"

A groom dashed in with one as soon as he could find what Rick needed.

"Now. Just light pressure as if he's skittish getting on the trailer. Alexandra, pull when we start pushing."

I understood, even with my brain addled.

"Alright. Un, deux, trois," I said.

Rick pushed. I pulled. We clucked our hearts out.

"Alexandra," Rick said, remarkably calm. "Sweetheart, can you just try again? Try one more time. Give him lots of encouragement."

I nodded bravely. We counted once more. The horse thought about it but remained unsure. Rick gave him a bit of encouragement, smacking him hard on the rear. Barney did not like this. He pinned his ears and lurched forward, managing to nearly nail Rick with his hind right hoof. It worked! My boy was standing again!

"See, the asshole has some fight left in him. Sorry, bud. I didn't mean to frighten you, okay?"

Rick patted Barney on the shoulder who pinned his ears in protest.

I showered the horse in praise. "Good boy. Very, very good boy. We're going to get the vet here and we will make you better. Promise. We'll stay with you until you're up and good. Okay?"

It wasn't over yet. We still had many walks to do. Colic was a long road. It wasn't over until the horse's gut caught up and decided to work again. We could only hope that with some medication and movement, Barney would work it out. I felt helpless, but Rick didn't give up. He stayed with me even if he didn't have to. Rick wasn't all bad.

"So, this guy, he's special then?" Rick asked.

We were in the middle of our third long walk with Barney. There were some good signs. If he didn't improve soon, he'd be on the next float to the equine hospital in Belgium. I wanted to avoid that. At Barney's age, he would be lucky to survive the surgery.

"He was my grandfather's favourite mount. And he's in his late twenties. He's one of the few reminders of Grand-Papa. When he goes, I will be broken. And this... it cannot end like this."

"Nah. It won't. He's too dignified and feisty an old man," Rick said.

I giggled. "He's still cross with you!"

"Well, it was all for progress. I am sorry, buddy. I will need to earn my way back into your good graces, huh?"

Barney was unimpressed.

"Okay, that's fifty minutes. Time to break." Rick turned off the alarm.

We put Barney in cross-ties. I slid down a wall to sit in the aisle. I looked at the horse, my chin resting on my knees. I wanted him to perk up so badly. He must pull through! It would destroy Ingrid to lose Barney.

"He's Ingrid's favourite, too," I said. "It wasn't just Grand-Pere. He is such a good old man, Rick. It would end Ingy if we lost him."

"I can tell. Everyone is pulling for him. Me included."

Rick sat next to me, our shoulders touching.

"I'm sorry. I don't want you to think I've imprisoned you here."

"Nah. At a stables? Impossible, Alexandra! I could spend all my days like this. Well, with better circumstances, but... I am happiest with the horses. I suspect you are, too?"

I nodded. "I missed this—the smell of the barn, the sound of horse hooves on the aisle, and the feeling of horsehair getting stuck in my mouth. This time of year—"

"They're always shedding like crazy. Yeah. Pumice stones."

I laughed. "For sure! Look, I am so sorry. This was a chance for us to get to know one another and... now what?"

"We've got nothing but time," Rick said. There was a sweetness in his voice. Was he warming up to me? I assumed yes.

"I guess."

"There is no better way to get to know someone than this. Well, if you're a horse person?"

"We're all a bit odd, yes."

He smiled, displaying dimples—glorious dimples! And then, his chin! He spoke, but I was oblivious. I now found him especially handsome—sweaty, dusty, down-to-earth. I tried not to let it show. Again, this was a ruse. We were doing this for legitimate reasons. I wasn't about to *fall* for him. He was the annoying prince, but I couldn't ignore the way his smile made me feel.

"You know, horse people are good people," Rick said. "I think we'll get on just fine."

"Uh-huh."

I had a sudden urge to kiss him. This was new! It was the way he looked at me. Maybe I was off-kilter or just delirious by this point in the evening, but I so badly wished to lean my face closer and graze my lips to his. I knew it would feel good. Certainly, Rick had kissed *plenty* of girls, so it's not like I would appal him, right? Then, as I debated what to do, we turned towards a noise.

Plop!

We both smiled.

"Well, fuck!" Rick chuckled.

I leapt up, elated to see horse manure in the barn aisle. Suddenly, all was well. I gave Barney a big hug and kiss. He snorted in my face. He was fine now. He'd live to see another day. I was so relieved.

Barney let out a long fart and we burst into laughter.

"Well, sorry. He's a bit rude," I laughed.

"It's okay. I'll take it."

"Sorry we wasted the evening like this, Rikard."

"It was lovely. No better way to get to know someone than in a crisis waiting for a horse to take a shit," Rick said. "I think we did fine."

"We made a good team," I agreed.

Twelve

Rick

Is Love in the Heir?

Prince Rikard was spotted in Neandia with none other than Queen Alexandra. They held hands and got cosy in these exclusive photos taken of the Prince with the twenty-one-year-old monarch. Not much is known about the until-now reclusive young queen. She is an enigma. Love between two royals is a sweet surprise. While both palaces say the two were merely out for a ride at the Queen's stables on the royal estate in the Neandian countryside, we call foul on that account. The Palace in Blavenberg says the Prince is in residence in Neandia in preparation for the Gold Cup polo tournament. Many foreign royals are expected to arrive from throughout Europe for the charity event.

Guilt befell me as I led Alexandra into a full-on fake arranged marriage. She lacked a complete picture of our circumstances, but she was down to play games with the tabloids that haunted our lives. Thankfully, our press were game. The agreement was that *Exclusive,* our big broadsheet in Lundhavn, would run all stories first.

And run they did! Without so much as a request, Alexandra and I were spotted outside her barn together with photographers staged in the bushes. Photos of us holding hands and looking oh-too-cosy were enough evidence. The press cover-up was a win-win for us both.

It worked. Alexandra was happier than I had seen her. She was freer, lighter. It was as if the floodgates were opening. After the night nursing poor Barney back to health, I struggled to lie to her. Something about her grew on me. The more she let me in, the more I liked her. And the more we successfully hoodwinked the press, the happier we both were. She came alive. I didn't expect to feel anything, but I was happy to be part of this story. We did it together, but Alexandra was the one who had the most to gain—a real, free life was waiting.

Besides our barn spotting, the press caught us having a casual dinner alongside her sister Astrid in town. We briefly held hands. It was above board because we had a chaperone. We had plausible deniability but it all felt a bit naughty. It didn't hurt that Alexandra was as happy as ever to be out, free, and eating a big dinner. Her enthusiasm made the mundane more interesting. And while holding hands wasn't inappropriate, it was a choice way to anger one's octogenarian oppressor.

Then, came the Gold Cup—one of the most important events of the season. While it changed hands every year, Neandia was hosting. My entire string appeared the week before the event. We were spotted arriving at the grounds the night before the event to check on my horses.

"I'm going to get flak for this," Alexandra said as we walked into the barn, always under the eye of a waiting telephoto lens.

"What?" I asked.

"The dress."

"The dress is fine."

"We altered it to pull the hem up," Alexandra said. "The minute she sees the papers and that I went out like this... she'll take it out on me."

"You look great. You're young, Alexandra. Celeste can't possibly think you should always dress like you're fifty."

Alexandra crossed her arms. I took her in—not seeing the issue. I came onto girls wearing far less. She looked saintly in the white floral number. It was perfectly serviceable for a Thursday evening out with friends. If anything, it was an improvement on her regular wardrobe. Apart from her gear for the barn, she often looked overdressed and buttoned up.

"You should be able to dress the way you want," I said. "Live a little! She can bitch all she wants, but you hold the cards here. They are salivating over you. It would be to her detriment to actively sabotage you."

I had the urge to put her at ease. It seemed appropriate to rub her back to comfort her. It might have been an overreach, but ignoring her felt wooden.

She looked at me, big blue eyes vulnerable. "You mean that? You don't care if we catch flak?"

"I will defend your right to wear what you choose, Alexandra. That's an essential part of being a person. You don't seem the type to parade around in a club dress. *That* will get you in trouble. Of course, if you did, I'd still defend you."

"Really?"

"It's ridiculous. You're a grown woman! People shouldn't care what you wear. I know that's easy for me to say, Alexandra, but I don't believe in telling women what to wear. It's contrary to how I was raised."

She smiled. "That's nice. We should visit Lundhavn soon. And then I shall buy *all* the clothes and be nothing but vindicated."

"We should, yes," I agreed.

She doted on my horses lovingly, satisfied somehow that I would stand up for her. It was heartbreaking in a way I didn't anticipate. I began to worry the other shoe would drop when she found out who I was deep down. All the while, my protectiveness of her and her sisters won out. She didn't deserve this. I may have been a prick, but I didn't think of women as property. My parents raised me better than that. Women were people.

We departed in the car.

"Can you not ever drive yourself as monarch?" I asked.

"I cannot drive at all," Alexandra answered.

"You do not know how to drive?"

"It sounds like a dream," Alexandra said. "But I never got the opportunity."

It was so sad. She couldn't drive. Independent people drove cars!

"I cannot drive a car. I cannot dance. I cannot do a lot of things normal people my age do. They let you drive?"

Celeste and her courtiers saw Alexandra and her sisters as pawns to control. They reduced them to silly girls over which to exert themselves. It was deplorable. I dug in. Three weeks in, I wasn't the man they wanted, but I was probably the man they needed.

"Of course. I normally drive at home," I said. "You really cannot dance?"

She shook her head. Something about that was even sadder. The girl was neglected. I suspected if her parents were alive, things would be different. I wish they had been there for her. I realised what I read as boring wasn't that at all. Alexandra never had the benefit of growing into someone with the opportunity to have hobbies and love things. She wasn't boring. She was clever but deprived. The more we spoke, the more I read her as quick and eager to learn. She was a sponge, wanting to feel everything and do everything. Alexandra deserved the chance to spread her wings.

"We'll remedy both," I promised.

"I will need to learn to dance. But drive?"

"Do you want to drive?"

She nodded. "And I would drive if only I were able to even get a moment to myself. I am not stupid, Rick. I graduated top of my class —early. I am clever and could easily drive a car."

"Of course," I agreed.

"Everyone thinks I am stupid. They underestimate me. I... I hate it. I know you don't know me that well, but... I don't want you thinking I'm daft."

"God, no! I don't think that, Alexandra. You engineered a plan to free yourself and the girls and ran in front of a train—all with a massive weight around your neck in the form of a complicated prince."

She snickered. "Well, as long as we're clear. I would like to learn to drive, though. All joking and whinging aside."

I squeezed her hand, instinctively. It was an urge that hit me suddenly. It was sincere. "I will teach you as soon as I can. If you want to learn, you should."

She grinned like the Cheshire Cat. It was infectious. I beamed back.

"Thank you! I want to do that. I cannot believe you'd... offer? Can you do that?"

"You tell me, Your Majesty." I chuckled. "What do you want me to do?"

"I want to learn to drive. I want to dance. I cannot think of much else now, Rick."

"Well, tell me when you find out," he said.

"I want to take up tennis again," she spitballed. "And go out to dinner regularly. I want to taste the best, most avant-garde food. I want to go shopping and have fun. I want to make friends. I want to do all those things."

It broke my heart.

"I am sorry I didn't believe you at the start. I couldn't imagine growing up like you did. You were locked up at a time when everyone else gets to spend exploring, making terrible choices, and learning from their mistakes. You didn't even get that chance to find yourself. It makes me sad, Alexandra."

She took my hand in both hers. They were tiny, soft, and warm. She was earnest.

"I appreciate that so much. Thank you for seeing me. But don't pity me, Rick. Just give me space to be myself and we'll call it even. That's the best you could do for me."

"I will," I promised.

"Why do you care? You don't have to."

"Because I like you," I said. "And your sisters. I want to see you all happy. I might be a dickhead. And yes, I'm getting something out of this, too, but I care about you, Alexandra."

She smiled. "I appreciate that."

I felt a pang of guilt. I was getting more than she knew. She was saving my ass. She was sparing my family an abundance of pain. And she also may still be in the crosshairs someday if it ever came out. I cared enough about her that I could worry, but not enough to spare her. She didn't know a thing and I was sure I'd take that to my grave.

"Don't worry about me, okay? Just enjoy the next few months of being the belle of the ball."

"Hard to believe I could be."

"You will be," I assured.

"And tomorrow?"

"We will put on a hell of a show this weekend," I said. "I promise you. The press will be eating out of our hands."

Thirteen

Alexandra

Rick and I played it cool for the first day of the tournament. We were only spotted together momentarily. I played adoring girlfriend from afar. I didn't particularly care for polo, but it meant I got out of the house. Astrid and I were invited to the polo association's tent to mingle with charity. I wrote a check, of course. Or, I had been told I had since I couldn't do anything much. I got to see the Belgians again.

I nearly tripped over the glamorous Brits. They were the most popular royals—the beautiful people. All their clothes were so posh and chic.

"We need to take fashion notes," Astrid said. "Look at them all. They're so fab."

"I am so jealous. I'm like the frumpy queen. Compared to the others."

"It's unfair. Natalie and Kiersten are sisters and Margaux is their cousin," Astrid said. "I'd never seen them with my own eyes. But look! Their family has deep genetic strength. They all look so alike."

"Right?"

"It's freaky," Astrid said.

"Asti, how do I find attractive clothes?"

"Ask Marta. Let's see what she can do. She's magical, right?"

"I hope. I am so out of it. What if I'm honestly harming Rick by bringing him down? He's far more glamorous."

"Nonsense," Astrid squeezed my hand. "You make a surprisingly attractive couple. I still am unsure of him. I am suss, but I can admit that much."

I looked out over the championship match underway. Rick was focused on the game at hand and couldn't have cared about me. However, every point he got, I had to act like I was jumping out of my skin. And, in a way, I was happy to play along with the handsome prince on a white horse narrative. It was easy given that the final horse he was taking out today was an almost white grey with lots of chrome. Of his entire string, I adored this mount the most.

"He is surprisingly dutiful," I said.

And handsome.

I didn't add that part. Not only was it obvious, but Astrid would tease me mercilessly. I couldn't get girlish. Not now. Not ever. I'd never been around men much and never any so handsome. The closest we came to attractive men was the tutor we'd had as teenagers—Rudy. He was handsome in a bookish way. Rick wasn't a nerd or an intellectual but was hot. He was a jock, and in a pair of breeches and a fitted polo, I couldn't deny he was swoon-worthy. I wondered why he bothered with me at all. Anytime he placed his hand on my back or took my hand in his, I marvelled at his size-. I had uncomfortable thoughts about other things his hands could do.

Rick was riding well. He'd had a great day which made the British-Norwegian camp nervous. They'd been the favourites coming in and had the most star power and money. Rick's team was a dark horse. Today, they were on fire. I became invested about the halfway point. I wanted to watch the underdog trounce the Brits.

"You are getting interested," Astrid said. "You want him to win."

"Of course, I do," I scoffed.

"No, you *really* want him to win."

I shrugged. "What is the harm in that?"

"I am just pointing out that it's a slippery slope. The lady wears the knight's colours and ends up in his bed after he triumphs at the joust. I'm just sayin'…"

"Don't be ridiculous! Where do you get this stuff?"

"Books, darling. Books are brilliant. You should read them. It's how I've learned anything about sex, I swear. Celeste thinks they are chaste. Covers can be deceptive. They aren't."

"I don't want to read your smut, sister."

Astrid snickered. "It's not smut. It's literature. People call it smut because female sexuality makes them uncomfortable. I embraced it. I love a happily ever after when a heroine ends up with a man who meets her every need. I suspect book boyfriends are better than real boyfriends, not that I would know…"

Her voice trailed. We were both starved for any male affection. And at this moment, while I was allowed to parade around with a man I had no business with, Astrid was stuck in the tower still. I broke her out as I could—to keep an air of chastity about—however, she couldn't even look. Of all my sisters, Astrid was the most interested in boys.

"Your time will come," I said. "And you will fall in love—properly—with the perfect man. Don't fret. I am working on it."

"Just don't fall for the wrong knight—really fall—for that knight," Astrid said. "I don't want to see you get your heart broken. Men like Rick… they'll break your heart."

"He means well. And I'm not jumping into bed with the wrong knight, Astrid."

"What does he expect?"

"We have clear boundaries, okay? You wouldn't get it."

I was frustrated. On one hand, part of me wondered if we would ever end up in bed. The thought terrified me. I knew nothing of sex other than the basic mechanics and suspected he knew a hell of a lot more. I'd never live up to expectations. On the other hand, he was gorgeous and the mere idea of exciting him made my heart leap.

I knew Rick could be an asshole and suspected he saw me as a charity case—feeling superior by helping us out—but I had the upper hand. Holding all the cards on what happened in our "romantic" lives, I'd let him play the hero, but I was the heroine of my own story saving the day.

He was the pawn, right? He agreed to it because of our mutual benefit, but could we have fun? Maybe in a year, we'd feel differently than we did now.

"I do get it. I know the stakes. Alexandra, when you play with matches—"

"Asti, I'm done talking about this with you." I left her to find another drink.

"Alex!"

I ignored her. Picking up a glass of champagne, I honed in on a piece of cake. Angry with my sister, I ate it in an act of protest. I would catch hell for my weight gain, but I neither feared Celeste nor cared. It suited me much better. I felt more like a woman—a happy woman. Celeste did not own me. I would savour every lovely bit of food.

I missed so much in life. Rick wasn't perfect—far from it—but he had a protective side that made me swoon. He was a kind-hearted asshole. Maybe I could turn him into a reformed scoundrel and kick the Rick the Prick moniker to the curb? We could rewrite our stories together. And I held the power to help him. Together, we'd take back our narrative. Or, at least, that was my assumption as I sat there.

"You think you own it," Astrid dug in. "And I hope you do. I just cannot help but worry about you, Alexandra. You are doing so much— so fast—and I fear Celeste's retribution."

"I know you do," I said. "But I am done living in fear because of her nonsense, Asti. And Rick won't put up with it. He's good for that much, okay? I trust him on that. And can you please trust me? I'm not an idiot, Astrid."

"I know. You're doing more for us than I would be willing to do."

"I doubt that is true, Astrid."

"No. I'd not want this. He's hot, but I am unwilling to tie myself down to anyone until I've had fun."

"I think he knows the stakes are high. I will grant you that he's flawed but deep down, I do think there is good in him."

Astrid looked across the field and shook her head. "I hope he's less wanker and more benevolent patriarch—for your sake and ours."

Fourteen

I played the best game of my life and had one of my greatest wins. I'd shown up to trounce the British and Norwegian princes in a legendary way and I couldn't have ridden any higher by my final goal. Triumphant, I celebrated with the rest of the guys before noticing Alexandra at the field's edge.

She sweetly cheered for us the entire weekend. She didn't know the game well but was a good sport. It didn't hurt team morale to have the Queen and Princess Astrid on hand. I couldn't complain. I trotted over to Alexandra's sweet face, hidden partially by a big hat.

Sweat be damned, she doted on my horse.

"A brilliant job," she cooed. "You were such a good baby. Such a lovely job."

"I get no credit?" I joked.

She looked up. "Yes, Rick. You do. You got the job done. I secretly love watching the British women seethe."

I grinned. "Ah, Her Majesty does have a dark side."

"I do, yes," Alexandra answered. "Now what?"

"We will get the trophy."

"Obviously," she said.

It was cute. She had no idea what was going on.

"They will award it and likely insist on you doing the honours. Which is great for our photo op."

"What do I do?"

"Just hand it over and take photos like a dutiful, adoring girlfriend. The press will go crazy for it."

Alexandra smiled. "Well, then, well done. You've given us a natural opening."

"I wish I could say my goals were quite so charitable, Your Majesty. I did it because I wanted to win and humiliate the Brits and Norwegians. But I will believe my win was chivalrous if you do."

"Oh, well, let's go with that then." Alexandra patted the horse. "You should go cool her off before she ties up."

"Yes, I should. I will see you shortly."

I departed, handing my favourite mare off to a groom.

The podium scene was a natural place to cause a stir. Typically, if a woman connected to a player presented the trophy, it was a sure sign they were serious. Moreover, it was customary to *kiss* said girl. I assumed that would be alright given Alexandra's endorsement. If I did not do so, the press would suspect we were on the rocks or not together. It was a must. So, I would give her a nice, chaste kiss to prove we were fine—nothing more. I didn't want to frighten the poor thing.

We returned for the awarding of the prize. And, no doubt, they pulled the Queen up to do the honours. She looked nervous but happy —basking in her moment in the sun. That was good for her. And we'd get bragging rights early in the season. I wondered if she'd be permitted to travel to Windsor for our next match. I suspected if we announced our engagement before that, it would work out for us. It would be odd if I travelled without her, wouldn't it?

Alexandra stepped forward to present the trophy in front of the waiting press. People clapped. And that is when I kissed her, our hands both on the trophy. I expected it to be a simple, quick gesture, but, to my surprise, she really went for it. She held onto me for a moment, wrapping her arms around my neck. It wasn't half bad. She knew what she was doing, so I didn't have to fake anything or whip it up. When I pulled away, it was clear she'd surprised even herself in the moment.

She quickly returned to ceremonial mode. As we filed out, my entire team gave me shit in our mother tongue about it. I wasn't even sure what to say.

"Good?" I asked.

"Good." She grinned. "I think."

We didn't get to say much more until we were headed home. She waited around for me to finish, playing the role of girlfriend dutifully. It was so strange. She was the Queen playing twenty-something polo girlfriend and she was good at it. It was believable—as believable as the kiss. She was coming into her own. We were selling it. By the time we were headed back to the palace, the press ate out of our hands.

"You're good at this. That was a convincing way to handle it, Alexandra," I said.

"Really?"

"Yes. Way to sell it. I didn't plan for it to go that well. I was going to be sweet about it and do it to make sure no one suspected anything. Nice call, Your Majesty. We fooled 'em."

She fell quiet.

"You alright? I didn't overstep I hope."

"No." Alexandra's body language closed.

By the time we made it back to the palace, she was silent and prickly.

Where had I gone wrong? I thought I'd behaved. I didn't chat up other girls or flirt with the member of the British delegation I'd slept with about a month before in a one-off in Brussels. I didn't so much as acknowledge her out of respect for Alexandra. What more could have I done?

I walked her back to her quarters, obligated somehow. Then, I wanted to know what I did to hurt her. I didn't like leaving her in this way.

"Alexandra," I said, "what could I do differently? You're upset with me."

"I'm not!"

"You are. Don't lie to me."

"I am cross because you act like you couldn't have *possibly* just kissed me."

"It's a ruse, Alexandra. We are on the same page—"

"Are we? Because I'm down with the ruse, but you acting like kissing me is such a laborious, awful thing is cruel! I thought you enjoyed it enough. I didn't realise you were so repulsed by me that—"

Oof. She had feelings for me. That was bad news.

"Alexandra, I didn't realise... I didn't mean..."

Her face indicated she was about to burst into tears. I was a dickhead. What could I even say?

"I didn't find it off-putting. Are we done playing a game?"

"Of course not," Alexandra said. "But you act like you don't even like me. Rick, we have fun. At least pretend you can bother to stomach this. I cannot continue to act like your girlfriend if you pretend like it's so ridiculous you could ever find me attractive."

I stepped forward, putting my arms on her shoulders. Despite being tiny, she was intimidating when she wanted to be. Her anger and disappointment worked effectively. I acted tough, but I didn't like hurting her. Something about her innocence and sweet demeanour gave me such nerves. So, maybe she was saying she didn't have romantic feelings for me, but she wanted to be respected? I could do that much. I hoped, anyway.

"It's not that I find you repulsive or any of this ridiculous, okay? I find you to be a fun friend. I like hanging out with you. It's not that. I just wanted to be clear—"

She nodded a little. It wasn't overwhelmingly positive.

"You are a sweet person, Alexandra. I don't want to hurt your feelings. I don't mind admitting that I'm lucky to be stuck in this with you. It would suck for it to be someone who made me miserable. You don't. You make me smile. I enjoy being stuck with you. Didn't expect that. Thank you for playing along and being such a good sport today."

"Really?"

"Yes. Look, I'm sorry I hurt your feelings or gave off that impression."

I tried to think about how to make it up to her.

"What do you want to do more than anything?" I asked.

"Just live, Rick."

"Okay. Well, I am going to... I'm going to do something. Eat dinner. Prepare yourself for something. I'll send word."

"What do you mean?"

"Just trust me," I said.

I was spitballing. Time to come up with another brilliant plan to make sure she didn't think I was using her. Sadly, I was. She didn't know it yet. I hoped she never would. I also didn't want to abuse the privilege too much.

FIFTEEN

ALEXANDRA

Rikandra Lives!

Exclusive! spent the weekend at the Gold Cup charity polo tournament in Neandia. We hoped to see more PDA between our royal favourites Prince Rikard and Queen Alexandra. Following some signs of interest between the two—lots of hand-holding and loving looks— we were treated to a royal reveal. In a surprise upset, Prince Rikard's team beat the British-Norwegian conglomerate with a severe handicap going into the game. Their triumph inspired a kiss for the ages after the match. When presenting the trophy, the Prince kissed Neandia's young monarch. If this isn't an official couple, we're surprised. Stay with us as we will wait on tenterhooks for an engagement announcement.

In bed with Asti that evening, I ignored anything Rick promised. I was cross with Rick, licking my wounds, and wanted to forget his stupid promises and stupid face. The problem was if I told her too much, she would say, "I told you so." As such, I only communicated the frustration of him kissing me. I wasn't giving in to him. He tried to redeem himself, but I was hurt. I wanted to believe that his kiss was more about wanting to kiss me than out of obligation.

As much as I denied my feelings, I had them. I didn't expect him to fall in love with me tomorrow. That was ridiculous! I needed him to say he found me attractive enough to kiss me. It was bigger than that. I *was* attractive. The more I dressed like a young woman instead of an elderly debutante, the more men looked at me. I owned this power. I felt more like the heroine in my own story and less like the wallpaper in the background. It thrilled me that people looked to *me* for style advice. They should not have, but that wasn't the point. I was good enough for them. I refused to accept he felt *nothing* for me—not even a bit of attraction.

"I just... I wanted my first kiss to mean something. I didn't think that much through. I wish it hadn't surprised me," I said. "It did."

"How did we get this far without kissing boys?" Astrid asked. "That's the real crime. You shouldn't have your first kiss on a polo field at twenty-one. I shouldn't still be un-kissed at twenty."

"It's all so screwed up," I said. "It's a damn mess, Asti."

"Was it good? Did it feel nice?"

I blushed. "It was nice."

"Lucky! I hate you. Honestly, I know he's an asshole but if I had a free pass to do whatever with a handsome guy, I'd throw caution to the wind."

"Astrid! That's not how this works! And you are the one who believed he was up to no good."

"Look, I want to be kissed, okay? I am sure it's fun. I could make it work."

"It caught me by surprise," I said. "I wanted it to be with someone I loved. That's all."

The truth? The kiss was better than good. It made my entire body tingle and my pulse race. I was desperate to do it again. I kissed hi-m back, wanting more. I wasn't ready to admit that to anyone, but it had been more than nice. I wanted to bask in it. I wanted my heart to continue fluttering. I wish he would have lied to me. I wanted him to want me—desperately. I never expected it, but I felt it.

Marta entered with a knock, holding a note, "A footman handed this off."

The scrawl was a mess compared to my nice handwriting.

> *Meet me in the ballroom at 22:30. Don't get caught.*
> *-Rick the Prick*

I stifled a laugh, reminding myself that he was, indeed, a prick. However, I was intrigued.

"I shouldn't go. He doesn't have my best intentions in mind. Why should I bother?"

"You protest too much and want to go. I doubt he's planning a hookup in the ballroom when he could come in here or invite you down there," Astrid said. "I am curious as to what he is doing, though."

"Can you come with me?" I asked.

"Nah. I don't need to be a third wheel. You don't need a chaperone."

"Maybe I do? Celeste will be livid about the kiss thing in the morning when she reads the papers."

"Meh. You two are about to announce an engagement, right? People expect it. She will have to get over it and live in this century."

Astrid brushed my hair as if I were a puppy. "I've got your back. Go, see the man. And if he's an ass, just leave."

I shrugged. I wasn't excited to let Rick get away with this—wanting to admonish him. If I fobbed him off, he'd probably grovel even more. Part of me loved that. Why? I didn't know. Being in control was fulfilling if not downright *hot*. Ordering an older man around unexpectedly resonated with me.

I decided to be honest and follow. I pulled myself together and left at the indicated time, sneaking through two back corridors and around the ballroom's rear. There, I peeked in.

"Rick?"

No response.

"Rikard, if this is a joke, I swear—"

"It's not, it's not," Rick said, coming into the light of the hallway. "I don't know how to make it any brighter in here."

"There's a lighting box somewhere," I said. "Come with me."

He held up his phone as a torch and we crawled through to a closet where I knew we'd find something.

"What were you thinking?" I asked, annoyed.

"That I would be able to switch the lights on like it was something out of the past two centuries, Alexandra."

"Well, next time, tell me."

"It was a surprise," Rick protested.

"Well, I don't like surprises, Rikard!"

"Women *love* surprises!"

"I'm not *women*!" I protested. "God! Who do you think me to be, Rick? I'm not some silly girl in a bad romance. I am not too stupid to live."

"Too stupid to live?"

"It's when the heroine is too dumb for her own good."

"I got that, yes."

It was dark, but I felt him pressed against me as he held the light too high. We were stuck in this tiny area, our bodies touching as I fumbled. I had a burning desire for him to drop the phone and pin me to the wall and was relieved my flushed face wouldn't show in this light.

"Hold it down a bit," I said. "You expect me to be a foot taller than I am."

"Fine," Rick complied, illuminating the light switches.

I flipped them, "Go check.".

"Check what?"

"To see if the lights came on."

"Oh, shit, yes!"

Rick raced out and returned. "We're good."

"Brilliant."

I went to the ballroom, unsure what this was all about. Rick was on his phone.

"Glad I came down here to watch you stare at that thing."

"You should get one."

"What? So she can monitor it?"

"No," Rick said. "So you can do fun things."

He turned the volume up on his speaker and played music. It was some old music. Something classical.

"I am going to try to teach you how to waltz," Rick said. "Now, I'm not the best dancer, but far from the worst. And I hope that as bright as you are, you'll outclass me sooner than you know. It's an olive branch. Are you game?"

"Sure," I agreed, surprised. "You will not die of embarrassment?"

"Should I?"

"No," I said. "Don't men hate dancing?"

"I don't. For one, it's plenty fine. Two, you will get a kick out of it, and I stuck my foot in it. So, come on. Let me abscond from guilt."

I took his extended hand. I was confused about what to do with the other.

"On the top of my arm," he said.

I did as directed. Rick pulled me much closer than I bargained for, putting his hand on my back. I looked up, surprised.

"What? You must be close to dance a waltz. I don't bite. I swear."

I nodded like an idiot, staring up at his brown eyes. His expression was calm, pleasant, and not at all grumpy. I loved his dimples. God, why must he have dimples? I was overwhelmed by how our bodies touched and the strong smell of his cologne. I worried my palms would get too sweaty. How was this allowable? It felt strangely intimate.

"You doin' okay?"

I nodded again and squeaked. "Uh-huh."

"Okay, so I lead, you follow. I go forward, you go back. You mirror me," Rick said as if this were simple.

"Just follow you. Got it."

Rick started. He stepped forward. I fell back, then forward as he fell back. I nearly tripped as he did something else. He caught me and pulled me back with him.

"So, it's a change step. 1-2-3, change, 1-2-3. That's it. And we just go around and round. We could do this all day. It's not difficult."

"I am far from good at this."

"Practice makes perfect. You've never done it before. In my family, you'd have spent a decade learning to do it right. You'd be bored about now."

"Maybe."

"You're doing great. Really," Rick said, encouragingly. "It suits you."

"Honestly?"

He nodded. "You are a decent dancer."

"You don't have to take pity on me."

"One, I have fun with you—"

"Because you have no one else to hang out with—"

He chuckled. "Yes, but I do have fun. I realised how much freedom I've had and how little you had. I am honoured to be your partner in crime, Alexandra. I'm putting my devious powers to good use."

I smiled, feeling faint as I had when he'd kissed me hours before. I was running on a high. I couldn't put anything into words. We stopped. I held his hand. We stood staring at one another, my mind racing, hoping he might kiss me again. Rather, dying for him to kiss me again.

Just when I felt his face coming closer to mine and we were moments from a genuine, real kiss, it all fell apart. My hopes were dashed. The fuzzy feeling turned to fear, and it all faded away.

Sixteen

RICK

Alexandra's eyes stared deep into me again. This time, I held her so near. My hand moved down her back to rest just above her ass. An urge to kiss her rushed over me. I knew I shouldn't. I knew it was bad for us. I suspected staring at her now that she *had* caught feelings, regardless of what she said. Maybe she had gotten her wires crossed or maybe there was something there?

The truth was, I was a sucker for a girl dressed down—much more than a woman all buttoned up. Somehow, in a pair of shorts and a tank top, Alexandra was more appetising than I had previously credited her to be. She was cute in a girl-next-door sort of way.

We were bonding, yes, but damn if I didn't want to kiss her. I suspected she wanted the same. With a whoosh, the doors opened. The Dowager Queen entered, flanked by footmen. She looked unamused.

"Alexandra, what are you doing?"

"It's my fault," I said. "She couldn't dance. I was teaching her a waltz."

Alexandra, by now, stepped back. She'd panicked.

"Need I remind you that he's not your husband, Alexandra? That he's not even your fiancé! He would drag your reputation through the mud as all men are wont to do."

I set my jaw in anger. "I swear. I was just teaching her to dance."

"Did you or did you not kiss her at the polo match, Your Royal Highness?"

"We kissed each other," Alexandra insisted. "He and I chose to kiss ahead of time. To give them something to talk about—rile them up, Grand-Mama."

"I do not like this," Celeste said. "He can do everything he wants to you, and you have—"

I cut her off, unable to stand seeing Alexandra twisting in the wind. I couldn't take it anymore.

"We're going to do the announcement. We've decided it is time, Celeste. But it's late. We didn't want to bother you."

Alexandra looked at me, eyes wide.

"Not sure how you handle things. But, generally, back home, we'd do engagement photos and an engagement interview with the press— all to do with that release."

"We do all those things. Of course, it has been so long," Celeste murmured. "You are getting engaged?"

"Yes. I planned to speak with you in the morning before I notified my father and decided on a ring."

"You needn't do that. Her mother's ring remains in the royal collection. It was willed to her," Celeste said. "That will do."

Alexandra's face lit up like a Christmas tree.

"Call your father," Celeste said. "At once. I will not have you bandying her about, wrecking her reputation for your enjoyment! It is sterling. We will figure out the engagement photos tomorrow and hire someone suitable. Until we make the final announcement and I can speak with the PM about my intent to terminate the regency, you are not to be alone with her. I will not have her sullied in the process."

Sullied? I only kissed her. I hadn't even slept with her. Hell, I hadn't even seen her tits yet! There was something bizarre about mentioning Alexandra's chastity before me like it was a prize. And, given the way the girl kissed, I suspected she had gotten away with something. She knew to hold me down when I got out of line. A quiet little virgin wouldn't know how to make a man grovel. She was wiser than Celeste gave her credit.

"I will now return you to your quarters, Alexandra," Celeste said.

Alexandra looked at me, eyes big. "Thank you."

I watched Celeste drag her granddaughter down the hall like you might a wayward dog or naughty toddler. I loathed it, looking the way to see Martin shaking his head.

"Martin, I worry for her."

Martin, pained, said, "I'm sure it will all work out, sir."

"I don't know. It will for us. If it kills me, I want to make sure of two things," I said.

"Yes, sir?"

"I need to find a way to get Alexandra a mobile phone. She protests but... I worry for her. My job is to take care of her. I cannot do that if I have no access to her."

"I do not think the Dowager Queen will approve, but I can do my best. Maybe make friends with her lady's maid or something?"

"That would be great," I agreed. "Can you handle the phone or—"

"We will sort it—send it to her in secret as best we can."

I smiled. "Thank you, Martin."

"What was the second point?"

"I don't need anything now, but I am hatching a plan to remove that bitch from the Queen's quarters. It should have been Alexandra's bank of rooms for ages now. If it kills me, I will evict her."

Martin chuckled. "You are taking this defence of the woman very seriously, sir."

"I am obligated—and not only to Alexandra, to her sisters. I don't like the way that woman pulls her around like that. She treats her poorly. Alexandra is a monarch—whether that bitch likes it or not—and I will not have anyone treating her like that."

My voice was hot. I had gotten myself surprisingly wound up. Martin had a satisfied look. He understood my righteous indignation and was glad to see it.

"Sir, we should notify your father of the engagement," Martin said. "You said after—"

"Yes, yes. Let me call him," I said.

We returned to my room where I called my father's phone and received the switchboard. Eventually, I was transferred. My father was already in bed. Despite their happy marriage, my parents always slept apart. I did not understand it but felt it was fine if it worked for them. The lore was that Pappa was a fan of reading late and Mamma was not one to tolerate late nights with any form of light. So, they didn't share a room in the evening.

"You doing alright? I heard the match went well," Pappa said.

"It was my best match to date. We surprised everyone. Couldn't be prouder of the guys. But that's not why I'm calling."

"Oh?"

"I'm ready to do it."

"To do what?"

"Announce the engagement, Pappa."

There was some silence.

"Sorry, just sitting up properly," he apologised. "You do? You are ready?"

I could have gotten into everything strange with Celeste or that things were messy. I could have explained that I was defending Alexandra's honour in a chivalrous way that surprised even me. Instead, I took the easy way out.

"I think it is a slam dunk and we need to make a move. Alexandra is totally on board and her grandmother has offered up her late mother's ring. I think it's a go."

"Well, I will work on a release with the press office. I am proud of you, son. Well done for getting yourself out of a jam. But need I remind you—"

"Don't fuck it up again. Yeah, yeah," I said.

"Alexandra is alright then?"

"She's very well, Dad. Extremely well. We are getting to know one another. Becoming friends, even. She's a nice person. I think I got off on the wrong foot with her. These people are boring, but she and her sisters are not. The younger ones are sweet, and she and Astrid are great fun. It's not bad. I never had sisters. It's nice to inherit some."

"Are you running a fever?" Pappa asked.

"Nah, I'm hopeful I've made it out alive. Things will settle the minute the wedding band is firmly on Alexandra's finger. Everyone will get their happy ending."

Everyone but us, I feared.

Seventeen

ALEXANDRA

"Do not try me," Celeste said. "Do not trifle me! I know what you are up to, and you are playing a risky game!"

Celeste waited until we were far from Rick to start. She was in a serious mood. I wanted so badly for Rick to kiss me and hoped he might come and rescue me. Still, there was no hope. He had no idea how angry she could be. She'd work on starving me for the next week or send me to my room without reprieve. It was always the same. I was biding my time before I could be free. Even if I didn't submit, I knew fighting did little good.

"Do you know what happens to women who go to bed with men? Do you know what happens?"

"Grand-Mama, I was not doing anything. He was teaching me to dance, which I need to know how to do! I must be able to dance at my wedding."

"We'll see if we even get that far. You hope he has your best interest in mind!"

I sighed, frustrated.

"He will get you pregnant, leave you, and take your virtue. It will destroy our family. His will remain just fine because he's a man. You don't understand it. He has you under some spell. Wait until the wedding night. No more kissing him!"

"Grand-Mama, if I am to marry him, should we not be close? So what if he kisses me? Won't he have to do much more on the wedding night?"

"We will talk about that when the time comes!"

"Grandmother, I know what sex is!"

She looked angry.

"Listen to me, Alexandra. You are a little minx as your mother was, aren't you? She and your father never struggled in that area. He always chose her because she had him wrapped around her little finger. That's good for you. You have beguiled Rikard. However, you are playing with fire running around with him unchaperoned."

"I will do as I please! If you don't believe me, put me on the pill. I would gladly take it!"

A look of pure hatred spread across Celeste's face. The pill was a badge of honour. By taking it, I'd buck all religious conventions and suggest to Celeste I refused to fall pregnant right away. It was me asserting my independence. She wanted none of that. That I had even genuinely solicited Rick's attention surprised both of us. Celeste found it offensive, but it thrilled me.

She wound up, ready to strike me when a voice spoke from the void.

"If you hit her, she'll have a bruise, and you won't be able to cover it," it said. "Bad for the pictures, yes?"

It was Astrid. She, Odette, and Ingrid stood there, pyjama-clad with crossed arms. They were all here to back me up. Celeste found herself outnumbered.

"And if his family finds out she's damaged goods, it will cause suspicion."

Celeste remained enraged but let this one go. She dropped her hand, thinking better of it.

"Be dressed early tomorrow. We need to measure you and your finger, and we need to prepare. There is no time to dawdle. If I catch you alone with him again, it will be your head. I won't allow you to marry him."

I teared up, suddenly feeling vulnerable and even more tortured. I wanted to spend time with him. This was a crush, but I was on the cusp of making it more than that. I fought my tears until she was out of view when I turned to Astrid. She carried me back into my room. I sobbed into her shoulder while all four of us sat on my bed. No one spoke. The little girls were confused.

"What did you do?" Ingrid asked. "You were alone... with Rick?"

"Don't ask stupid questions!" Astrid told her.

"He invited me to the ballroom. It was all innocent. He's teaching me to dance. I need to learn. He was very sweet."

"Can he teach me?" Odette asked. "In exchange, I could play on the piano. I would so love that!"

"Let's not all overwhelm Rick with requests for dance lessons," Astrid said. "We'll scare him off."

"Well, I will need chaperones now," I groaned. "All we were doing was dancing."

"We knew she'd go ape after you made out with him at the polo."

"You did what?" Odette asked.

"You made out with him?" Ingrid chimed. "What was it like? Did he kiss you?"

"Was it like totally amazing?" Odette asked.

"We didn't make out. We had one kiss." I blushed. "It was nice. He is a good kisser."

"Would you do it again?" Ingrid asked.

All the blood rushed to my face.

"She would!" Odette laughed.

I giggled. "Okay, yes, I would. I would do it again in a heartbeat—and would have if she didn't show up and start screaming."

Astrid slapped my knee. "I told you that you'd regret not going."

"He's so handsome. I hate it. And he's so good at dancing. I don't deserve someone who can dance."

"You do, too!" Odette said. "Oh, darling sister, this is what we all need."

"I do *not* need a man!" Ingrid protested.

"I would not throw a man like that out of my bed," Astrid said. "I wouldn't marry him. I'm not interested in anything like that, but I am not you."

"Well, you aren't about to marry him, are you?" Odette asked.

Astrid shrugged. It was like she was telling me to move forward and just do the thing.

"I... we have... fallen for one another," I said.

Astrid and I had not told the little girls what was going on. They wouldn't understand and while they couldn't gab to anyone of importance about it, we knew it would confuse them. So, even to them, I kept up the ruse. It hurt me in the pit of my stomach. It was a white lie but a lie all the same. Saying all of it also made it feel *real*.

"So, given that I'm Queen and life is complicated, we've decided to marry," I said.

"How did he propose?" Odette brimmed.

I froze.

"He didn't," Astrid said. "Funny story. She proposed to him after the polo. Sort of off-the-cuff. He accepted. He's cool like that. Secure in his masculinity. It's the twenty-first century!"

Well, that would be interesting to tell him. I was unsure that would fly with Rick. He did not strike me as the type of man who would tolerate a woman proposing. However, I loved Astrid's original assertion. This was a fairytale I could get behind.

"So cool!" Ingrid brimmed.

"That's so... not what I expected. Where is the ring?" Odette asked.

"They are fitting it," I said. "I will have Mamma's ring. It was willed to me."

They stared at me, tears in their eyes.

"I'm sorry," I said. I felt even more guilty for using the ring for this sham marriage we had agreed to.

"No, no, it's beautiful," Astrid said. "You should have it and keep it in the family. She wanted you to have it. Papa would be happy, too."

I teared up again. "I wish she were here. I wish he was, too. I miss her every day, of course, but I need her here for this."

"You have us," Astrid said. "Always and forever. Okay? We will make it through. We will get out of the regency and help you get on with your life. A real life."

"Yes, a life with a wedding and a husband and babies," Odette said.

"Maybe in a bit on the babies," Astrid winced.

I nodded in agreement.

"Will he sleep in here with you?" Ingrid asked in a sweet baby voice. "Does that mean we cannot come in here anymore?"

"Oh, sweetheart," I said. "He will be here sometimes in the future, but you are always my sisters. He won't come between us. He likes you three. We will have a different rhythm someday, but we're always sisters, okay?"

They nodded.

"Now, it's bedtime. We have a full day tomorrow of preparations... whatever that means. So, off to bed!"

The little girls scurried off. Astrid remained.

"Stay with me," I asked. "I don't want to be alone."

"Okay," she agreed.

Astrid pulled the sheer curtains of my canopy bed closed so we were in a dark tent. When we were little and Mamma was sick, we'd do this. And when she passed, we did this, saying it warded off evil spirits. Namely, we lied to ourselves and said it kept Celeste away. Cuddled together in the dark, we tried to fall asleep.

"You fancy him, don't you? Admit it!"

"I do. I thought she would wring my neck. I wanted her to leave. I wanted him to kiss me again. This time, it would have meant something. Astrid, the way he was holding me... it made me feel faint. It made things... tingle. But if he'd even so much as asked me about sex, I would freeze up. I know nothing. I don't even know how to learn?"

"Books," Astrid said. "I will give you some of my favourites and you can learn everything."

I was doubtful that her books would teach me anything. However, they couldn't hurt as I was a rank amateur, and must figure it out in a few months. I'd soon be lying in bed with a man who knew far more than I did.

PART TWO
THE TEAM

Eighteen

Rick

Several days after I committed to marry her, I entered Alexandra's room. It was a first to make a it month before seeing a woman's bedroom. I expected it to be sterile expanse, but it was a sanctuary of sorts—lovely and homey. Pinks and florals peppered in with ivory. It was very feminine.

She looked up, a bit nervous. Her sisters surrounded her as her maid watched on.

"Could you all give us a moment?" I asked.

"Rick, I cannot—"

"Just a minute," I said. "I want to chat before the big to-do."

We were about to take engagement photos. I hadn't seen her in a couple of days. We were kept apart. But, this morning, I was told I would spend the day with my future wife—yes, wild I know—taking photos and acting like the perfect couple we were supposed to be.

Marta nodded, smiling kindly. I gathered from all Alexandra said about her that she was a trusted person. To date, she hadn't done anything to raise suspicion. Marta left the door cracked as the others left.

Alexandra stood and stepped towards me.

"I have a gift."

"Ah," Alexandra said. "You didn't have to. I got the ring."

"Did you?"

I reached for her left hand. She smiled and held it out. Girls in Neandia wore their engagement rings on their left hand—the opposite of Lundhavian preference. It was a holdover from old Scandinavian traditions—Vikings being contrary.

The ring was beautiful. It was a big, shiny rock shaped like an emerald. I didn't know much more. It made her finger look even smaller. It shone like the sun in the morning light. She treasured this heirloom.

"It's nice," I said. "Very nice. Fitting."

She blushed.

I handed her the box. "Here. May you wear this if you so choose."

Pulling the wrapping back, she unveiled a pretty ruby bracelet.

"It's the same colour in both our flags," I said. "And I thought you might like it."

"I love it!" She smiled broadly.

It was infectious when she got excited like this.

I bent closer, "Check under it."

Alexandra looked confused, then set the bracelet down. She peeled back what she suspected was the bottom of the box. Instead, she discovered something below it. She looked up at me. I put my finger to my lips, suggesting she remain silent.

She whispered, holding the phone in the box, "How?"

"In case you need me, my number is in there. For any of you. Hide it well, but call or text if you need something."

Alexandra gaped, then nodded. She looked surprised but didn't protest.

"Should we make everyone believe a fairytale, then?" I asked.

"I thought you'd never ask."

She instinctively took my hand and dragged me excitedly into the living room. I couldn't help but adore her suddenly. She was excited. In her shoes, I would have been frightened. She'd been locked up for two days—hidden from everyone. I could only imagine she was used to it and had nothing more to lose.

Her hair, now in pretty curls that fell past her shoulders, bounced behind her as excitedly as her gait. I caught up, matching her determined stride. She squeezed my hand like she didn't want to let it go. We proceeded down to something called the Jade Room. Inside were big, luxurious curtains, cream couches, and a unique fireplace inlaid with jade. It looked out onto the gardens. There, we were met by a man I'd not seen before.

"Hello, Your Majesty and Your Royal Highness." He bowed.

"Hello. I was told I would be meeting Louise," Alexandra spoke French.

"Louise will be on leave indefinitely," the man confirmed. "I am your new Private Secretary in the meantime. My name is Lord Jacques Matin. It is so nice to meet you. You look lovely this morning—far prettier than in pictures."

He stared at her as if I didn't exist. She mooned back at him like I wasn't there—dreamy-eyed. Dropping my hand, she laced hers together in front of her body like a surprised schoolgirl who was hot for teacher. I should have ignored Alexandra's flirting, but the asshole was practically eye-fucking her as we stood around for engagement photos. It was beyond ridiculous!

"Well, you're too kind. Are they not yet ready?" Her voice was soft and breathy.

I hated it.

"Not quite yet, ma'am. Can I get you anything in the interim?"

"I'd like a coffee, Lord Jacques," I announced. "Thanks."

He looked up from her, glared, and then fixed this expression. "Your Majesty?"

Alexandra stared like a guppy.

"Your Majesty?"

"Oh... what?"

"Anything to drink?"

"No, thanks," she answered.

Her eyes followed him as he left the room.

I shouldn't have cared. This should have made me happy. Maybe she could have a go with her private secretary, leaving me to have fun with someone else on the side. Instead, I was lit on fire by the gall of a man who flirted in front of her fiancée! And he didn't even know we weren't an actual couple!

"You don't need to trip over him," I said.

"What?" Alexandra asked.

"He's not that handsome."

"Have to agree to disagree, Rick," Alexandra said.

She thirsted!

"What is it about him?" I whispered.

"He has fabulous shoulders," she stammered. "A kind face."

"And I don't?"

"I never said that. No. You don't have a kind face. You look quite serious and a bit like you might cut someone most days. You have nice shoulders. I am not insulting you. I'm not about to run off with him. I was merely observing—"

"That he had nice shoulders?"

Alexandra shrugged. Whether she knew it or not, she was riling me.

The asshole moving in on Alexandra under my nose brought my coffee back. He glared and immediately turned to a totally obscure topic.

"This room is lovely, ma'am. It will do well for photos. Do you know about the wallpaper?"

"I can assure you it's not laced with arsenic," she laughed.

I didn't follow.

"I loved the block printing style, though. I love textiles. That's why I studied them," Alexandra said.

"Oh, did you?"

He was full of shit! How he found this out about her, but I did not, was curious. I suspected the old bat of a grandmother had it in for me. She figured if she could insert a handsome ringer, then I might fade away. She'd continue maintaining power over Alexandra. Who would be that crazy? A sociopath, I guessed. This family got weirder and weirder by the moment. What was the plan? To prolong Alexandra's agony and make it worse? To embarrass me in front of my family? No, the old bitch wouldn't win this one.

"Do you know anything about the preservation of tapestries?" I asked, trying my damndest to keep up.

"Of course. Well, preservation of all textiles. God, I love talking about this, Rick! Stop me if I bore you."

She rambled. I was bored immediately. At least she looked sweet as she smiled and explained. Then, she stopped.

"So, that's how you do it. Well, one process. I love that you both enjoy this stuff. Fascinating, really," she said.

"For certain."

The photographer moved us into place. I handed my coffee over. He lined up the shot, then paused to address something.

The photographer called Jacques the Dickhead over. He went. I had one moment to impress Alexandra. She looked up at me again with those big, blue eyes of hers. Damn if they didn't sell me at this moment! I needed to do something good. Alexandra was distracted by some exceedingly average asshole who was here as a plant. I needed her to fall into my spell—and quickly. Kissing her worked before, so I tried again.

I gambled. And, at first, I thought I'd lost.

Alexandra pulled away, staring. Then, to my surprise, she dove back in. The woman could kiss! She wrapped her arms around my neck as I pulled her closer. And, despite the thirty or more idiots in the room, we kept going. This began with practical, strategic motives but I soon found myself longing to push her up against a wall. What was that about? We were completely wrapped up in whatever this was. As a shutter clicked and clicked, we pulled apart.

"That's lovely, but won't do for the official ones," the photographer said.

"I'm sorry. You didn't... catch us did you?" Alexandra looked nervous.

"Young love," he said. "It's beautiful. I figured I would capture it for you. People usually fear having to kiss and be romantic in front of a camera. But the two of you are naturals."

Alexandra blushed. I squeezed her hand.

"Perhaps a little less of that then? Focus on the official photos?" Jacques declared.

"I can't help myself," I said. "I just... couldn't fight it."

Alexandra shook her head and bit her lip, her eyes never dropping my gaze. I realised that here, dressed like a normal young woman, and in a different light, I liked her. She was beautiful like this. I admired her legs and the way the curve of her hips felt in my hands only moments before. I wanted so badly to grab her ass. That would be satisfying.

"Well, shall we get on with it?" Jacques barked.

So, we did. We gave them every bit of a show.

NINETEEN

ALEXANDRA

Rick was intent on finding *any* opportunity to kiss me. He couldn't keep his hands to himself. While I was flattered and luxuriated in the way his lips met mine and how our tongues felt tangled together, I was clever enough to know this had something to do with the arrival of one new courtier.

Lord Jacques was a tall glass of water. He had hazel eyes, a brilliant smile, and dark brown hair. His eyes complimented his remarkable tan. I immediately thought of the man I had read about in one of Astrid's tawdry novels. A man who was always shirtless and tanned but kept running into the heroine in the oddest ways. I wondered if he looked good with a shirt off. I suspected he would. Either way, he was far better than my previous Private Secretary who was nearly eighty. She was a sweet woman, but Lord Jacques was about the same age as Rick and much nicer to look at than Louise.

I was convinced Jacques wasn't interested in me. We could keep it professional. Rick, meanwhile, was upset—even jealous. His ramped-up desire on full display was an act of claiming me. I hated it. I wasn't a trophy to be won—even by the man who would marry me. Still, the kissing felt so good! I didn't want it to end. The more we did, the more natural it was to wrap myself up in him and enjoy it.

As the pictures finished, we were assured that the best ones would be retouched and sent over by morning for our approval. The announcement would go out soon. I knew that Celeste would mastermind it all. She'd keep any of the beautiful ones of us kissing and lay it on thick far out of sight. Still, it was nice to know that somewhere they existed. We weren't in love. We weren't a real couple. We only played along well.

"You can calm down," I said as Rick walked me to my side of the house. "He's not going to edge into your territory. One man is enough, I can assure you."

"You wouldn't have two if you could do so no questions asked?"

I flushed.

"What, you wouldn't want us both to cater to your every need?"

I was too flustered to answer. "Would you have two women?"

He grimaced.

I was appalled. "Don't answer that, Rikard. Or as I should say, *Prickard!*"

"That's great, actually," he chuckled.

"Astrid came up with it."

"Nice one. I will have you know I'm not jealous."

"Uh-huh."

We stopped at my door.

"Really, Alexandra. That's not it!"

"Then explain it," I said.

"I'm not. I just... I was overcome."

"Uh-huh." I wasn't buying it.

As he turned, I sang the chorus of the Gin Blossoms "Hey Jealousy."

Running his hand through his blonde curls, Rick asked, "What are you doing, Lex?"

I was surprised by his shortening of my name, though not opposed. I also wasn't sure why this song wasn't on his radar. Yes, it was a very old song, but it wasn't completely unknown.

"The song. I'm giving you a hard time," I said.

"How?"

"Hey, jealousy?"

"The words are 'Hey, Chelsea!' Aren't they?"

I snickered. "God, no. Hey, Chelsea? Who is Chelsea?"

"How the fuck would I know, Alexandra?"

I shrugged. "You're wrong. Look up the lyrics on your pocket oracle."

He smiled and shook his head. "I should but I won't."

"You always want something but are never willing to do what you need to get it," I said.

He moved closer in a way that made my body quake. I couldn't explain why. I felt warmth in unmentionable places.

"I cannot help it if most things just *come* to me," Rick said.

His hand grazed my cheek. He pulled my chin towards him.

"I usually get what I want. I am lucky to have people willing to do the work *for* me. And that includes women who are willing to do my bidding. Even if only to Google song lyrics."

"Must be nice," I said, pulling back a bit.

He put his other hand on the small of my back, drawing me in.

"What? What do you want, Alexandra, that you aren't getting?"

I wasn't sure how to answer. I wanted *everything*. I wanted him. I wanted this. It physically pained me now to be here, so close to my door, knowing I could not bring him in with me to do... well, I wasn't quite sure what I was going to do. But I knew it was something and I knew it involved the part of me that was presently tingly and warm. His hand made it further down the small of my back now onto my bum and I shuddered.

"What? Cat got your tongue?" Rick ran his thumb over the small cleft of my chin.

His finger was close to my mouth now. I had a sudden urge to bite his thumb. What was that about?

The closer we stood, the stronger the smell of his cologne and the harder his hand gripped my backside, I wanted more. I wanted all of him. That was what it was. I knew I shouldn't want it. It was a terrible idea—and one that could end in bad consequences—but I wanted him to run me into the bedroom right now.

I had no words for what I wanted. So, I gave into the only sort of language that seemed to work for us both in these scenarios. I kissed him hard. He pressed me against the wall. I bit his lip. I don't know what the impulse for biting was, but I was a woman unhinged. Rick responded by pushing me into the wall hard and running his hand down over my breast. It was the first time a man had ever even bothered to make mention of my breasts. I moaned. It was uncontrollable. Where were these impulses and noises coming from?

I didn't know, but I wanted to do a lot more.

TWENTY

I pressed Alexandra against the wall of the corridor. She wanted to entertain me this afternoon. Had I finally broken down the walls with our fair princess? She moaned as a ran my hand over her breast. *Moaned.* I was sex-starved and on a roll here. If I was to keep her away from the asshole plant sent to disrupt our happiness, I had to do something.

I was not about to let this one go. I wanted her to beg. I wanted her to plead and say "fuck me" more than I ever imagined. She'd never say it, but maybe she didn't have to. She bit my lip and ground up against me. We both wanted the same thing. I worried the old bitch might castrate me if she found out, but I figured that my odds were good to come out unscathed. No one was around.

"Maybe we should... go inside?" I asked.

Alexandra looked wide-eyed at me. She was *panting*. Her face flushed as if I'd ripped the band-aid off and was the only one who could cure her ills. She nodded and dragged me inside, slamming the door behind her. I dove to sweep her up in another kiss. Suddenly, it felt deliriously good. The forbidden of it made it so very hot.

We fell back on her bed, all askew. I was pressed on top of her now.

Alexandra moved to make herself a bit more comfortable. Her skirt was a mess, flipped up. I wanted it gone completely. I wanted to see all of her—naked and willing. She was now so beautiful as she lay there, nostrils flaring, looking up at me as I kicked my shoes off and tossed hers aside, too.

I kissed her again, running my hand down to her centre. I put my hand in between her legs, running my fingers over her panties and tights. She shuddered again. I continued to run my fingers over her clit. It was swollen. The wetness seeped through her panties. She moaned louder. It was like the ultimate high to make her get loud. Alexandra was controlled, quiet, and so *good* but I gave her the ultimate pleasure. Her body begged for me—*needed* me.

"You want me, Alexandra?" I asked.

She nodded.

I kissed her again, this time on the neck. She let out a sweet little moan as I played with the elastic on her tights, wanting to pull them down. Or rather, indicating I wanted her to. Alexandra responded by pulling her tights down slightly. I did the rest, tossing them aside. She moaned, louder now, as I ran my hand around the top of her panties. I was torturing her, and she was loving every second of it.

The more she moaned and begged, the more I wanted to be between her legs. My cock braced against the zipper of my trousers so uncomfortably, I had to adjust myself. I wanted to ask her if I could just get to it, but I was also enjoying toying with her more than she knew.

"You like that, don't you?" I asked.

Alexandra nodded, looking out of it in the best way. She bit my lip again and we continued kissing. I ran my hand inside her dress to play with her nipple. She let out a growl. I liked that. I was about to finally pull her panties aside and get to work when a noise spooked us.

"Your Majesty!"

We panicked.

Marta and Martin both stood there, staring.

"Shit," I sat up. "It wasn't... we were just..."

"Overcome?" Alexandra asked in French.

She was as bad at covering up as I was.

I looked over at her and nodded. We sat there like teenagers interrupted by our parents in the middle of a make-out sesh. I hadn't felt this way since before I could drink. It felt like a special treat. It was exactly what I needed. This thing was naughty but oh-so-good. And she was *gorgeous*. Her hair was a mess, her lipstick smudged. I'd made her that way. I'd left her completely devastated. There would be more of this. We'd make it work eventually.

"I'll be going," I said. "We should... chat later?"

Martin nodded as if he was desperate to pull me out of there.

"Check the song."

"What?"

Alexandra giggled. "Hey, Jealousy. Check the song."

I forgot. I checked my phone as an excuse to cover my shame upon leaving the bed. I let out an exasperated sigh. She was correct.

"Fine, you're right."

She smiled, satisfied.

I was about to depart but needed to remind her about the plan I hatched before we returned. I'd lost my mind at some point, forgetting my intent to break the princesses out tonight. Suspecting an excursion could earn me the trust of the woman I now lusted for, she needed reminding to check her phone. Otherwise, coordination would be impossible. She needed to check the box with the bracelet.

"Don't forget to check in on your bracelet. Wear it," I said.

"What?"

"Wear your bracelet. Think of me," I said.

Twenty-One

ALEXANDRA

"Wear your bracelet, think of me."

Rick smiled and stepped out, Martin herding him. Marta stared, confused. I didn't have time to explain what she'd just witnessed. I was out of words.

"Ma'am, I think we need to have a chat," Marta said.

She sat on the bed next to me, like a mother or big sister might.

"Ma'am, I will be frank with you because I care about you and worry. What you almost did... could have... consequences."

Embarrassed, tears welled and I flushed bright red. "We weren't... nothing happened."

"Your Majesty, I am not upset with you. Nor should you be guilty," Marta's tone was sweet and kind, maternal. "Things can escalate fast. And men may not always think of what happens when they do, ma'am. There are consequences—"

My embarrassment turned to fear. "Please, please do not tell Celeste. She might kill me this time!"

"Oh, darling, no!" Marta exclaimed.

I cocked my head.

"My sweet, I am here to help you. To care for you. I would never turn you into Celeste. My concerns are about you and your safety. He is very handsome and things whipped up quickly. Everyone has been there a time or two, ma'am. It is okay. I want to talk to you about it, so you are... aware."

I was relieved. "Oh... okay."

"What can begin as just kissing can quickly turn into... far more. And I know you are not... well you are not as prepared as you should be to keep yourself from suffering one of the most obvious consequences."

"Pregnancy?" I whispered.

She nodded. "Among other things. But in your case, that is the primary concern for the next few months. Have you ever considered getting on the pill?"

"I screamed at Celeste and threatened to do so recently, yes."

Marta chuckled. "Oh, dear. Well, we might need to see about taking care of that. If you are prepared, you will be able to make better choices."

"You wouldn't tell on me?" I asked.

"I cannot promise that the halls would not talk, Your Majesty, but I plan to keep your secrets as well as I have any great lady I worked for. I vowed to care for you as I would my own and I continue to do that."

"It's not a moral failing? We aren't married. What if we do it and he drops me—"

"I suspect His Royal Highness cares little about the status of a woman's virginity. I think he fancies you. And, given what I saw, would be only too willing to go a lot further than he just did."

I blushed.

"Make choices when you are ready. You are young. Life is long. If you want to do more, you should, but let us take care of the practical problem first. I will get the pills."

"Thank you," I said, relieved.

I would be taking matters into my own hands. God, it felt glorious to do that! Every day, I would take a pill and stick it to Celeste, the Church, and the old men who told me what to do with my body.

Marta left me to sort myself. I revelled in the way it had felt when Rick touched me. I wanted more. I had no idea it could feel so good to have him run his hand between my legs. I wondered if we might do it again soon, but I suspected I should wait until Marta was able to procure the pill. I would have to try hard to avoid him. I still felt the pleasure of his fingers rolling over my nipple. I wanted him so badly.

I snapped out of the fantasy. I remembered Rick's words. He didn't seem the sentimental type. I found the bracelet box, still closed and undisturbed. The phone was inside, switched off. I locked the door, flicked the phone on, and waited for it to boot. The logo came on and I went through the steps to set up. I prayed no one bothered me. It took so long. No wonder why these things were impossible!

After minutes of trying, I got a message from someone I assumed was Rick.

RICK

Tonight, be ready to flee. I have a plan. Bring A with you.

ME

How?

RICK

Dress like normal people going out. Dress down, okay? Jeans.

ME

You're mad

RICK

I'm not

I changed the caller ID to Rick the Prick. I'd played on these before since Astrid got one without any access to making calls or texting years ago. We used it to stream movies late at night sometimes when we were too lazy to get out of bed. Not that it mattered. After all, who would we ring? We knew no one.

ME

Okay

I smiled and powered the thing off, shoving it inside a big box of tampons. No one would go in there.

Twenty-Two

RICK

Martin was my ear to the ground for the past few days. He made nice and shared information with Alexandra's lady's maid. Marta appeared trustworthy, knowing about the phone but saying nothing. Obligated to care for the girl and help her along, Marta was the last staff member remaining after Alexandra's late mother's death. Marta was crucial for the weeks ahead. With the channels open, we pushed forward.

I heard the Dowager Queen was about to skip off for a few days. It was time for us to break out of the asylum. I planned to show Alexandra—but not only Alexandra—more of the world. We would bring Astrid, too. I liked Astrid and knew she brought Alexandra out of her shell. Astrid was also Alexandra's key ally. If I was to keep Alexandra happy, I also had to keep Astrid happy. What better way than taking them both out for a night on the town?

I felt new pressure to bond with Alexandra as Celeste's spies became even bolder. I wasn't sure why Celeste intervened, but I would ensure Alexandra remained far from the clutches of Celeste's nerdy plant. I was not about to lose her to that dolt.

I spent time reading about wallpaper. I learned more than any man should about the stuff. It was exhausting keeping up this ruse when I could spend little time with Alexandra. But in the limited time we had, I needed to make a better impression. Before, I assumed that merely agreeing to the ruse was enough. However, if Celeste sewed doubt or caught me in a lie, Alexandra may pull back before we even got started.

Yes, my motives were strategic. I remained steadfast in this plan. I needed to focus on Alexandra. She needed me. And together, we could still rule the world. I just had to work a bit harder to do that. I couldn't get lazy or complacent now.

I texted her.

ME

Do you copy?

ALEXANDRA

What?

ME

Are you receiving this?

ALEXANDRA

Yes.

ME

Meet me in the garden just after nightfall. Celeste is out of the palace. Take a walk with Astrid. Bring her.

ALEXANDRA

What for?

ME

We are going out. Put on your most normal outfit. We will have a good time.

ALEXANDRA

What?

ME

We are going to drink like normies. You'll see.

She sent a thumbs up and I was satisfied.

Martin and I found the two women under a tree in the back garden around 9:30. They were dressed down in jeans. There was no way out. I decided to walk out the front and bring security with us claiming we had a late dinner reservation. The girls were doubtful.

"It won't work," Alexandra protested.

"I will make it work. I planned it, right?"

Alexandra and Astrid rolled their eyes. They acted more like one person than two.

"Anyone have a better idea?" I asked.

"No," Alexandra replied.

"Sir, if I may," Martin interjected. "You and Her Majesty do have a right to eat dinner. I doubt they will stop you for that. You've done it before."

"Alexandra, you are the one in charge," I said. "You can tell them—"

"They will not listen to me. Martin or you, yes," Alexandra said.

I looked at Astrid. Her arms were crossed and she appeared defeated. I hated that the girls were probably right. We had no business ordering anyone around, even if that should be Alexandra's job.

"Come on then," I pulled Alexandra by the hand, leading the two to the service entrance.

"Where are you headed?" Alexandra's guards asked.

"We need to go downtown," I said. "Dinner reservations. Sort of... last minute."

"We will wait while you clear it," Martin added. "It is authorised on our side."

"Is there an issue?"

Alexandra stared in a quite intimidating manner at the head of security.

"Because I am getting cross standing here. And... well, Rikard has been so darling to offer to take us out to dinner. We were fed scraps tonight since our grandmother is out. Would you have us starve?"

She laid it on thick, now batting her eyelashes. She knew what she was doing. I resisted the urge to laugh. I handed it to her.

"We were just so hungry. Second dinner," Astrid played along. "You know how it is."

The head of security looked doubtful, but his men were completely captivated by the women. Their distraction was evident.

"Please?" Astrid said. "It would be so lovely."

"We'd be forever grateful," Alexandra added. "If it won't be *too* much trouble."

They flirted. I was dying laughing inside. I was proud of them for this bizarre act of defiance. Baby steps. The head of security relented, calling us a car. We were off.

"Don't have them drop us right at the restaurant," I told Martin. "We can take detail, but I'd rather fly under the radar."

The restaurant was a casual place—a brewery with a kitchen that was second to none among the small group of Neandian hipsters. The fact that there *were* hipsters confused me. Neandia was an odd place. Upon arrival, they dropped us in an alley 2 blocks away, our rendezvous point if we weren't seen. Martin informed us that if we were spotted and things got messy, we'd be swooped out of there before we could scarf down our food.

The girls and I walked into the bar and asked for a table. No one questioned it. Alexandra and Astrid were unrecognisable in street clothes. Astrid had a very casual demeanour about her on any day, but even Alexandra was always buttoned up. Tonight, she waited for a table, her hands in the pockets of her painted-on jeans. It was good to see them enjoying themselves. I couldn't imagine having lived twenty or more years, never to see the inside of a bar. The drinking age in Lundhavn was a tender eighteen. Great, boozy celebrations were a rite of passage before one went to university.

"Can you tell me what to order?" Alexandra whispered at first but raised her voice because the place was loud.

"What do you mean?"

"I don't know what to drink."

"What?"

"We don't get to drink beer—ever," Astrid explained. "We have no idea."

"We can get a flight."

They cocked their heads in unison. The resemblance unnerved me.

"It's six beers. Tiny ones. You can pick and choose. Let's get two and split them. Choose what you think would be good."

The girls chose based on beer names. Some were slang terms I didn't understand. My French wasn't the best. Now around French speakers day and night, I admitted my French needed improvement. I was assured that our engagement interview would be conducted in English.

The beers arrived along with the huge basket of fries the girls ordered as a starter—as they were starving. Finally, our burgers arrived. The way they dug in, it was as if this was their first time tasting food. They inhaled the frites, ordering even more. It was as if they just escaped a bunker or a cult. I felt grateful to have a somewhat normal childhood.

As we finished our burgers—which they devoured in about five seconds—a man approached and sought out Astrid. Sitting on her own across from us, she looked up, keyed into the fact he was hitting on her. Meanwhile, Alexandra was confused and acting like the world's greatest cockblock.

"What's your name?" Astrid played with her hair.

"Tim."

"You from around here?" Astrid knew full well he wasn't.

"No, the UK," he said in poor French. "I'm in a band."

He laid it on thick, but I had to hand it to him.

Astrid changed to English, taking pity upon him. "I'm Asti. I'm from here. And I speak English."

"Brilliant. Nice to meet you."

"This is my sister, Alex, and our... friend... Rick."

I hated being the friend—more than I was willing to admit.

He nodded. "Cool, cool. So you want a beer?"

"We still have some," Alexandra said.

"Go, go," I gestured to Astrid. "Get another. We can finish these off, babe."

I sensed Alexandra's confusion. We'd never done pet names.

"Um sure," Astrid jumped at the chance to grab a drink with a musician.

"Why? We have perfectly good beer, Rikard!"

"He was hitting on her."

Alexandra again cocked her head like a spaniel.

"Chatting her up?"

Alexandra nodded. "Oh, got it. Really?"

"Yes. That is a normal adult interaction at a place like this."

She looked hurt by my words.

"I'm sorry," I said more tenderly. "I didn't want to hurt her chances. I know this is new for you."

"Do not baby me, Rick!"

"I won't. I'm not."

I needed to distract her. So, I tucked some stray hair behind her ear. Alexandra remained still. Our eyes met, stuck on one another for too long. I couldn't help but edge closer—much closer. The urge to kiss her grew stronger. So, I went for it.

Alexandra kissed me back the same way she had earlier—in a lusty, not-so-chaste way. She got more adventurous now. She bit my lip, pulled away slightly, and stared back. Then, she dug back in, gripping my shirt tightly. If we were putting on a show, we were doing a damn good job. If we were not, we were still doing a damn good job.

"You are being very naughty, Lex," I said.

"I thought my name was babe?" Alexandra asked.

"I got caught up in things."

She smiled. "If you keep kissing me like that—enough to make me lose myself—you can call me whatever you want."

"Challenge accepted."

I kissed her again. Had we not been who we were and *where* we were, I might have suggested we slip away. Shortly after that thought came, Astrid and Tim returned.

Tim and his bandmates asked us to follow them to another bar. Despite my desire to push Alexandra up against a wall and do *much* more, I wasn't going to cockblock my future sister-in-law. Astrid was quick not to hold Tim's hand in public. She was smart. Meanwhile, Alexandra disregarded any sense of propriety, and I adored her for it. I wanted people to know I was with her. I wanted to claim her in a way—not as an object, but as the woman I was about to marry. Any man would feel the same. Alexandra felt more mine than ever. But, for the first time, I hoped she might see me as hers.

Twenty-Three

ALEXANDRA

Is a Royal Wedding Happening?

Last night, Prince Rikard and Queen Alexandra were spotted leaving a bar in the entertainment district in Neandia walking hand-in-hand. Rikandra were spotted with the alt-rock band, Riot Elephant. Walking with the band's frontman, Tim Sheers, was Princess Astrid.

Onlookers said that Rikandra spent time at the club they were seen leaving "all over one another" and stated that the Queen was spotted showing off a very large diamond on her left hand. This seems the new normal for the royal couple who have been inseparable since they were first spotted together weeks ago.

To add more to this plot, photographers caught Queen Alexandra heading to the barn with Prince Rikard the next morning sans-diamond. The jury remains out with Rikandra showing no signs of waning. We are waiting with bated breath for official news.

"Alexandra, we need to talk *now!*"

Celeste returned. I was about to atone for everything I got away with. It was a glorious two days. Rick took us out on the town. I danced in public. We'd barely been apart for more than five minutes. No, we did not get into any trouble. With people around, we'd not have time to avoid getting caught. Still, we did what we could. We ate in the dining room this morning like independent grown-ups and went riding this afternoon. It was freedom again, but I knew I would pay mightily for it.

I stopped. "Yes?"

Rikard stood to my right. I expected him to scurry away, but he stood fast.

"You're dismissed, Prince Rikard," Celeste said.

"Dismissed?" Rick played dumb.

"Dismissed. Go on. This is a private conversation."

"And Alexandra is my fiancée. So unless that has changed, I'd rather stay."

His tone was fierce. He'd gone from laughing to a growl in about a minute. It was hot and no one else defended my honour.

Celeste set her jaw.

"I am here to help, as always, if I can answer any questions, Your Majesty," Rick said.

"Did you take the girls out last night?" Celeste demanded.

"They were hungry, ma'am. Yes."

"You realise I should wring your neck for that?"

Mouth agape, I turned. His face remained neutral.

"Well, you can do as you please. However, I made sure they stayed out of trouble and returned in one piece."

"You might say that, but the press are saying that you were canoodling with musicians of all people! And that the two of you couldn't keep your hands off one another. I won't have this, Prince

Rikard! You haven't married her. Not yet anyway. And you won't get anywhere—"

He played dumb. "Is it my fault if I find my future wife irresistible? Apologies, but I am a weak man."

"You should not take her out and kiss her in public. And you should know better, Alexandra!"

I was unsure how to respond.

"Hormones are a dreadful thing! Can you two not wait a few months? In my day, we didn't so much as kiss before a wedding."

I stifled a snicker. It was all a bit harmless. We were supposed to be madly in love, right? What was a bit of light snogging on a night out? That was normal for any other person my age. I wanted to push back.

"We will be good," Rick said.

"I doubt that. Nor can I trust Astrid to properly chaperone you. What will I do? Her reputation is destroyed by this point."

"Grand-Mama, nothing happened with her. We made some friends. It was all very innocent!" I rushed to Astrid's defence. "She didn't kiss him. She didn't do anything."

Celeste was enraged. "It doesn't matter but your reputations do."

"Or else, will we not be marriageable?" I asked. "Because isn't that what you mean? That a man—or his family—won't find us worth it?"

"Of course!"

"Excuse me, but have we entered the Twilight Zone?" Rick interjected. Celeste glared.

"I would say most parents don't prize chastity in this day and age. Mine do not."

"The church does! And your marriage must be sanctioned by the church—as will Astrid's."

"I know Catholics can be conservative, but I doubt kissing defies any requirements," Rick protested.

"You all did this behind my back! You waited for me to leave."

Celeste grabbed my arm, digging her nails into me. "You want something to go wrong. You want this all to end up an embarrassment, Alexandra! You aren't taking this seriously!"

"How am I not? I have done everything asked of me," I winced.

"You're whoring yourself around town with him."

I fought tears.

"Your grandfather would be so disappointed to see you lack any degree of character! I think it is time to call it all off."

"What?" I asked.

"The wedding," she said. "You're not mature enough to keep your head on you."

"No, no!" I pleaded. "Don't say that."

"We're going through with this," Rick's voice was strong and posture aggressive.

Celeste glared. "You will not. I must authorise any marriage."

"What if your hand was forced?" I played my *last* card. "Because our release is set to go out tomorrow morning."

"It doesn't matter! We can scrap it."

Rick stepped closer to the old bag. "The photos will be ready. I am not asking. I am telling you that I will make it so—that *we* will make it so. And, as Alexandra says, force your hand."

"Your parents—"

"Will understand that we want to get married and support it. Celeste, the entire world is watching Neandia for the first time in however long. This is something the people want and need. You'd anger them. I won't stay quiet if you do this to Alexandra. You are punishing her for acting like a woman of her age. This is what people our age do—and much worse!"

Given the way he defended us, I *wanted* to do a lot worse. He wanted this. He was defending *us*. Someone cared enough about me to have my best interest in mind. I wanted to kiss Rick more than ever. His defence of me changed things. I trusted him now. My stomach had butterflies. I gripped his hand tightly. I needed him to know how much it meant.

"Don't test me, Celeste," Rick said. "You had your side of the bargain, we had ours. We sold this completely. I adore Alexandra. And my duty is to her—not you. To her and the family but not your whims."

Celeste backed down. "Fine, have it your way. But mind yourself.

She is a precious commodity and if you don't treat this seriously, I will make sure your family suffers a blow so great—"

"I would never do anything to hurt your family unless you give me a reason to. Don't try me," Rick's voice boomed through the hallway.

Celeste left. We stood hand-in-hand watching her depart into the abyss. After she turned the corner, I turned to Rick.

"That was... the sexiest thing anyone has ever done," I murmured.

"She can die in a fucking ditch, Lex. I mean it," Rick said.

I wrapped him up in a great big kiss. Everything felt different. It was brighter, more authentic, and sweeter. I wanted to try and do everything. I wanted to trust him and believe he would always have my back like this. It was amazing!

Twenty-Four

For Immediate Release-

His and Her Majesty are excited to announce the engagement of His Royal Highness Prince Rikard, 29, to Her Majesty Queen Alexandra of Neandia, 21. The couple have been dating for some time, having met at an event with mutual friends. They will wed in Neandia in the autumn. We wish them many happy years together and are overjoyed to welcome Her Majesty on an upcoming state visit next month.

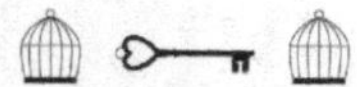

From the Desk of the Queen Regent-

Her Majesty Queen Alexandra, 21, will wed His Royal Highness Prince Rikard of Lundhavn, 29, son of the King and Queen of Lundhavn. The pictures released this morning serve as the official engagement photos for the couple. An engagement interview will follow on Thursday evening.

The nuptials will take place at St. Veronica's Cathedral in Ville de Neandia 2 October. A reception will follow at Neandia's Royal Palace.

This is the first royal wedding since the marriage of the Queen's mother and father twenty-three years prior. A request to end the Queen's regency will be entered into parliament at a time agreeable to all. The Prime Minister will ultimately sign the dissolution of the regency into law.

It's Official!

We have a royal wedding planned in October! Prince Rikard managed to land the young Queen Alexandra in a surprising redemption arc usually reserved for shady politicians with good senses of humour. There are few details available apart from the wedding date of October 2nd and that it will take place in Neandia City. We will be there to follow this wedding every step of the way.

Photos released by the Palace in Neandia show the couple smiling happily in front of an intricate fireplace in what is known as the Jade Room. The princess chose a red dress by Belgian designer Marie Lacroix. The prince wore a grey suit. They looked very at ease and cosy together. It was clear they enjoyed one another's company.

Exclusive! will have the exclusive scoop and will cover this wedding, being the official Lundhavian press outlet to cover the couple's upcoming engagement interview later this week. We are fortunate to have a front-row seat in this proceeding.

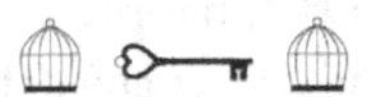

Following Celeste's incident in the hallway, I threw my weight around more. Celeste lost power by the day. Moreover, worries about Sexy Nerd Boy faded as Alexandra became more wrapped up with me.

I am not saying I relished misleading the girl. I was sure for years I had no conscience. Now, though, I felt guilty. Alexandra and her sisters expected me to stand up for them. The little girls treated me like I was their saving grace. I was the hero of my own story—despite my shady behaviour. Alexandra trusted me. Suddenly, I prayed that she and I would get out of this unscathed and I wouldn't break her heart. I suspected if she found out about the coverup it would wound her beyond help.

I now had strong feelings for Alexandra even if I was unsure where they came from. I wasn't in love with her. She wasn't the first girl I'd kissed. I'd never seen her naked or taken her to bed. And yet? I felt obligated to her. Was this labelling theory in action? Maybe since I knew Alexandra would be my wife, I treated her differently. I found myself smiling at her involuntarily. That wasn't like me!

As we prepared for our engagement interview like students cramming for a test. On this beautiful spring day, we sat on a blanket at the creek's bank taking notes and quizzing one another over things that were bound to come up. Alexandra's distracting presence took away from my normal quick-wittedness. I found myself looking at her cleavage as she reached over to pick up a new pen. She colour-coded everything. I should have found it annoying, but I could only stare.

It was terrible. I was in puppy love with the girl I was supposed to marry. Normally, this would be fine, but our marriage was arranged. It was a joke, right? So why did I want to spend the time doing nothing but kissing her?

"Okay, so proposal. The girls were told I proposed to you," Alexandra said.

"Huh, what?" I shook myself out of my stupor.

"Yeah, so Asti told them. She made up a whole thing because they were asking and—"

"Shit. No. I wouldn't let that happen."

"Oh, you wouldn't?" She set her jaw defiantly.

I wanted to kiss the subtle scowl off her lips.

"I wouldn't, no. I'd ask you properly. Maybe both could be true. You broached the subject, and I insisted I would do it properly."

"Okay, I like that." Alexandra scribbled notes. "But... how did you do it?"

"Maybe we were on a picnic. Cosy little day. I decided to keep it simple."

"You are the least inventive man!" She giggled. "You mean like right now?"

"Newsflash—men don't come up with big proposals like you see in the movies. This is nice. It's intimate. I adore you, Alexandra."

She looked at me lovingly. "Alright, fine, picnic."

"And we met at a royal gathering," I clarified. "Royal gathering. No more, no less. Mutual friends. Blah, blah, blah."

Alexandra nodded. "Yes."

She paused, biting the pen. "When did you know?"

I was temporarily distracted. Something about that was sexy. This very bookish version of her was driving me crazy!

"Know what?" I asked.

"When did you know I was the one?"

I tried to come up with an answer when she bit the pen again. Throwing caution to the wind, I kissed her. Tossing her notebook aside, Alexandra kissed me back. I pushed her down against the blanket—my body pinning hers to the ground. I stopped to look down. Alexandra stared back up. Her eyes were wide with surprise, but a smile presented at the corner of her full pink lips. Her hair fell against the blanket, framing her sweet face in a golden halo.

"Riding horses," I replied. "The barn."

She giggled. "What?"

"When we went to visit the horses. That's when I had to know."

"Oh, oh." she smirked.

Alexandra pulled me back in. I kissed her again.

We spent the next few minutes clawing at one another. I wanted to take her then. Before, the thought hadn't crossed my mind that I could just fuck her out here. Ever since the fateful interruption, we'd not managed to find a full moment to go back down that road. I'd fantasised since then about the way she shuddered and the sound of her little moans and growls as I ran my hand over her panties. Now, with her body lying beneath me and her hips pressed to mine, I knew I would have done it if she asked.

We heard laughter, and I looked over to see Odette and Ingrid staring. I pulled myself back onto the blanket, hoping that my interest in this situation was not telegraphed by the outline of an erection showing through my pants. It had been so long since I was with anyone that the mere thought of fucking Alexandra had me running wild. I sat back, allowing Alexandra to pull herself together.

"Do you all not have something better to do?" Alexandra demanded. "We are busy preparing wedding things."

"I'm sorry, but you two weren't up to anything important," Ingrid snickered. "Unless you're practising for the wedding night. If so, get a room, Alex!"

Alexandra grabbed her notebook back and glared at her sisters. "Run along, girls!"

The girls snickered and left. I couldn't help but chuckle.

"They're so annoying. I'm sorry," Alexandra said.

"Nah. It's sweet. They care about you. They're young and idealistic. They look up to you."

"Do you look up to your brother?"

"My brother and I don't get on. He's a social nightmare. I'm just a nightmare. We have almost nothing in common. He hates sports. He hates going out. He's just not like me," I said.

Alexandra looked sad. "I don't know what I would do without them, honestly. I know they will all fly the coop eventually. I want that for them. However, it breaks my heart. Because I will miss them."

"They're not gone yet," I said. "We've got them for a bit longer."

We. God, I used we in a not-at-all-royal sense. What was happening to me?

Twenty-Five

ALEXANDRA

The more time I spent with Rick trying to cram in every ounce of our life stories into our brains, the more I fell for him. It was impossible to avoid. I wanted to know everything. We spent nearly twenty-four hours together learning everything we could. At least, that was what we said because it also led to us snogging like teenagers behind the schoolyard. Not that I would know anything about that. I didn't have my first kiss until I was standing on a polo field faking a relationship with a dubious prince.

Still, the more I kissed him, the more I wanted of him. When we'd been there on the blanket in the garden, his body pressing mine into the soft ground, I felt things I never had. My body tingled. My knees weakened, falling apart. I wanted him to envelop me and I wanted to envelop him.

On the day of the engagement interview, I didn't have to fake adoration for Rick. It was genuine. I stared at him like he was the moon and the stars because he was at that moment. I admired his jaw and adored his blond curls. I longed for his hand on my thigh, slowly going north.

"When did you fall for her?" The interviewer asked Rick.

We'd prepped for all of these. Rick was going to nail it.

"I was dancing with her," Rick answered, going off-book. "And just looking at her... I couldn't help but fall. She's wonderful."

He was being *honest*.

"And you, Your Majesty, as well?"

I stammered. "No... different time. We were at the barn. He was adorable with my horses. He is a sucker for animals. It endeared me to him in a remarkable way."

My answer was canned, but it worked. I couldn't be the wild one. That was Rick's role. He was the carefree, romantic hero in this story. I had to be Queen first and foremost. It was a tough tightrope. All I wanted to do was pull Rick into another room and kiss him again. I wanted him to press me against the wall and do far worse. I couldn't explain these feelings to anyone else. They were all-encompassing and came out of nowhere. One moment I was fine. The next, I wanted him to do something but wasn't sure what that something *was*.

"And how did he propose?" The interviewer followed up.

"She sort of proposed first. In true queenly fashion," Rick joked.

"But he wasn't satisfied with that," I said. "No. He wanted to do it properly. To treat me well. We had decided on it happening, but... he wanted to do something special. So, he took me on a picnic and proposed there. It was lovely."

"She deserved better than a handshake agreement, don't you think?" Rick asked.

Oh, the irony!

"And this ring is beautiful!"

I nodded. "Yes. This was my late mother's engagement ring. My father had it made for my mother."

"The Dowager Queen was very gracious in letting me use it to propose," Rick said. "It is a beautiful piece."

I smiled. "And it wasn't just that. He also chose a bracelet for me. Something old, something new."

"A bracelet?"

I nodded, holding my hand out and showing off the rubies on my wrist. "Stunning, right?"

The interviewer nodded. "He's already a good gift-giver. My husband could take a cue."

We snickered.

"I cannot complain." I shrugged. "He gives me no reason to."

Thinking back on it, that was insufferably cute. At the time, I meant every bit. I fell all over myself around him. Sometimes the feeling seemed mutual. Rick was more experienced, but I knew he felt *something*. If he didn't, why would he rush to defend me? Why was he always there to protect us? He had felt something, too.

"Of course, I don't," Rick said.

"So, what is next? Wedding plans?"

"Next... state visit to Lundhavn and wedding plans are in full swing," I answered.

He nodded. "But easy for me. I'm excited to go home and introduce Alexandra properly. But when I return I don't have to deal with much of the preparations. No one cares what the groom does most of the time."

"I care." I laughed. "You get to have opinions."

"She and her sisters will override me. That's alright, I don't care. The girls are so enthusiastic." Rick rubbed my knee.

"They are very excited. All my sisters are," I explained. "And I am so happy to be visiting Lundhavn. I cannot wait to meet Rikard's family properly and to engage with the Lundhavians a bit."

It was true. I wanted to learn everything. I wanted a family to include me. I was so excited to meet Rikard's parents, brother, and sister-in-law. I hoped his sister-in-law and I might be close. We'd be queens together someday. Our children would be cousins, right? Of course, that assumed Rick and I might have children. However, right about now, I was convinced that would happen. We were falling in love. I started this off, worrying I could never see myself going through with it. Now, I wanted him to throw me on a bed and... well, beyond that, I wasn't quite sure. But I wanted something.

"They will be so happy to meet her," Rick said.

"Been homesick?" The interviewer asked.

"Sometimes," Rick admitted. "But I enjoy it here. The outdoors are lovely, but I miss the mountains. I hope that she will love it there. We can visit whenever we want."

"Is it important for your children to understand both your Lund-havian and Neandian customs?"

We looked at one another, unsure how to answer.

"Well, you will be having children, right?"

"Naturally," Rick replied, looking a bit nervous. "Not in the immediate future, of course. I think we will raise them with an appreciation of both of our cultures."

It was a diplomatic answer.

"I would like them to speak both my mother tongue and his."

Rick agreed. "That would be good. I'd like them to be connected to their first cousins."

"We're all family now. It will work out." I smiled.

"Most people are over the moon about this wedding, but some are concerned about the age difference and the fact that you are so young, Your Majesty. Some would bring up that the regency still hangs over your head. Are you ready for this?"

I nodded. "I think so. I don't think anyone is ever completely ready for any big life change. They get that way over time. The regency is ending and while there is an age difference, it doesn't feel important to us."

Rick shook his head. "No. We're both happy together. She's a lovely person. I hope we get to spend many, many happy years together. She'll keep me young, I'm sure."

I snickered. "Or I will run you into the ground."

Rick chuckled. "It's a choose-your-own-adventure, Alexandra."

The chemistry now was undeniable. You couldn't fake it. We were a real couple. We could lie to one another, but... it wouldn't work.

TWENTY-SIX

RICK

The Royal Tour Begins

Today, Queen Alexandra arrived in Blavenberg looking adoring on the arm of her soon-to-be-husband, Prince Rikard. The two are in the Prince's home country to visit his parents and conduct royal engagements. This is the first tour abroad for Her Majesty. The Royal Palace in Blavenberg has provided the itinerary for the couple.

In their short week in Lundhavn, they will attend a sailing race, open a new exhibit at the National Museum, meet with children at an international school, and open a European trade summit.

The couple is on the heels of their engagement interview where we saw their incredible sexual chemistry in full glow. We couldn't love them more if we tried. Stick with *Exclusive* for more dirt to come.

"*Min skat*," my mother gave me an embarrassingly long hug as if I had been at war.

"Mother, he is getting married, leave him be. Don't steal him from dear Alexandra," Mikkel said.

We stood in the family sitting room, having only arrived in time for luncheon. Alexandra was trying to play along, but everyone forgot she didn't speak our dialect.

"Welcome to Blavenberg, Alexandra," my father said. "It is lovely to have you and finally meet you properly."

"Thank you for having me," Alexandra said a bit quietly. "My grandmother sends her best regards."

"Of course. Of course," Mamma said. "Come, come, sit. How do you take your coffee."

"As black as her heart," I joked.

It was true. Alexandra took her coffee black, but I was also trying to get her to come out of her shell. She looked nervous.

"Be nice," my father said to me.

Meanwhile, Alexandra snickered.

We settled in for coffee. Marie, whose English wasn't the best, tried to engage with Alexandra. Alexandra was either ignorant or otherwise disinterested. It occurred to me I had little to go on knowing how my future wife would handle normal social situations. She struggled when confronted with a man hitting on her younger sister. She wasn't sure how to read it. It hit me that this all might be overwhelming.

Alexandra did not lack manners. She was pure perfection but could be wooden in social situations. I knew she was capable of being funny and charming when she let her guard down, but she had little experience talking to outsiders and tended to freeze up.

Meanwhile, if she was reading the room's vibes, she fed off how awkward this was. My brother was noticeably agitated. His wife was acting off. My parents were trying to make the best of it. It was not helping.

"I heard you called off Windsor," Mikkel said. "Best season of your life and you called off Windsor! What a dumb idea!"

I shrugged. "Not a lot of time for polo when you're about to get married. You know that."

Truth was, I was disappointed about missing it but also wanted to save the family name. That required Alexandra and I to be open to speed bumps. She wanted to go, too. She desired a big international week away as much as I did—far from both of our families. And, selfishly, I thought if we'd managed it, things might have taken off.

"How are the wedding preparations... happening?"

Marie was nervous about her English.

"How are they going?" Alexandra asked, voice kind. "So far, we're talking to dress designers. All my sisters are excited. We had a meeting with the bishop."

That was awkward as hell. But, for the first time in my life, I could add celibacy to a list of held virtues. Although, I was struggling with that more than ever. Since the beginning of adulthood, I had sex quite regularly, never contemplating holding back. The more time we stole away, the more I prepared to lie to the bishop about being on good behaviour. While I feared Celeste's wrath, Alexandra became more and more tempting. The fact that we hadn't done much was odd but also made me want to do a lot more in a big way. Maybe there was truth to some things being worth the wait?

"You met with the bishop. Will you be converting?" Mikkel joked in our mother tongue.

"Look, it may be funny to you, but it must be done," I replied in English. "And no. I don't have to convert. We must go through this awful conference process. I don't much care for it."

"Neither of us does. A box to tick," Alexandra said. "I loathe that."

"You are not very religious?" Mikkel asked.

Alexandra shook her head. "Afraid not. Piety is a virtue beaten into our heads by my grandmother, but I find it tiresome. Anything that is reinforced primarily by guilt seems unfair."

Her candour surprised me. It was also kind of hot. I loved off-the-cuff Alexandra. Whenever she came out to play, I encourage it. I squeezed her knee to let her know I concurred. She met my gaze with a devious smile.

Mamma changed the subject. "If we can be of any assistance with the planning, please let us know. We are very excited for the wedding,

Your Majesty. I am sure you have things under control. I also remember being a royal bride and the extreme pressure."

"It is very much," Marie said.

"It's not without stress. The good news is, as a monarch, you sort of do what you want. And please, call me Alexandra."

It was partially true and partially not. I suspected we would cross bridges that Celeste would fight us on. We hadn't hit an issue she much cared about yet. I was surprised we hadn't gotten more pushback. It made me wonder what the old bitch was up to.

"Well, we are happy to have you with us," Pappa said. "Alexandra, we have put you in the apartment directly next to us. If you need anything—"

"She will not be coming back to Blauhus with me?" I asked.

"The request made by the Palace—the official demand—was the Queen must be stationed here for security reasons," Pappa answered.

I assumed we'd have a bit of an awkward first evening together sharing a bed before things got off to a roaring start. Since Alexandra couldn't keep her hands off me, I wanted to get the show on the road. She was ready, but my plans were thwarted.

"It's fine. I can stay here. I don't want to leave you alone, Alexandra." I said. "That seems unfair."

"We do not want there to be allegations of impropriety," Pappa said. "So it is best—"

"They lived together!" I waved in the direction of my brother and sister-in-law.

Alexandra squeezed my knee. "It's got to be Celeste up to being Celeste. It's fine. We will just... we don't want to put your family in a bad position."

I was angry, but I also couldn't tell her why. After coffee, she decided to settle in and direct the dressers and maids assigned to her. Meanwhile, I hung out in her room. We would be alone sparingly on this trip.

"I wanted to spend one-on-one time with you," I lamented.

"I would like that, too, but you know Celeste," Alexandra said. "Darling, whatever happens, she is going to find out and punish us. She could do all manner of things."

It was the first time she'd used a pet name for me. It was unexpectedly heart-warming.

"Can we not wait a bit longer?" Alexandra laughed. "Just a bit. And I promise you... it will happen."

Her tone was earnest. I couldn't help but trust her but also wanted to throw caution to the wind and take her right there. I assumed if we fucked, it would already be worth it. Inversely, Alexandra made a good point. Celeste could wreak havoc. The risk wasn't just to me but also to my family. It was for Alexandra and her three sisters who never asked for any of this.

"Okay," I agreed. "Just know that... I do want to... do more."
She blushed. "Same."
"And I hope this place suits you and all is well."
"Your family seems... normal. So far, they are lovely. I adore that your mother refers to you as *min skat*. Mamma used to do the same to us, Rick. It was sweet and it hit me in the feels."

"I thought it was embarrassing."
"Don't. Your mother loves you and you still have her! Sometimes I wonder if I will ever remember her another day. Mamma was the best sort of person. Asti and I remember her. We miss her."

"I am sorry for that, Alexandra," I said. I never thought about how much it must hurt. "Doing this all without your parents must be difficult. Weddings... they're emotional, right?"

"It's hard, yes."
"You can always tell me about it," I said. "I don't know how I can help. I'm not good at this stuff but I will try."

"I disagree. You can be very sweet and understanding," Alexandra said. "You describe yourself as if you were some sort of monster, but Rick I do not see it that way. You're wonderful. You are capable of being compassionate. Don't convince yourself you're a monster. You love hard."

It was the first time a woman acknowledged what my mother had done alone for all these years. She always said I was her sweet one. And, compared to Mikkel the Emotional Vacuum, I was. No one saw that—not my father and not past partners. After spending my entire life being told I was just an attention whore, I gave up and dug into being the monster other people saw me as. I was the bad boy. I was the rake.

"Thank you for believing that but I don't know if I deserve it."

Alexandra took my face in her hands. "You deserve it for as well as you take care of me and the girls. Okay? You may have done some bad things before, Rick, but... you are a good person deep down. Tell yourself you are worthy of love. You are."

There was a knock. "Sir, your father and brother are going out on the sailboat. They request you join them."

"Alright," I agreed. "Thank you, Martin."

"You should go," Alexandra said.

I nodded, not wanting to. "I should. Never alone."

"I will see you later. Enjoy the time, darling."

She gave me the sweetest kiss. Alexandra was so good and pure. Lying to her was wrong. Yet, what she didn't know wouldn't hurt her. And I hoped she would never know.

I left her room, joining Martin in the hall.

"Apologies, sir. I did my best to keep them at bay. I figured you might want some time alone with Her Majesty."

"You did your best. I appreciate it."

We continued down the hall. I shook my head.

"What is it?" Martin asked.

"I'm so guilty! She's so good and sees me as good. But this scheme with the press? My lies about why I agreed to the engagement and how we engineered it? She still doesn't know. She must never know, you understand?"

Martin nodded. "Sir, I think she would understand, but I gather some things are best left hidden. I see how much you enjoy your time with her. I know it is genuine. You shouldn't feel guilty about that."

"I am doing the best I can to make a life for us—but also to save the family. It's selfish. I hate lying to her. It never bothered me at the start, but now..."

Now I knew what was going on. My feelings for her grew stronger by the day. Alexandra was now my greatest confidante and champion. I worried if she thought this was all put on, she'd never forgive me. Yet, telling her risked her not understanding how much I adored her and wanted her. I couldn't tell her. Lying seemed more compassionate now.

"Now, you just want to make her happy," Martin said. "It is good. I wish you both much happiness."

Twenty-Seven

Alexandra

Blavenberg was a cosmopolitan city with progressive ideas. Women sunbathed topless and no one said boo. People left their babies in prams outside of coffee shops unattended. Fathers often played a role as primary parents, hauling two or three little ones through the street. It was charming but different.

The language I only half got—grateful to speak a bit thanks to Mum and her past. Their dialect differed from what I knew, but it slowly came back. My language skills proved enough to make me *dangerous* but not a lot more.

Marie spoke shaky English and while I understood much of her mother tongue, I spoke little. Rick pointed out she tried to bridge a gap. Mikkel complicated it by admonishing her as she struggled to find the right words. The guilt churned my stomach. I always spoke kindly as she tried. I appreciated the effort, but neither of us knew the words to communicate effectively. I was even more out-of-sorts.

The staff at the palace were lovely as ever but I was a fish out of water. The customs differed. Celeste called ahead to make sure Rick and I would not spend a single night alone, which to some degree, made me expect we wouldn't.

At the same time, I wanted to. Thankfully, I packed books. I was devouring a series written by one of Asti's favourite authors. I hated to admit how much I lived for the moment one of the people fell. And, sadly, I was began to relate to those poor tortured souls waiting for the other to turn around and say I love you back.

The books were a distraction on my lonely evenings after Rick left. When his parents withdrew, his brother and sister returned to their apartments. It was so eerie to be so alone. I wanted to cuddle with my sister. And while I'd like to say the same about Rick, there were other problems.

I wanted him. Well, I wanted him but for what I wasn't sure. Rick was glorious, dashing, and made me feel things in places I never felt them—things I realised were normal the more romance novels I consumed. The wetness that appeared between my legs after we spent ages kissing was easily explained.

It was a version of *arousal,* a word I didn't yet understand. The more time we spent, the more I wanted *something*. I wanted to feel what the heroines in my stories described almost as rocketing to heaven. I wanted the clouds to part, the sun to rise, and fireworks to explode. I wasn't sure how to get there, but I craved it.

I suspected Rick wanted the same after his reaction to the sleeping arrangement snafu. He brought it up every day we were in Lundhavn. Such was the case one morning when he climbed into the car with me to depart on a royal engagement at the National Museum before flying back to Neandia.

"How were you?" Rick asked. "Bored to tears?"

"I tried to speak to Marie, but Mikkel kept interrupting—even worse than when you were there. I'd like us to be friends, but he seems hell-bent on ruining it."

"I wish I were there." Rick squeezed my hand. "I'd tell him to calm down. My brother is awful at socialising."

"I thought I was bad."

"You have been clever and charming. Disarming. He is mostly anti-social. Mamma always does the heavy lifting with Pappa, but he lets her do that. He acknowledges her social suitability. Mikkel ignores all else. He is insufferable!"

"You two don't get on?"

"We aren't like the Deschamps girls, no. I am jealous of the way the four of you connect. It's nice."

I nodded.

"I missed you, though," Rick said, voice sweet.

I wished he would kiss me now, but we were arriving at the engagement.

I grinned. "I missed you, too."

And with that, we stepped out. Continuing the engagement looking very much like a couple, we listened to one another. Rick guided me through passages and crowds with his hand politely on the small of my back. It was a sign of ownership. Rick had no idea how much I relished the feeling that he had chosen me. Even if he had only partially chosen me, it was tremendous.

When we left the museum, the new exhibit was official. People cheered. Flashbulbs fired. Unfortunately, that was it. We had one more evening here. Rick stayed for dinner and then we all broke off again. It was so odd. I missed my sisters and fought homesickness like mad the minute Rick left.

I read a bit and took a walk. The idea of wandering was a novelty. Here, I was safe, but also free. It was odd. Yes, the palace was like a giant prison in lockdown, but here I could walk as I pleased. I paraded all around, taking stock of the dark corridors. The dark didn't frighten me the way it did others. I loved the calm.

That was when I ran into someone.

"Oh, darling, are you just out here wandering?" Rick's mother asked.

"Queen Karolina." I bowed in a Pavlovian response. "I am sorry. I was restless."

"Come, come." Karolina wrapped her arm around mine as if we were sisters.

I followed her down to a tiny room. In it were two sofas, a television, and a small kitchenette.

"I will make you a hot cocoa!"

"*Takk*," I thanked her.

"Why are you still up at this hour, my dear?"

"I usually have more company," I said.

She blushed and I did the same, realising she thought I meant her son.

"Not Rick," I said. "No, my sisters and I are close. And my sister Astrid and I often stay up late talking or reading. It makes it feel like home to have her with me. But... it's odd to be in this scenario where no one needs anything, and no one wants anything."

"You could have said he visited you and I would not have minded," Karolina assured. "You two make a lovely couple. He's protective of you. He doesn't like that you are here, and he is there."

"He's protective of my sisters, too. I don't understand it. He is a good person. I know some might disagree, but he has a good heart," I said.

Karolina smiled. She came back with two hot cocoas.

"You see the good in him. That is sweet. He is a good boy—a tender boy. Most do not see it. I am grateful you do."

I nodded.

Karolina let out a long sigh. "The next time you return, you will be wed."

"It's wild. A bit mad."

"It is good. You will have a lifetime with one another still. You are young and have many good days left."

I supposed she was right.

Karolina shrugged. "Marriage is hard, but gratifying. You need to do your best for one another, but that's all you can do. It will never be equal or perfect at all, but still wonderful."

"What is the best part?" I asked.

Karolina smiled. "Having someone who is yours—in your corner alone. Having that one person who will always stand up for you and care for you. It is beautiful in that way. August always takes care of me. Treasures me, really."

I beamed. "That is sweet."

"Your mother loved your father fiercely," Karolina offered. "I don't know how much you remember?"

"Enough," I answered. "Papa was a complicated man. Mamma

tried. She did love him very much. And sadly, he loved her more than I think she ever knew. Without her, he couldn't go on."

Karolina nodded. "Your mother was a bright spark in the dark. You are, too. And I see the way Rick takes to you. It is beautiful. You are wonderful for him."

"He is good for me as well. I am learning to stand up for myself and talk to people. I was raised very sheltered. He is the opposite. Maybe he can be too much, but I need an overcorrection to appear normal."

"That is a good way to put it."

"I suppose it's like that for Mikkel and Marie."

The Queen snickered, covering her face playfully to avoid my gaze. "Mikkel would do well to let her manage his social affairs, but he fights her. He struggles. It annoys her. Let Rick be the talkative one. Enjoy the work you don't have to do," Karolina said. "Don't do it for the sake of control. Sometimes, it is nice to give it over."

I admitted it sounded attractive to hand over some degree of control to Rick. I trusted him. I supposed if I trusted him, it made it okay. Back when I hadn't, I worried he was out for anyone's interest but mine. Now, I knew we were united against Celeste. That was all that mattered. Or so I thought.

Twenty-Eight

Rick

"Sir, Miss Morgen is on the phone for you. Should I patch her through?" A butler asked.

I was at my own home missing Alexandra when my ex rang me up, wanting to chat. It had been months and now I was engaged. She had no business calling. Struggling to resist, I agreed to take the call and waited to hear her sexy, husky voice on the other end of the line.

"Hi," she said.

"Hello." I tried formality.

"Well, I'm legally divorced now."

"Congratulations?"

"Yes, indeed. I am free of the man who has made me miserable for years. Rikard, you know—"

"Very little. Very little of you. And that is for the best."

"Don't you realise—"

"Bridget, we aren't together. I am engaged. I am living abroad—soon to move to Neandia permanently."

"Are you? Because we could run away together. Wouldn't you like that?"

It was so tempting. Even two months ago, I would have left forever.

Now, I thought about my parents and their earned happiness. I thought about leaving my brother with an exploding box of kittens if I did that—the scandal that would haunt this court forever and a day. But mostly, I thought about breaking Alexandra's heart in pieces. It hurt. I was sure if she knew I was speaking to my ex, she'd be upset.

"This is risky even—us talking."

"Rick, I miss you."

"Bridget, you must stop calling me, okay? Like... I don't know how to put this. In my time of need, you hung up on me—"

"My settlement was on the line!"

"Alexandra's heart is on the line! She is a sweet, kind person who believes I am capable of being good deep down. I cannot hurt her, Bridget."

I listened as she had a good belly laugh at my expense.

"Yes, poor little Alexandra. Baby Alexandra. I know you have no interest in her."

"I do," I said. "And we grow closer by the day."

"Is she there then?"

"No. Official policy is the bride must stay separately. No concerns of impropriety."

"So you aren't fucking?"

I didn't like her tone. No, we weren't. I wished we were. I gathered so did Alexandra. I hated the idea of a few months more with celibacy but damn if I didn't think it might be fun at that point. I wanted to unwrap her like a birthday present. God, the idea of it conjured up more than feelings these days. I never imagined I would find myself attracted to Alexandra, but she lived in my brain rent-free. Our time apart only hammered that home. I worried about her.

"Whether we are or aren't isn't your business, Bridge."

"Hmm... well, since you've gone soft on me, I am done. This is your last chance. If you want—"

"Bridget, I could blow up my life for you, yes, but I don't want to. What I want is to try to have a redemption arc where I stop lashing out and hurting people. You deserve the same. Take the time to find someone who treats you well for once. Cherish that, okay?"

"What?"

"Just..." I wasn't sure what to say. "Goodbye."

I hung up.

I paced, wanting to scream. I was shaking. Torture was seeing her dangled in front of me. I knew she was no good, but I couldn't help myself. I headed down to the garage. Hopping in my car, I drove like a madman through the streets.

I arrived at the palace and padded down the hall to find the person I longed to see. Press and parents be damned! I needed to do this.

"Rick... what are you doing here?"

Alexandra opened the door to her room in a dressing gown. It was not sexy, but I sensed maybe there was something sexy underneath it.

I pushed my way into her doorway, still reeling. The bed was unmade. She'd been cosied up with a book by the looks of it-— one with a half-naked cowboy on the cover. Interesting choice, but I couldn't fault her for reading.

"I... I wanted to tell you that I missed you," I said.

"You said that earlier," Alexandra said. "Are you alright?"

"Alexandra, I want and need you in my life. We started this off on odd footing, but I need you now. You see good in me I do not. You believe in me when I have no hope in hell of doing anything right."

"That's not true."

"I care about you, Lex. I just wanted you to know."

"Okay, well, I care about you, too, but our hides will be tanned if—"

"Oh, fuck them! Celeste cannot control us forever—"

"Celeste can hurt me," Alexandra's voice was nervous.

"Alright, I won't stay," I agreed. "I want to, but I won't."

I opened the door to the hall and stepped across the threshold.

"I will be here for you—no one else—until you tell me otherwise," I promised. "You and your sisters can trust in me. Now and forever. I'm here to help."

Alexandra smiled broadly. I couldn't help but want to kiss her. God, she looked so adorable! I leaned in, my lips grazing hers. She pulled me closer by the collar of my shirt. I dug in, pushing her against the door jam. We stood halfway in the threshold. I ran my hand down to cup her ass. As I did, she leaned harder into me. As I cupped her breast with my other hand, I was delighted to find it was surprisingly full. I wanted to bury my face in her tits before running her off to bed. She moaned. I wondered if getting her off counted against us.

That was until I heard a voice behind us.

"Dear brother, what are you doing here?"

I stopped, backing away.

"I was saying goodnight to Alexandra," I said.

Alexandra nodded, as if in a trance.

"Well, you should be mindful. There are rules and you are about to break them. Goodnight, Your Majesty!"

He called as he crossed back to the wing Marie and he shared.

"Goodnight," Alexandra called back politely.

"I should go," I said, shaken back to reality.

I loathed it but he was right.

"Why do they live here but you don't?"

"Mikkel doesn't do well on his own," I whispered. "And I think Marie needs Mamma to run interference."

"What? Why?"

"He's out there. And he and Marie don't get on like us," I said. "Believe it or not, we're friends. They aren't. It's all a bit odd."

She giggled. "We're friends?"

"A bit," I agreed.

Alexandra leaned back to give me a sweet kiss. "It will be okay. We are friends, yes. But I think we will have a lot more to be happy about. Let's get home, get married, and do all the things we need to get to freedom."

TWENTY-NINE

ALEXANDRA

Celeste did her best to separate us. I longed to keep up this back-and-forth of attending engagements with Rick, but it was not to be. Celeste ensured we were assigned separately most of the time. Going out with my future husband was a rare treat. She said it "preserved the mystery" but I doubted her reasoning.

Matters became further complicated when his sister-in-law announced her first pregnancy only two weeks after we landed in Neandia. She had complications very early on. When she landed in hospital, Rick's father requested that he return to Lundhavn -to help them manage engagements. Marie was the social butterfly. She was the one people wanted. And, as I well knew, Mikkel was dreadful before a public audience without her.

Rick would come back to Neandia occasionally, but we never had much time together. I didn't fault him. Nor did the girls. We knew he was taking care of his family. We admired him for it. However, the house was lonely without him. Rick was teaching the girls how to waltz. So, since Asti and I had gotten quite good at it, we continued this. I spoke with him on the phone daily. Everything about our relationship felt surprisingly normal.

The girls and I busied ourselves with royal wedding planning. Odette took great pride in putting things together and planning out "looks" for everything from flowers to colours to motifs. She even helped me choose our wedding march and monogram. Rick cared not what I picked there. He trusted me. He would always joke that I could put him in a pink tuxedo, and he would simply arrive and do the thing. It was our agreement, but it was also just Rick. He had no interest in micromanaging wedding plans and otherwise loathed being home and alone, having adjusted to Neandia.

Rick arrived back in Neandia for good a month before the wedding. He returned this time *with* his parents. Mikkel and Marie were still grounded, but Karolina and August were free to travel. Neandia hosted a state dinner for the King and Queen. It doubled as our engagement celebration, tripling as Rick's birthday night, and quadrupling as my official coming-out party.

To prepare, a designer prepared a beautiful red dress—the prettiest I had ever seen. It sparkled in the light. It was a traditional ballgown, but the bodice was the most age-appropriate thing I had ever worn. And, to top it off, Rick's family presented me with the most spectacular tiara—a traditional gift for a royal bride. It was the first time I had worn a tiara, and I was still getting used to the weight and pain of it boring into my skull.

Astrid and I prepared for the evening with a long bout of hair and makeup. The girls little joined us, bubbling with excitement. *God, I loved to see us all so happy together!* It filled my heart in the biggest way. I dismissed them while I took a moment to soak up everything I felt. I also needed to do the thing I needed to do every day now. I grabbed the package of birth control pills I hid inside a hollowed-out book on my bedside table. It was brilliant to give the old bat the middle finger. I was now a warrior for my cause—and that of my sisters—and this was another step. I was called more every day to take charge.

All a-dazzle, I reported to the line-up by the ballroom to lead in the rest of the family on Rick's arm. It was the first time we had spoken all day. As I raced down the hall with Astrid, I found him there with his parents trying to ignore Celeste. He looked bored but dashing in a tuxedo that brought out his shoulders. I was flustered thinking about him.

Rick's eyes met mine. He did a double-take. I still wondered why he saw me attractive enough to bother with. I knew I wasn't his type as he preferred thin, leggy brunettes. If you did some research and saw the women he dated, they all fit that mould. I was curvaceous—something Celeste loathed—and short. I stopped to his right, letting him take me in.

"You look... magnificent," Rick stammered.

I blushed uncontrollably. I wasn't sure if he was generally impressed or just surprised I could ever look this good. I didn't blame him if it was the latter. I was surprised myself.

I said, "Thank you. You also look very nice."

"Nothing compared to you."

He gave me a quick kiss. Celeste cleared her throat, annoyed.

"Let us be on good behaviour, shall we."

"Oh, that's harmless, Celeste. We're among family," August said. "It's nice to see the two of them happy, isn't it?"

Celeste feigned satisfaction but it was clear she was irate at Rick's handsy-ness. Even now he stared at me like I was a steak. I was suddenly the only woman in the room. I wanted to kiss him and do a lot more. I was prepared for it. There was something magical about this evening. I was willing to throw caution to the wind. He'd returned to me like a hero. I wanted to do anything with him. I wanted him to want to do everything to me.

We entered the ballroom and took our seats for dinner next to Celeste and his father. It was customary to sit apart once married. So, this would be the last time we got to do this. It was the first and last— sort of bittersweet. Crammed into this dress, I could not eat much. I saved most of my room for the torte delivered to me at the end of the meal. Rick was in a brilliant mood, and I couldn't stop smiling. Celeste opted *not* to give a toast, which was disheartening. I felt a loss. She didn't care to talk me up. Thankfully, August did.

"I am grateful to Her Majesty and the Dowager Queen for hosting my family today," he said. "It is wonderful to see our son so happy and making a meaningful commitment not just to his future wife, but to the people of Neandia."

Many clapped. I looked over at Rick, feeling nothing but adoration. He looked back at me as if we were alone here.

"Marriage is challenging sometimes but always rewarding. There are more good times than bad. You both will learn from one another as you go, but you can always rely on one another. Rikard, support her. That is your job. You are her right hand. Alexandra, ask for help when you need it. You do not walk alone."

I nodded.

"We are very excited to be back here next month for all the festivities. But now, let us toast them. May this month go as smoothly as it can."

People raised their glasses to say their declarations of best wishes. *Skol was* the Lundhavian choice. *Santé* rang out from the Neandians. We sipped and stared at one another. It was a surprise to make it here. I wondered where the time had gone—finding myself deliriously happy in the meantime.

After dinner, Rick and I danced a beautiful waltz. It was a test run for the wedding. I was impressed at how well I was doing.

"You look so beautiful, Alexandra," Rick said as we stepped across the floor. "Really and truly. I would like to do far more than I am permitted to do at the moment."

I shook my head, unable to stop blushing.

"You want me to, though."

"I... I do, but... I cannot speak of it here," I protested.

"We will... chat... later."

"Uh-huh," I agreed like an idiot.

My heart soared.

It would happen! We would be together in every way. Everything else could wait until we'd done all the things. It was worth the risk suddenly. All the dreams of what I had desired came to mind as he dipped me and pulled me back in. Our bodies seemed closer than before. The music ended and we parted ways. I only got a moment to catch my breath before August cut in.

"Alexandra, could I have a dance?"

"She's all yours," Rick patted his father's shoulder.

I nodded. "Of course."

We picked up again. Around and around we went. He was a good dancer, though not as light or nimble as his adept son.

"I am so happy this worked out. And you... you are more than we could ask for, Alexandra—for Rick and the family."

I shrugged. "I don't know. I am fine."

"It takes a brave woman to willingly engage in press intrigue. And you must love him to go along with everything so quickly. I almost didn't believe him."

"What do you mean?" I asked.

His words confused me.

"Just the cover-up. That you would be willing to go to the mat for him to cover up the affair."

"What?" I asked, more confused.

"The affair. He had an affair. Your wedding is saving us from the press coming after him. You agreed to—"

"Oh, yes, of course."

I cut him off, not wanting to hear anymore. I held it together by a thread as the song ended. Cover up? Did Rick use me all this time? An affair? With whom? My brain scrambled; my limbs suddenly fell lip. I wandered off the floor and took a seat. I stared back at the floor to see Rick going around with Astrid now. I wanted to smack him. I hated that he was with her. Was he more interested in Astrid than me?

It was as if everything was suddenly a lie. The happiness and adoration we shared only an hour before was gone. All peace left me. No longer did I want to crawl in bed with him. No longer did I want to kiss him or say sweet things. I didn't want him to be sweet or to dote. I wanted none of that. I had no choice but to power through this and move along. The mission was freedom.

I wasn't here to fall in love or for something romantic. I focused again on the end goal I previously identified. It would be enough.

Thirty

RICK

I found Alexandra suddenly cold. She protested that she was tired. She said her tiara gave her a headache. Still, she was curt. I was confused. Before all this, I thought we were about to jump into bed. I thought finally I might get to have her. Instead, I realised not only was that not happening, but something was wrong.

We left the ballroom. We couldn't go unescorted, so of course Astrid accompanied us as we proceeded. Alexandra remained quiet and Astrid was prickly. We'd all been laughing only hours before. Now, the humour was gone. What could have happened to make things so sterile and odd?

When we arrived outside Alexandra's door, she asked that Astrid leave us. We were now alone in a mostly dark hallway. I made out the pained expression on Alexandra's face. Gone was the beautiful smile on full display earlier. Her tiara picked up tiny bits of light but seemed dull suddenly.

"I don't know what happened. Can I get you anything?" I asked. "I'm worried about you, Lex."

She shook her head. "I'm fine."

She was lying. I reached for her hand, and she pulled back.

"No! Do not touch me!"

"What?" I cocked my head. "Alexandra, what is happening? I thought all was well. We had such a lovely evening—"

"Rick, I cannot... this is not happening. Maybe you thought you might land me tonight. I am, after all, just a pawn."

Her face pulled, as if in pain. She started to cry.

"No, Alexandra. You aren't. I don't think that—"

"I'm not? So, I'm not part of the attempt to subvert the media and cover up an affair? What affair, Rikard? What happened? What are you lying to me about?"

Her voice rang, loudly. I was busted! I felt terrible. My stomach churned. My heart sank. It broke. I realised I'd been living a fantasy— caught up in very real feelings about her. Alexandra suddenly slipped away. Love in her eyes was replaced with contempt.

"It's not like that," I insisted.

"Your father said—"

"Alexandra, I do not care what he told you, my feelings are genuine!"

"So there was no plot with the media?"

"I didn't say that!"

"Who is she?"

"She was no one to you, but I did love her. She was married. Her husband blackmailed Pappa and then lied. He went to the media anyway. *Exclusive* was willing to take a deal if they could cover every-thing first," I said.

Honesty poured out of me in a way I never expected. I wanted to tell her everything. I wanted to start over. I wanted everything clean. She didn't trust me. I should have worried about my situation if she left me, but my greatest fear was that I would break her heart.

"I'm a dick, okay. I'm Rick the Prick. I'm sorry. Or I was. I.... Alexandra, I love you."

The words flew out of my mouth. I wanted her face to soften. I wanted her to believe me. It was the truth. I *did* love her. I wanted her to grab onto me. I longed for an exuberant kiss. Instead, she sobbed.

"Stop lying to me. It hurts worse!"

I tried to comfort her, but she backed up, unable to even look at me now.

"Alexandra, baby... I'm... I'm so sorry."

"Don't baby me. You have been lying to me—"

"Not about my feelings. Not about how I love you. Not about how you make me feel, Alexandra. No. I want you. I need you. I want to marry you."

"I know. Because it will save your family's skin," she sobbed. "Fuck you! You don't deserve me!"

"We agree on that, yes."

She shook her head. "Don't worry. I'll not break it off. You and I will do the thing and look the part. But this is it. We are teammates with the same goal. Your job is to ensure Celeste goes her merry way. We will keep everything above board, so she suspects nothing. And the girls will be free. Do you understand?"

She smashed my heart.

I quietly agreed to her plan. "Yes, Alexandra. Anything."

"I don't want you to think anything is ever going to happen between us," Alexandra said.

"I...I will always follow your lead, Alexandra. I am sorry I hurt you. I am sorry I ever lied. I wish I would have been honest with you because you don't deserve this. I don't blame you, but I do love you."

"Stop saying that!"

"I cannot."

"It's contrived!"

"Alexandra, I never meant to say it. Saying it is frightening. Baby, I do love you. And because of that, I will wait. As long as it takes. And Lord knows we have an eternity to wait it out."

She crossed her arms. "No. Nothing will change. You can wait, but this is where it stands. That is your folly."

"I have the audacity to believe it will work out," I said.

"Just... forget I ever said anything to you about wanting anything real," she said. "I didn't. I lied."

But she didn't lie. She felt every bit of the same for me. I had broken her heart. And now, I was breaking my own. This was all my fault. I had—once again—destroyed my happiness. She was right. I didn't deserve her. However, I believed this time I might have a second chance. I had nothing but time.

"I will wait. And always take care of you and the girls," I promised. "Hate me all you want, Alexandra. That makes two of us. But I will take care of you all to the best of my abilities. That cunt won't win."

I expected at least a snicker out of Alexandra, but I got nowhere. So, I turned and left. As I did, I could hear her body racked by sobs in the echo of the vast hall. It killed me. I could not have hated myself more if I tried at that moment. I vowed to show here through all my best intent that we could make it work.

THIRTY-ONE

ALEXANDRA

"Darling, I know you are upset. I understand why. He doesn't deserve you. However, you're getting married, and we have a million plans. You cannot simply lie in here all day and ignore everyone. The entire house is getting nervous the longer this goes on. They will suspect something."

Astrid sat on the edge of my bed. It was the week before my wedding. Rick's family were about to arrive any moment now and we still barely spoke. Tonight, we had to open the opera together. I dreaded it.

"It doesn't matter. Everything will work. It must. He has everything to lose," I said.

"She is set to hand the documentation to end the regency off to the PM," Astrid informed me.

"How do you know?"

"I overheard Lord William running his mouth to someone in the hall."

"You were snooping."

"What do you care?"

I didn't. Or, rather, I shouldn't.

"We must try on your dress anyhow."

I shrugged. "It doesn't matter. It's all a joke."

"Let's have lunch, then go to the fitting. It will be nice. At least enjoy looking beautiful if you don't enjoy anything else."

I grumbled. It was hard to think about my wedding dress when I was so broken. I had spent three weeks licking my wounds. Rick and I were seen together just enough. I hadn't kissed him since greeting him the night of our banquet. I couldn't even look at the engagement picture he gave me. That day, he brought it to me along with the tiara his parents bestowed. It was lovely. I couldn't wait to wear the new diadem with my reception dress but now the idea disgusted me.

"You will get to wear Mamma's tiara," Astrid said. "It will look lovely. The little girls don't understand any of this. They want to see the two of you live out the fairytale. And they are desperate to see you in your dress."

I sighed. "I guess I can do it for them."

"Exactly. That's the spirit! Now, come on."

She pulled me out of bed, forcing me to put on actual clothing in preparation for our luncheon. Celeste had us come down more often these days. I loathed any day spent with her, but she was more withdrawn than usual. I attributed it to her taking the win. She seemed pleased that Rick and I were in a bad way. She preferred me miserable.

"She wants it to be like this," I said to Astrid on our way to luncheon.

"Like what?"

"Me and Rick hating one another. She wants me to be so broken—"

"I know," my sister said. "I know."

"So you don't want me to give her the satisfaction?"

"No, I do not."

We arrived at the dining room to find Rick seated, having an awkward conversation with our great-uncle Hubert. God, this was going to be the longest week of my life! There was no doubt about that. I tried not to look at him, but it was nearly impossible. I had to sit across from him. I had to look at his strong jaw and his big brown eyes. I must put up with the smile and those goddamn dimples. The situation forced me to endure the look of him this afternoon—his stubble perfectly imperfect. It made him look rugged *and* put together. I hated him for it.

"Good afternoon, Alexandra. You've been very busy today," Rick said. "I've barely seen you girls."

"Well, you know how it is," I said. "Uncle Hubert. How are you?"

"Quite well, thank you. I have been talking to the groom about planning."

"Ah," I said.

I was confused about what planning they discussed. The only planning Rick had was a very basic understanding of how the ceremony would go and the parade route. Tomorrow, I would have to play act through the whole thing with him several times. I hope he read the information that Jacques provided.

"You are trying on your dress today?" Rick asked.

"Yes," I said, confused.

"I read the schedule, Alexandra."

"Ah."

He was trying *so* hard, but no bother. Nothing he said or did mattered.

"Is Celeste coming to join?" I asked my uncle.

"No, darling girl. She has caught a cold and has taken ill. She met with the Prime Minister this morning and went to bed. Shouted at me to leave her alone when I attempted to bring her tea."

"She met with the PM?" Astrid asked.

"And Prince Rikard, yes," Hubert said.

I glared across the table at Rick. How was *he* invited?

"Oh, was there a changing of the guard to sign my life away into your hands?"

Hubert chuckled. I wasn't joking, though.

"No. I was there to ensure matters were closed. I insisted she invite you as well, but... she didn't." Rick's voice quieted and he looked down. "The bill was handed off. Parliament will sign off this afternoon, Lex."

Astrid was bursting. "Really?"

Rick nodded. "It has been done. You could watch Parliament

working. I am sure there is a channel here to do so. We have that in Lundhavn."

"It is not so common here," my uncle explained. "We are not as open."

"Well, it will be done. It was a good conversation."

Rick smiled.

I did not return it, nodding. "Good."

"You are not so exuberant today as you were upon your engagement banquet," Hubert said. "Are you feeling well?"

"Just nervous," I lied. "Wedding jitters. I must try on my dress. I am worried."

Lunch continued. Astrid and Hubert yammered on. I would occasionally catch Rick looking at me. It killed me. He was still hopeful. Why? He never mentioned trying to save the thing with the press. He never pleaded with me to stay. He always just told me he wished me well. Yet, I could not get over how much he hurt me.

It was the first time I had loved anyone and the first time anyone had ever hurt me quite as intimately. I'd never thought about being with anyone before Rick. He'd made me think such dreadful things all the time. And then, he'd shattered it. He made me feel stupid. He betrayed me.

It was one more desertion. My mother and father left me so young. I wanted the person I married to stick around for good—to be honestly invested. At the start, I told myself I was hardened against loss. Now, I knew better. I yearned to trust my husband. With Rick, there was no trust. I had nothing with him. I wished he would have been honest, but could he even be honest? I wasn't sure.

We navigated down to the salon where my dress was waiting. My sisters crowded me, excitedly. I had long awaited my duchesse satin beauty with its long, gorgeous train and its sweetheart neckline. I wanted so badly for it to be perfect. If there was one thing I could have, it would be to look beautiful on my wedding day in front of millions. The dressers took me behind the screen to do the unveiling.

Sadly, something was wrong.

My ivory gown was replaced by a sad white disaster. The sweetheart neckline was now closer to a square that came up to just below my collarbone. It looked matronly. I began to cry. The dress was all wrong.

"What happened to it?" I asked.

"There were changes made at your request," the designer said.

I cried, standing in front of the mirror now. All three of my sisters gathered around me. Astrid held me up as I broke down.

"It still looks beautiful," Odette said.

"I look like a bloody nun," I cried. "It's ruined! She ruined it."

"Did these changes come from our grandmother?" Astrid asked.

"They came from the palace," the designer said. "We were told to raise and alter the neckline and use the white satin instead of the ivory originally ordered."

I shook in anger. She'd kept me in the dark this whole time. Normal royal brides would have had three or four fittings. She swore this was fine, but as I compared notes with Marie, I knew it wasn't. I suspected something was up then, but this was next level. I was beside myself.

"I'll be back in a minute," Astrid said.

Before I could tell her not to go, she ducked out. I worried–if she tangled with Celeste, it would blow up in our faces. At the same time, I knew it couldn't get worse than this. Standing in a dress fit for a sixty-year-old religious virgin, I felt hideous and ridiculous. Anymore I didn't care. If I emerged in this number, I'd be the laughingstock of Europe. If Neandia was already known as conservative and weird, it was about to get much worse.

Part Three
Partners in Crime

Thirty-Two

RICK

The door to the dining room burst open and Astrid strode in. She looked out of breath but determined. Uncle Hubert looked at her, confused. I wasn't sure what to say. I knew she was about to read me the riot act. She stood at the head of the table and banged her fist as if she was about to call us to order with a gavel. For such a little thing, she terrified me. Neither of us dared utter a word.

"There is a wedding emergency—an *emergency*—and you are needed urgently, Rick!" Astrid said.

"What?" I asked, confused. "You were just here—"

"I was. We were. Come with me," Astrid said.

I excused myself, following the princess into the hallway. Again, she outclassed me by walking a million miles an hour. My brain couldn't function with my feet moving so fast.

"Astrid, slow down. What is happening?"

Astrid stopped, turned, and glared with hands on her hips.

"Alex needs you. Terribly. The least you could do—"

"Alexandra does not want my help."

"She may not want it—at least not openly—but she needs it."

"The bitch signed the papers. You all are safe," I said. "I was there to ensure—"

"And I am grateful for that, but this isn't about freedom. This is about Alexandra's happiness and self-esteem. This isn't strategic. This is because I know you love her and want to help her be happy. She is in a puddle of tears. This is me giving you an olive branch. It is your job to help and not fuck it up."

"What?"

"Her dress is a disaster. I am not sure what we can do. It's your chance to hold the cunt accountable for her actions, okay? Be the white knight. That's what Alexandra needs right now. I find it insufferable, but she craves it. She'll never say it."

"I don't want to poke the bear."

"Do you want a happy bride? A happy wife? A happy life?"

"Of course."

"Then bloody well grow a pair, Prickard!"

I snickered. "Okay, okay. Go easy on me. I am trying to figure it out. What is the issue?"

"The dress is all wrong. Celeste interfered. She says she looks like a nun. Even the colour is wrong. It's arctic white. She wanted ivory."

"Fuck! Wait, does she look nunnish? Is that even a word?"

Astrid rolled her eyes. "I don't bloody well know! And... never tell my beautiful sister, but yes. She's understandably and justifiably broken right now."

"What can I do? I'm no seamstress," I said, annoyed and confused. "I know nothing about women's fashion apart from what I find attractive."

Which was certainly not bridal gowns. Those held no appeal to me. No matter what Alexandra wore, it would be fine, but I'd rather have her in tight jeans or a short skirt any day of the week.

"Maybe, fight for her? For the both of you? She's still hurt and livid. I also think you strangely love her. She loves you. Where there are challenges, there are opportunities. Be the knight in shining armour and fix it. At least try. Stand up for her. Make her realise how much you care."

Astrid was emotional. Tears welled. She wanted us to succeed, too.

She'd been my biggest concern. She was her sister's best friend and strongest protector. The key to getting back with Alexandra was to take this olive branch. I had to fight like hell for Alexandra if I wanted her. Astrid was helping me.

"Of course I love her! I mean that. I promised to wait."

"Stop waiting and burn it all down for her. Go get your wife, okay?" Astrid said. "She lives for grand, romantic gestures regardless of what she tells you."

I nodded. I knew that by now. Alexandra wanted to be fawned over, even if she swore up and down she did not. Truth was, I enjoyed it.

"Got it," I said.

I strode down the hall to find the witch tormenting my bride. I entered the Dowager Queen's sitting with nary a request, annoying a footman who chased me. He missed the mark and soon I was there, in the room with her ten cats, glaring. My pulse raced. I was determined to defend Alexandra's honour above all else. I had no idea how to fix this, but I would.

Hands balled in fists, I demanded, "What did you do to Alexandra?"

"Excuse me, can you not please address me formally?" Celeste groaned.

"I don't much feel like it. And given Alexandra runs this household as of thirty minutes ago, I have no reason to fear your wrath!"

"I did not want to see anyone. Come back another time when you have calmed down."

Celeste didn't look ill. I realised she was licking the wounds of signing power over to Alexandra. She was upset—unable to watch Alexandra ascend. Her hand was forced. She was backed into a corner. Yes, I could throw my weight around and empower Alexandra to do the same. However, it would not fix the wedding dress a week before the wedding. Nor would it temper my rage or fix her emotional distress over something so important.

"I am not leaving until I have let you have it," I said. "My family will arrive within the day, Celeste! And they will find the bride beyond help. She is a mess right now. Her dress is nothing like she imagined it.

She feels she cannot walk down the aisle. She will, of course. We agreed. We will marry but damn it I don't want her to feel so ugly! A bride deserves to feel beautiful on her wedding day!"

"Brides always whinge about such things—"

"Not Alexandra. She has accepted almost every constraint you have placed on her like a champ. She's taken things on the chin. You don't get to claim refuge here. You made massive changes to her dress. Did you not?"

"I made some tweaks. I needed to ensure it was acceptable for a church wedding."

"I doubt that this is the case. She claims it will be a great disappointment to the crowds. I trust her."

"And you two are speaking now?"

I sputtered. "Well, we have been better, but it will all be sorted out. She's taking some time—"

"And you are in a bind? You need to get her under control, Rikard. This is a perfect time—"

"I will not break her spirit," I said. "Celeste, I do not own her. She needs a partner, not a dictator. She deserves that. You can trust that we will take care of the institution."

"I can call the PM right now."

"I specifically requested news on the matter. The bill was passed and signed. The PM made a formal comment on the matter. He cannot go back. I will not let you rule her with fear now. This ends now!"

Celeste's face twisted. She knocked a cat off her lap and stood, meeting my gaze.

"You are getting yourself in a heap of trouble, young man."

"Fuck it. I don't care," I said. "My allegiance remains to Alexandra. It always has. It always will. And in a week, I will codify that in front of millions. I love Alexandra—truly love her—and I will do anything for her. You won't win Celeste."

She chuckled. "And you can fix this with a week to go?"

"I may not succeed, but I will try. I will do everything I can to help. You destroyed her dreams here, Celeste. See if she ever speaks with you again. I know I will not."

Lord William arrived. "What is the issue, Your Royal Highness?"

"Celeste has ruined the bride's dress. I am lighting into her over it."

"She has two dresses. She has a much less appropriate second dress for your reception. She can be happy I didn't edit that one. I did this for her own good. Her first dress was too wild."

"I don't care what you think about the dress. It was never up to you to alter!"

"Her Majesty always does what she can to guide Alexandra," her henchman said.

"Well, that's over. The bill is signed. We're in charge. Now, Alexandra wants these rooms for our use," I said. "You may confirm that with her, but it is true. By the time we return from our honeymoon, I expect the Dowager Queen to vacate the Queen's quarters or there will be hell to pay for all of you. That includes you, Lord William!"

Neither said anything.

"I will be here until I die," Celeste said.

"No, you will vacate. Be gone! This is our right. I refuse to be across the palace from my wife or to share space with her younger sisters. We need privacy."

"It will be fine."

"Do you want grandchildren? We have been patient and we need space."

Celeste had no reply.

I reinforced my statement. "The Dowager Queen will move across the palace to where I am presently staying. I will move into the King's former quarters. Alexandra will rightfully take up these quarters. So help me, Lord William. It will be done by the time I return."

Thirty-Three

ALEXANDRA

The doors suddenly opened, revealing my breathless fiancé. He was livid—the vein popping out in his neck said it all. I was a crying mess and in no mood to fight, so I hoped he was cross with someone or something else. I longed to crawl into a hole somewhere.

"Sir, you cannot be here!" Marta said. "It is bad luck."

"We have had enough bad luck, Marta. Alexandra, Celeste has been lit on fire. I perhaps overstepped, but I couldn't give a flying fuck about that," Rick said. "How do we fix this?"

I wasn't sure if he meant *us* or the dress. Either way, I wanted the help more than ever.

"The dress is ruined. I have no idea how to fix it. Just look at me."

He approached, looking me up and down, curious. Rick shook his head.

"You are beautiful as ever, but this thing does you no favours. You will always be stunning, mind you, but if this is not what you want, we gotta fix it."

His words made me melt. I wanted to kiss him again, to hear he loved me, and I wanted to love him back. That spark wasn't dead, but I remained frightened to jump in again. Still, his admission seemed genuine. He thought I was beautiful even in this hideous, dreadful dress. Maybe I needed to hear it more than ever or maybe I was miserable without him. I figured it was a bit of both.

"How can we fix it?" Rick asked.

"We cannot. The dress is cut," another woman said. "We would have to pull it all apart. That would take a month or more."

Rick shook his head. "That won't do. Hmm... there is a second dress?"

The women nodded.

"Rick, it's strapless. I cannot wear that in the cathedral," I said. "I hope it is beautiful, but it will not do."

"We might be able to make something to go over it," Marta said. "Use lace or another fabric to cover her shoulders?"

The designer nodded. "I will come up with a few ideas. You are alright with wearing that all day?"

I nodded emphatically. "If it is the same dress I ordered, yes."

"It was unchanged, ma'am," a woman confirmed.

"Then, try it on," Rick said.

"Rick, I'm not going to do that standing here with you. Go. If it can be salvaged, I don't want you to see me!"

"Why? Because you care?"

He was smirking. I wanted to slap him. I also wanted to thank him.

"Go, go. It's bad luck to see the bride," Astrid said.

"Fine. Call me if you need me," Rick said. "I love you."

I wasn't ready to tell him the same yet. He'd have to wait. I nodded. "We will notify you if we need something."

Two dressers forced him out, closing and locking the doors.

"You owe him," Marta said quietly. "Your Majesty, he just did battle for you."

"I know," I murmured. "But why?"

"Why do you think?" Ingrid rolled her eyes. "He *loves* you, Alex."

"Does he?" I deflected.

"That man loves you. He may be misguided, a bit of a dickhead, and very self-obsessed, but he loves you," Astrid said. "Give him credit, Alex."

"Men get credit for everything—for doing so little. I refuse to praise him for the bare minimum!"

"Normally, I would agree with you, but you have done nothing but light into him for weeks now. He's been admonished but never goes away, never doubts you," Astrid insisted. "You love him! Deep down you adore him. Everyone makes mistakes."

"Yes," Odette said. "And isn't it better that people do better than to be punished for trying to make it right?"

I groaned. "When did you all become such romantics?"

"When we watched you fall in love. And it gave us some hope," Ingrid said.

"Ingy, you are too young to speak of such things," I said.

Deep down, I thought her admission was sweet.

The women zipped me into my second dress, strapless with a corset-style bodice. The boning snatched in my waist. The base layer was a stretchy buff colour with an overlay of beading that looked like a meteor shower. I glittered in every possible way.

Despite having temporarily stopped crying, I teared up looking in the mirror. *This* was the moment I wanted. *This* was what I needed.

"We can make a cape. We have more fabric to make the overlay. It will be tight, but we can make it slip over your shoulders," the designer said. "And if you want more volume—"

"I do. The dress is magnificent, but it must fill a cathedral."

"We can make a train out of more of the overlay and tulle and it will be full as a ballgown without the weight of satin," the designer assured. "You are beautiful. It suits you so well."

I smiled. "Thank you. So much better. It's mine."

"It is," Odette said. "But we're forgetting the biggest thing."

She brought my mother's wedding tiara to Marta. "The final touch."

Marta and the others fastened the tiara temporarily atop my head. Settling it in would take twenty minutes, but here it was for effect. It hit me like a sack of bricks. I sobbed big tears out of nowhere.

"Oh, darling, it is going to be a happy day. We will fix it all," Odette assured. "Please don't cry."

"No. Sweetheart, I wish Mamma was here. I wish she was with us today. She would be so happy, I think."

"She would," Astrid agreed. "Because you are beautiful. And you two will be happy."

"I am so lost," I admitted.

"Everyone feels like that the week before their wedding," Marta said. "It is expected. Even your mother did. But it will get better. He loves you. It hasn't always been easy, dear, but you have a lot of life ahead of you."

"And freedom." Ingrid grinned. "Freedom to be yourself."

I cupped Ingrid's happy little face. "You will go to school—properly. The both of you will."

"He won't police you," Astrid said. "The man *needs* policing."

I snickered. "He's aware."

"Mamma would be proud of you, Alexandra," Astrid said. "I miss her. It makes me sad she didn't get to see you this beautiful, but she knows. She knows."

"She does, yes, Your Majesty," Marta agreed. "She would be proud of all of you for making it out of this. Let's think only happy thoughts."

"Okay. Time for me to take all of this off!" I dried my eyes. "I have things to do."

Much as I wanted to stay in my beautiful dress, there was much to do before greeting Rick's family for dinner. I left the salon to retreat to my room. That was when there was a knock.

"Come!" I called.

Rick popped his head in. I stared, not sure what to say.

"I come in peace," he said. "I just wanted to make sure the dress—"

"It will be down to the wire, but the dress will work," I said.

"Good. Okay great. I wanted to give you this before things get to be crazy."

He brought over a small box.

"Rick, you don't—"

"It's okay if you're still angry with me. I don't expect things to be perfect overnight. However, it *is* your birthday. They are a big deal in my family. Usually, you get cake in bed, but seeing as I don't think we are anywhere near there at present, I am satisfied with you accepting this token of my respect and reverence."

"Reverence?" I joked.

"I tried, Alexandra." Rick's voice was deflated.

It made me sad. If I didn't give some credit, I was cruel.

"Sit." I patted the bed "Sit. She won't run in here now."

"And even if she does? She can go fuck herself. I told her as much."

I gaped.

"Yeah, I went off on the old battle-axe. Sorry. The woman is a lying piece of shit. And she ruined your wedding dress. Fuck her! Also, we'll be getting her quarters. I made that demand and said it was yours. I swear I did it for you, but... I couldn't allow her to sit up there so smug while you're back here with the girls."

I was surprised. "Well, I suppose it makes sense."

"I'll have the other set of rooms. You'll have yours. There is no pressure—"

"Understood."

I peeled the paper back to see the mark of a local jeweller.

"Rick, you needn't spoil me always," I said.

"I vehemently disagree with you. If I cannot spoil you? Who can I spoil, Lex?"

I blushed upon opening the package. I unveiled the simple silver necklace with two pendants. One was a birdcage with the door open. The other was a bird flying away. I picked it up and looked at the inscription behind the birdcage.

Be Free. -R

I teared up, staring at him, eyes welling. He got it. This wasn't about the press or about ticking a box. It was about Rick loving me. It was about him waiting for me—patiently. I wasn't back to where I had been before, but I was *seen*. I realised that I still loved him. I believed the feeling was mutual.

"Is it okay?" Rick asked.

I nodded. "It's lovely."

"Good," Rick said. "I was hoping it would suit."

"More than. Thanks," I said, turning from him. "Can you help me? I'd like to wear it."

"Sure, sure," Rick said.

I sputtered, unsure as his hands brushed my shoulders. "I feel dreadful since I ruined your birthday and you're being so sweet about mine—"

"I fucked up my own birthday, Alexandra. I did that to me. It's the least I could do for yours."

He paused as if he wasn't sure what to say. Then, he leaned down. Ever so gently, his lips met my neck. He kissed me and a shiver shot down my spine. It was so simple, yet more intimate than anything I'd felt to date.

"Sorry. I was... I uh..." Rick retracted, stepping back.

I turned, checking my necklace, to face him. "It's okay."

He shrunk towards the door. "I'll leave you to have a moment to yourself. Be aware I have a great big cake on order for dinner, so save yourself for the final course, okay?"

I smiled, "Of course."

Thirty-Four

The night before our wedding, we hosted many foreign dignitaries and royals at the palace. I struggled to keep my eyes off Alexandra for even a minute. She was stunning, carefree, and glowing. We no longer fought. We weren't back in the place where I was sure we'd fall into bed together, but we made progress. We were back to being friends. Her sisters were wild and exuberant. We allowed all to attend. You could have thought Alexandra and I hung the moon by the way Ingrid told it.

The only person doubting it was Celeste. She sat in the corner glaring as people mingled. Still, it couldn't keep Alexandra down. This was her palace. These were her friends now. This was her life. I watched from the sidelines, but I was proud to call her mine tomorrow.

"She's happy as ever," my mother said. "Beautiful."

I nodded. "She is glad to be almost done with this. We both are."

My mother shook her head. "Not what I meant. She's lighter than last time."

"She's free. And really... I dunno... it's as if I am, too. It's the exact opposite. I am tying myself down. Seeing her like this, though, brings me even more happiness than if it were me. I mean, look at her. And look at the girls. I was part of that."

Mamma chuckled. "Don't give yourself too much credit. But she is beautiful—beaming. And you helped. She sees you, Rick. She understands you, *min skat*."

I smiled. "I know."

"Take good care of her," Mamma said. "And those girls. You're their big brother now. They need you, too, as she does. You're taking on a lot of responsibility."

"Of course."

"But I think it suits you."

I snickered. "Never thought you'd say that."

"You make a good patriarch given the chance to get your act together. Don't tear yourself down. You worked hard to help the girls and Alexandra. And if she makes you happy—"

"She makes me happy."

She did. I spent a month getting back in her good graces. I was grateful to have a second chance. I wasn't taking it for granted. But she made me glad to be alive. I loved her. I don't know how I managed to feel this about anyone. I adored her. It was everything at once.

"Well, you should consider retiring soon, *min skat*. Big day tomorrow. You both need your rest."

I agreed. "You're probably right. She and the girls won't sleep, of course."

"Probably not, but you will. You'd sleep through a disaster."

I laughed. "I'm going to find her."

I walked through the crowd to discover Astrid and Alexandra talking to a Belgian. She looked at me, confused. I motioned to my watch and mouthed "It's late" before she caught on.

"Ah, yes, it's getting late. We might want to turn in."

I nodded.

"I'll make sure the little ones get back," Astrid said. "Go ahead."

Finally, after a week of little time to even say a word to Alexandra, I again got to take her hand and walk with her. It was a relief. She linked her hand with mine as we walked towards her room. Little was said. We felt out the words. What do you say to someone who you love and will marry after only a few months of half-hearted courtship? What do you express to someone you care about the night before your wedding? What do you say after a huge blowup? Do you clear the air? I was unsure.

"It was a nice evening," she said. "Not bad. I was worried I might be bored."

"Hard to be bored watching Odette and Ingrid lose it over every little thing they've never done before," I said.

She smiled, her face softening. "Yes. They are good for that."

"I never had sisters, Lex. It's different. I was the baby. It's nice to be a big brother to them. There is something sweet about it. They're a hoot."

She chuckled. "A laugh, yeah. I will miss them. We've never been apart for more than a week—only when I went to Lundhavn with you. Can they handle it?"

"It will be okay. They are safe here. Astrid has them under control. They will go to school. I've never seen two children so excited about school as they are."

"They have never attended a proper school. It is all new to them."

We stopped by her door. I knew I must leave her. Or must I? Did it even matter anymore? I thought we'd thrown away impropriety the night of our engagement dinner. Then, it all fell apart. I figured now was not the right time.

Alexandra looked at our intertwined hands. "Rick, I am sorry that I cannot jump right back to where we were. And maybe... it's for the better. Because we were so deep into whatever rolled over us that we were blind to any semblance of sense."

"That's true," I said.

"But I think we can get back there," Alexandra said. "At least I hope we can. I... I don't want this to be a sham. When we say those words tomorrow, I want them to mean something. We're starting on a clean slate, right?"

I nodded. "If you want that, I want it."

She smiled. "I do."

I needed a lot more than just a sweet smile. I wanted to run Alexandra through the door and deposit her on the bed. I longed to watch myself undo her and feel her nails dig into my back. I tried to avoid thinking about it, but it was no use. That attraction for her came rushing back.

"I love you, Alexandra."

"I know," Alexandra said.

She didn't say it back. I didn't want to admit how I longed to hear it from her. I was hook, line, and sinker. I had given her all my heart to stomp on before. She wasn't stomping but she wasn't reciprocating, either. I was powerless, but it was all worth it if someday she returned my feelings.

She stared up at me with her beautiful, sweet eyes. I couldn't help it. I went in for the kiss. In true Alexandra style, she pulled me in even closer. She kissed me harder. I stuck my roots into the ground to stay upright as she gripped my lapels. We stood there for a bit, slowly kissing. At some point, our animal brains took over.

Pinning her to the wall next to the bedroom door, my hands roved. Rather than display any degree of disagreement, Alexandra pushed her hips towards me. She quivered, her body pressed against mine. As I kissed her neck, she gasped.

She asked, "Do you want to... come in?"

I thought she'd never ask me. Rather than reply, I kissed Alexandra again. We made it back into her bedroom and onto her bed. She pulled me onto her and toyed with my belt.

"I want you," Alexandra said, breathless. "I want you to make me feel everything."

She stopped.

I looked back at her, confused.

"What? Is that weird? Oh, God, I made it—"

"No," I whispered, kissing her sweetly. "Lex, I will give you everything you ever wanted. But right now, all I want is to watch you lose yourself while you scream my name."

She nodded at me and bit her lip. I was about to finally have all of her. I continued to kiss her, running my hand up her dress. She shuddered again, pulling away as I reached the edge of her panties. I ran my hand over them, feeling her wetness.

Then, as I was about to toss them aside, we heard someone

rummaging through her closet. The door was closed, but the light was on. I sat back up. Alexandra did, too. She put her finger over her mouth and crept over towards the closet. We heard a man's voice. I panicked, worrying we should call for security. I hopped up, disregarding the neglected erection in my pants, and attempted to defend her from... what?

She took one of her shoes off and held it over her head as if the heel would spare us. I grabbed a paperweight from the adjacent desk. Neither of us well-prepared, we braced.

"Where could it be? It's in *none* of these bags," a male voice said.

"How should I know, Bill?" Another said.

"Lord William," Alexandra and I whispered in unison.

Alexandra didn't wait for any sort of signal at that point. Annoyed, she pulled the door back and glared at the men.

"What are you gentlemen doing in my walk-in wardrobe?"

The men looked very frightened. They both bowed quickly and then stared at her in utter fear.

"We were... securing the area, Your Majesty?" The littler of the two asked.

"Yes. Securing it. Rightly so," Lord William lied.

"I think Martin and my team were quite satisfied with it," I said. "They have secured it without you bumbling fools!"

Alexandra stood, arms crossed, not buying it. No one would. It was a ridiculous statement. Her glare was so steely. It only made me want to kiss her. All my wires were crossed right now.

"What are you doing? Let me ask you once more before I call the police in here and have you both removed and arrested!"

"Alexandra—"

"Is that how we address the Queen, boys?" I asked. "Really?"

Lord William glared, wringing his hands nervously. "Your Majesty, we were sent here."

"By whom?"

"Your grandmother. To check... on your wedding dress."

"It is with the designers," Alexandra said. "I don't have it here. They are keeping it safe."

"We all feel it would be most secure—"

"What, in the hands of the woman who destroyed the first one?" I asked. "It's not going to work. Whatever game you're—"

Alexandra put her hand on my arm, signalling this was her battle. I backed off.

"You won't find it here. Moreover, if I ever see you in my quarters again—two unattended men who should not be in here—I will ensure neither of you *ever* returns to a crown property again. Have I made myself clear?" Alexandra said.

They dispersed. Alexandra shook her head.

"I thought it would stop."

"So did I. That's fucking crazy," I muttered. "Alexandra, where is your dress?"

"It's in Odette's room. It's hidden in a trunk," Alexandra replied. "We worried about this—Asti and I."

"You're clever. I'm sorry you must worry about any of that."

She shrugged. "It's my life. And apparently, it remains so."

"We will liquidate things when we return, my love," I said. "I promise you. I will do it myself if you give me a mandate."

She wrapped her arms around my waist, pressing her face into my chest. "I will give you a mandate, Rick."

I kissed the top of her head, lovingly. Yes, we'd been disturbed. Nothing would happen tonight. However, I now knew the woman I married tomorrow had my back and I had hers. There would be time for much more tomorrow. Or so I thought.

We went round to Odette's room to ensure the dress was fine. I ducked out while Alexandra checked to make sure it was still locked tight and perfect. Then, she returned to the hall and nodded.

"I will take it to my room," I said. "I won't open it. I promise you. But I don't trust it here."

"How will you protect it?"

"Don't worry about that," I assured. "But I would feel better if it were with me."

"Fine," Alexandra said.

"One question, though."

"Yes?"

"What was the endgame with the dress? What made you worry?"

"She asked for the other dress to be returned to her. Our worry was she would destroy this dress and force me to wear the other."

"But why?"

"Control, embarrassment, maybe to make you not marry me? She would have loved the humiliation you leaving me at the altar would have brought."

"The other dress wasn't you, but you weren't ugly. And I'm not so shallow, Alexandra. I am marrying you, not the dress."

"Didn't you think I was plain when you met me?"

I shrugged. "I didn't know you. And you had no right to choose anything for yourself. You were subdued by that cunt. Come on now! I don't feel like that anymore."

Alexandra wrapped her arms around my neck and bit her lip. "I know. You don't mind me."

"Not at all," I smiled.

She kissed me. It felt like before—normal, simple, true—and we were back to a good place. I was affirmed.

"Okay, take the dress. You can be my knight in shining armour again. I will send Marta to get it from you in the morning."

I chuckled. "I will defend it bravely, Your Majesty."

"Of course you will. Get some rest. You will need it for the marathon tomorrow. We both will."

And that is how, with Marta and Martin helping, we arranged for a housekeeping cart to take the massive garment bag down the hall to my room. I tucked it into bed right next to me still clueless as to what was in the bag to my left. It was ridiculous. And yet? I knew she'd look beautiful as ever. I would have married her in either dress, but I hoped she'd be happy in this.

Thirty-Five

Alexandra

I stood before the mirror, full regalia on display, when the doors opened, and the bitch emerged. I couldn't have wanted to see anyone less than I did her. However, I also couldn't have wanted to rub anything in her face more than the way I looked at this moment. I was beautiful, elegant, and confident. My womanly hips were no longer hidden as if shameful. My breasts could just *be*. I loved this version of myself—this unapologetic, brave, feminine version of myself. I was a beautiful bride.

Astrid stepped nearer to me, squeezing my hand.

"I would have liked you in white," Celeste tried to sound sweet. "But this will do."

"As if you didn't try to sabotage my dress last night," I cut back. "Not that it matters. Because the dress was spirited away well before then. I found your lackeys in my wardrobe."

"It was for the protection of the dress. I know how much it meant to you."

"Oh really?" Astrid raised an eyebrow.

Celeste ignored Astrid, as per usual. "It is good you have someone to manage you and your... moods, Alexandra. You think things up that are most incredible. A wild imagination."

"It's not an imagination," Ingrid said. "You destroyed her first wedding dress. She's beautiful, despite you not because of you."

"She's fine," Celeste said. "I wish you were more covered. I am sure the priest will, too."

"I think he'll be fine," I said. "And I will be myself."

"What is the point of this conversation?" Astrid demanded. "Why are you here, Grand-Mama?"

"Because I came to give her advice," Celeste said. "Have babies soon. You won't always be so young. You're a plain girl. You won't age well. Have them now when he's still interested in you. Before his eyes linger on someone else."

A pang of sadness hit. She didn't know Rick from Adam. He never gave me any reason to believe he chased another. Even in the beginning, I'd told him anything discrete was fine. Still, he never appeared to care about that. I figured he wanted only me. Now, though, I worried. We never clarified. And we were about to wed. Suddenly, I needed that clarification. And I needed it directly.

"I... there is much time for that," I fobbed her off.

Still, the rash creeping up my neck gave me away to Astrid. As soon as the old bag left, Astrid asked what was wrong.

"You alright?"

"I'm... I need to talk to Rick," I said.

"He cannot see you, Alexandra," Odette insisted. "It's bad luck."

"It will be fine. That's a superstition. Has he left for the church yet?"

"I will check, Your Majesty." Marta rushed out to speak with the event staff.

"It's just jitters," Astrid said. "You look beautiful. It will all be fine."

"Not if he comes here—"

"Odie, sush!" Astrid said, annoyed.

Marta returned. "He is still here. About to leave, though."

"Can you—"

Before I could finish, Rick came around the corner in his tuxedo. I could have melted into a puddle. He was terribly handsome. I was dying just looking at him.

"What's the matter?" He stared at me, nervous. "What now?"

"Nothing," I answered. "Can you all just give us a minute?"

The rest of them faded out. I took his hands in mine, but he was all over, taking me in.

"I need to know that whatever we do, we're together—but just us," I said. "I... I said I'd be fine with there being other people, but that was before I... I want to confirm we're just us."

"Exclusive?" Rick asked. "Yes. I thought... well, I was sure we'd already decided that?"

"Really?"

"I had, I guess?" He shrugged. "I'm a scoundrel, but I'm a loyal one, Alexandra. I will make trouble with you and only you for the rest of our days if that is what you want."

I nodded.

He brushed his hand along my cheek. "I should kiss you, but I won't. Not now. It will mess your makeup up. But I want to."

"Uh-huh," I agreed.

"You're stunning. Beyond my imagination, Alexandra. And well past what I have ever deserved. You are so wonderful. It's bad luck, but I don't see how."

I smiled and kissed his hand. I'm not sure what possessed me. I had to do *something*.

"I am glad you got to see me, Rick. Because we never get a quiet moment. I want more of those."

"I hope we will have many more. I feel like I've done something very naughty to see the bride before everyone else."

"She's yours to see," I said.

Rick kissed my forehead. "I love you, Alexandra. I must go. Just know it's you. It's you forever. I will see you soon."

"I will see you, too," I agreed. "And it is only you, Rick. It will be forever."

He smiled and ducked out. We'd be together soon enough.

"Good?" Astrid poked her head in.

I nodded. "Perfect. This is a happy day."

"The groom is off to the church," Marta said. "The bride will follow soon. Are we ready to greet the world?"

"As ever," I answered.

It took several footmen and Astrid to shove my dress, veil, and train into the coach. The four of us were transported to the cathedral up the block. We waved and smiled at the massive crowds that went on as far as the eye could see. The little girls vibrated with the sheer excitement of being out in the world. Their exuberance kept us all going—nerves or not.

We arrived at the foot of the cathedral steps. There, Astrid and the footmen helped sort out my dress and veil once more. Now, the fun began. Astrid took my arm as my escort. Odette and Ingrid, both looking too grown, played bridesmaids, carrying my train upstairs into the cathedral.

We stopped before the grand primary doors to the cathedral. The organ played. Footmen helped the younger girls give my dress one final once over. Astrid fluffed my veil. Then, it was time. We four moved out into the aisle as the great oak doors opened. Rick turned to me. I held onto Astrid's arm, fighting tears in a big way, as we walked. His smile melted me.

The girls stayed with me as my escort until we stopped near the choir. Astrid kissed and hugged me before handing me over to Rick.

She whispered something to him as she ducked out. He chuckled and held my hand tightly as the girls disappeared. A song picked up with the strings present—a song written just for us. There was no time to talk. It wasn't until we approached the altar, and the priest flubbed the next part, needing to double back for the rings that there was a time for speaking.

"Hi," Rick finally said.

"Hi. I love you," I responded.

The words spilled out uncontrollably. I wasn't afraid. I wanted to tell him. I needed to, perhaps.

"I love you, too." He grinned uncontrollably. "Let's get married."

THIRTY-SIX

RICK

The Wedding of the Century

For Neandia, it has been more than twenty-three years since a royal wedding took place between Queen Alexandra's late parents, Crown Prince Christophe and Princess Linnea of Denmark. Almost twenty-three years to the day, Prince Rikard of Lundhavn and Queen Alexandra of Neandia tied the knot in the same place—St. Veronica's Cathedral in its capitol's old quarter.

We write from just outside the cathedral as the ceremony is conducted. The groom arrived with his family shortly before the Dowager Queen. She looked a bit teary-eyed over the idea of losing her beloved granddaughter. The Queen was escorted in by her three sisters—Princess Astrid, Princess Odette, and Princess Ingrid. She looked beautiful in a sparkling ivory and buff gown by Anna Lux. We are told the dress is convertible with a cape and train added on for the ceremony that will be removed for her reception look. Atop her head, she toted the Danish Starlight Tiara, a gift given to her late mother on her wedding day.

We cannot wait to keep you posted on the departure of the royal couple in a short while. They will endure a full mass, so it might take

a bit, but we will keep you updated online and via our live stream of
the ceremony.

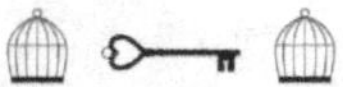

It was surreal standing before a thousand-person congregation holding
the hand of a woman I first met six months ago. Having just been
pronounced her husband was even more bizarre. Realising that I woke
up this morning and married a twenty-two-year-old queen was perhaps
the strangest of all. Yet, as I grinned like an idiot, I couldn't fight my
happiness. I couldn't pretend I didn't love her. The way she looked at
me was unlike any way a woman looked at me before.

And her first I love you had come moments before our hands were
bound together for what seemed like an eternity. If I wasn't a romantic
sap before, I was now. Alexandra radiated happiness. We stepped
forward, proceeding up the aisle and back out towards the waiting
crowd. Above us, the Cathedral bells peeled. The doors opened to the
mad world outside. People screamed as we stepped out into the light of
day.

Before I could negotiate whether we would give the people a show,
Alexandra already went for it. She wasted no time kissing me. And it
wasn't some little chaste kiss. I wasn't even sure this woman knew what
one of those was. She laid it on thick.

We pulled back and continued waving. I said nothing. I was taken
aback by her bold move. Rather, I liked it. I liked it a lot. I would have
taken her home and done terrible things to her. I'd gone half a year
without sex. I wanted it badly but didn't want to rush. We'd never
done it before. I'd never even seen her naked. In the past, I'd gone for it
without a second thought. Now, I didn't want to use Alexandra for my
pleasure alone. She was precious to me, and I owed her everything.

We climbed in our carriage to parade through the streets. The
crowds teemed and screamed. We smiled idiotically at one another, but
it wasn't contrived. It was precious. We were in love and living an
actual fucking fairytale. We waved until our wrists hurt. It was insuf-

ferable but necessary for the things that followed. We had to tick the boxes.

This going through the normal motions of a royal wedding included the attending monarchs' photos and many family snaps for release by both houses. Our candid shots would take place after our afternoon break. Before that, there was the balcony appearance.

The balcony wave was the crown jewel of royal wedding photo ops. For well-wishers, it was a beautiful opportunity to cheer for the fairy-tale couple. It was a scrap we tossed the normies—usually requiring a good, honest kiss. Most people would go for something simple. Alexandra, as I said, is incapable of this. I didn't bother going in slow and sweet. She would turn it into something more intense within seconds anyway. It was a full-body, romantic experience. Despite thousands of screaming people in the street and our families around, we went for it. Celeste glared. I'd find that out when photos of the event were released.

Even with the crowd, the moment was ours alone. After our big kiss, we had precious downtime. She would bust out of her dress momentarily to do her outfit change, have a bit of lunch, and we'd relax. I hoped to have a couple of drinks and get precious time alone with her. It was all I wanted just to chat.

I didn't expect what happened next.

As her sisters followed us into the next room, she announced in serious French.

"Ladies, we're going to take some time to ourselves. We'll join you again as I'm changing into my evening look."

"Oh." Ingrid was sad.

"Let's leave them to relax," Astrid said. "They won't have any time together tonight. Come on. We will have to change as well."

They left.

"You broke their hearts, Lex!"

"We're married. Forgive me for being selfish," Alexandra said.

Marta joined us to help bust Alexandra out of her headgear and to put the dress up. I kicked my shoes off for a moment and tossed my tie and jacket aside. I was relieved. I'd have to change into my new evening attire shortly. Alexandra's tiara was unsewn from her head, giving way to beautiful blonde curls that cascaded. She brushed her hair back as

Marta worked on the strings of the corset. It was quite involved. I had never dissected a woman from a dress with so many steps.

"Should I... step out?" I asked, realising I'd not yet seen Alexandra half naked let alone completely undressed

"No. You can stay," Alexandra said. "Even the Pope would permit it."

I tried not to stare too much. Layers came off, leaving her standing there in nothing but a tiny pair of panties and a rather pointless bra.

"Marta, can you just... give us some time to... decompress. Maybe bring us food in an hour?"

Marta bowed slightly, "Of course, Your Majesty."

Alexandra followed her to the door, locking it. As she did, I couldn't avoid staring at her ass. I wanted to grab it—to throw her down on the bed and take her from behind.

"So, what are you up to, Lex?" I asked, slightly confused.

"Whatever I want to be," Alexandra said. "What? Are you bothered by it? Or would you rather have eaten first?"

I had a feeling that whatever we were about to get up to, I'd rather do before my belly was full.

"No, no, I don't mind any of this. I am... this is... I..."

"What, you have no words?"

Alexandra stood in front of me, her arms wrapped around my neck. I stared her in the face, trying to avoid looking at her tits that were just *there*. They were better than I anticipated. I didn't expect to be disappointed, but they were beyond my imagination. I pulled her closer, grabbing her ass. She kissed me again, but with even more energy than she had earlier. She was as desperate as I was.

I flipped her back on the bed, pinning her. Alexandra looked up, eyes wide.

"I don't need words, do I?" I asked.

She shook her head.

"I think we understand each other. Yes?"

She nodded, biting her lip. The view of her looking almost angelic in the moment didn't hurt. I had been fantasising about this for months. Ever since the time in the garden when we'd been all over one another unexpectedly, I wanted to do this again—to pin her and make her lose her mind.

I kissed her neck. She gasped and shivered. She moaned as ran my hand down her body. I wanted to see her naked.

"Take this off," I pulled on the bra. "It's useless!"

"Okay," she agreed, breathing heavily.

I pulled back as she sat up and tossed it aside.

Meanwhile, I took in Alexandra's breasts in all their glory—paying one nipple attention, then the other. She pushed her hips towards me and moaned more. Her breathing picked up.

I looked up, "That's good?"

"So good," she gasped.

I played with the top of her panties suggesting she should take them off. That was where things ground to a halt.

"Rick," she said, her tone no longer so breathy.

"Yes, baby?"

"I've never been... with anyone. So if I'm like... bad at it... I promise I am... green. I can learn."

She said it as if she were describing a showjumping prospect. *Green*? I was confused.

"You're a... virgin?" I sat up, confused.

It wasn't her inexperience that surprised me, but it was her total lack of experience that did. Who made it to twenty-one without a round or two? How did she even have the restraint to avoid it? And how had we made it this long without her telling me? I wasn't prepared to deal with her neuroses. I'd expected we'd hit the ground running now that distractions were minimised. But now I was responsible for deflowering her? *Fuck!*

THIRTY-SEVEN

ALEXANDRA

Rick's expression wasn't one of excitement at the prospect of having a pure, virgin, unadulterated human. It was panicked. My entire life, I'd been told to prize purity above all else. Celeste ensured I remained white as the driven snow until my wedding day. No man in good standing wanted a woman who ran around. That was all I knew.

Rick looked concerned. We both went from 60 to 0 like an ancient Concorde on landing. Paranoia set in. Was he regretting his decision to marry me?

"I didn't lie to you," I said. "You never asked."

"I expected it to come out sooner than this, Alexandra," Rick said, astonished.

I tried to hide being upset, but I began to break down. My throat got that familiar itch. My lip quivered. Tears welled. I brought my legs to my chest. I wrapped my arms around them and buried my head in my knees, wanting to crawl into a hole and die.

"Oh, Lex, don't cry, baby," Rick inched closer. "I don't want you to be upset with me."

"You think I'm stupid. Ridiculous."

"No, baby," Rick said sweetly. "I'm... concerned because I don't want the upper hand here. I don't want some weird power dynamic."

"Rick, I am telling you I *want* to have sex, but I need you to be patient with me—understanding."

"I get that. And I would be. You can always tell me to stop. If it hurts, we stop. If something bothers you, we stop. That's never in doubt. But I want you to feel some sort of agency."

"Don't men fantasise about this?"

"Some men. Not me," Rick said. "It's a kink I don't get. I don't prize virginity. I would much rather corrupt you as soon as possible because sex is fun. I'd love to fuck you, but I don't want to feel like I am your everything."

"What? Of course you are. You're my bloody husband, Rick!"

He winced. "I just... you don't feel like you're going to miss out on something?"

"Do you?"

"I have experience, Lex. I do not doubt that we will have plenty of fun. I wouldn't have committed to you if I had even a single doubt. Truth is, I'm a prick. I'm also a serial monogamist."

I snickered. "You aren't a prick."

"I am, perhaps a reformed one?"

I looked up. He looked sweetly at me.

"I love you," I said. "So much. And I want this. I'm also a bit frightened because... I have no idea what I am doing. And you might think I'm boring or disappointing?"

"Impossible! No. Right now, I am staring at you—mostly naked— and wishing I could devour you. You're beautiful. I've been thinking that all day. And this? Fucking you? I've been thirsting for it since our engagement photos. Then behind the brook. Then in Lundhavn. And then last night? I couldn't want you more!"

I blushed.

"What... you didn't want it?"

"No, I did. I would have done it all with you before I found out your dirty little secret," I grumbled. "I was going to do it. Then, I wanted to strangle you."

Rick chuckled. "We had a lot of false starts."

"Last night killed me. Yet another missed opportunity," I groaned. "Even now."

"It's not. I was thoroughly enjoying you regardless of what happened," Rick said. "Here's an idea. Why don't you get yourself off? I'll watch."

"What? Why would I do that?" I was bothered by his suggestion.

"Because I want you to show me so I can take care of you," Rick said. "I want you to be comfortable. I want to please you."

"But what good would that do? You won't have fun."

"I will have plenty of fun watching you," Rick kissed my shoulder. "Trust me. I bet listening to you cum will make all the time I've spent in a tuxedo today worth it."

Without my months of romance novel education, I wouldn't have understood what he meant. The word "masturbation" was banished from my daily life. I'd been told it would send me to hell. I didn't buy any of that.

"I don't... know how."

"Have you never had an orgasm?" Rick sat up tall, shaking his head in disbelief.

"No," I winced. "Look, I don't think this will work."

I hopped out of bed, looking for my dressing gown. I was mortified. I didn't want him to see me naked.

"No, no. Come back here, Lex. Please." Rick patted the bed sweetly. "Come on. Just trust me. Do you?"

I shrugged and returned to bed. "What can you even do? I'm like beyond remedial."

"It's okay. You're clever. You will catch up quickly. If my dance teaching skills are representative, I am an excellent educator."

I blushed and lay down. "Fine."

Rick leaned in and kissed me again. He cupped my breast, running his thumb over my nipple. It sent a tingle down my spine. I couldn't control the involuntary movements my body made, nor could I stop the noises that came out of my mouth. It was primal. Mortification soon faded to pure bliss!

He ran his hand down my body again, playing with the sides of my knickers.

"Take these off," he said.

I complied, nervous. What if he saw everything and ran away? I'd only recently discovered what my vulva looked like in any real way when I'd gone for a wax and had to confirm it all looked right. I'd lived twenty-two years in my body and felt disconnected from this part of myself.

Rick didn't flinch. Instead, he ran his fingers between my wet folds. I'd been thinking about this since the night before. I gasped and pushed my head back into the pillows as he hit a spot that set me ablaze. It must have been my clitoris. Without the educational foundation laid by Astrid's dirty books, I'd be out of my depth already. God, I wanted him to keep touching me!

Rick looked satisfied with himself. "You like that?"

I nodded, breathing shakily.

"You try," Rick said.

"What?"

"Go ahead. I want to watch."

The way he said it sent a chill down my spine in the best way. I found my way back to the core of my pleasure, rubbing gently first and picking up speed. I wasn't sure where I was going. The more I did it, the wetter and wetter I became. I was high on this feeling!

"Here," Rick pushed my hand aside for a moment.

He put two fingers inside me. I moaned as his fingers tickled me and shuddered in pleasure.

"Yeah?"

"Yes," I answered. "God, what are you doing? It's amazing!"

"It's your g-spot. You can do the same," he said.

Rick wanted me to try. By this point, we were both naked. I looked over to see he was touching himself at the same time. The hungry look he gave me—watching me watching him—made me even hornier. Having never seen an actual penis in the flesh before, I was relieved to see his was no disappointment. It was bizarre and spectacular.

I moved my fingers in and out, reaching that spot. My palm rubbed against my clit all the while. I panted now, feeling slightly sweaty. My face flushed as if on fire. I looked over at his dick, wondering what it would be like to have it inside me.

Thinking about it sent me on a journey. My body tensed as I got closer and closer. It was like I climbed the most glorious hill. With each stroke, I neared its peak. I felt tighter and tighter. Finally, the release washed over me as a whole-body experience. I twitched and fell back onto the bed, feeling like I had run a marathon. It was the most delicious thing I'd ever felt. I panted, waiting to come down. When I looked for Rick, he'd disappeared. Instead, I felt him part my legs. I looked to see him kissing my right thigh.

Rick played with my now-swollen clit. "You're really wet."

"Just... do it," I pleaded. "I want you to have me."

"I wish I could," he chuckled. "But I'm spent. Watching you cum made me explode. You must wait a bit. Probably until tonight. Unlike you, I can't get off back-to-back. That's a superpower women possess that I don't."

I pouted.

"Oh, she wants to go again? Are you greedy now, Your Majesty?"

I giggled and playfully kicked my legs "I am a little greedy."

"Good girl," Rick kissed my thigh again.

He lowered his face until it was in between my legs, his tongue now on my clit.

I twitched. "Rick, is that even... good?"

He looked up. "It's fucking beautiful, Lex. Do you not want me to do it?"

"No, it feels good. I don't want to take advantage."

"Why?" Rick asked. "I want to taste you. It's my job to serve you, is it not? Am I not your very loyal husband?"

It was hot.

"Then do it," I told him. "And don't stop until you have succeeded in your mission."

Rick chuckled. "Okay. She gets what she wants."

THIRTY-EIGHT

RICK

Rikandra Remain Royally Amorous

Upon emerging from St. Veronica's Cathedral in Ville de Neandia, Queen Alexandra and Prince Consort Rikard were all smiles. The newlyweds stopped to wave at adoring spectators. And then, we got a big, wild kiss. To our surprise, it wasn't Prince Rick who did the honours. Instead, it was the Queen who went for it. They kissed again on the balcony. Neither kiss was even remotely subdued.

Not everyone was pleased. Dowager Queen Celeste scowled at the unusual display of royal love. Public displays of affection are unexpected with royals—stranger still for a sitting monarch. However, Rick and Alexandra seem too hot to stop for even a moment to smell the roses.

Per attendees at the royal wedding reception, the two remained wrapped up in one another. The newlyweds released a short clip of their first dance on social this morning. They looked completely absorbed in one another. Prince Rikard spun his bride out at the end of the song before wrapping her up in a swoony kiss. It was a particularly candid moment to be shared with the masses. We couldn't love them more.

As the couple departed in the early morning hours of their honeymoon, they waved at well-wishers crowding the gates of the airport in the dark. Hand in hand, they stopped at the top of the steps for another sweet kiss, lit only by the lights from the plane. We expect royal babies sooner rather than later.

When I finalised our honeymoon plans, as any groom might, I wanted to capture the spirit of things. At that point, Alexandra refused to speak to me and gave me 'fuck you' faces across any table we were required to sit at. So, I decided to pack our schedules full of solo activities. I wanted to make it less weird—for me—and not light a match on a smouldering dumpster fire.

In the process, I cockblocked myself. To begin with, whatever we started in bed before our wedding reception never continued. We were exhausted after our reception. We took a plane in the wee hours to our undisclosed location—a Swiss chalet high in the Alps. A long ride from the airport got us there at sunrise. It was beautiful, but Alexandra missed it. We had spent our first night together in transit and now she was exhausted.

Instead of having any interest in sex, I carried my very drowsy wife into the chalet and tucked her into bed. I didn't dare disturb her. I fell asleep on the couch, trying to stay awake and failing. She arose around noon, waking me.

Our itinerary started with ski lessons in the mid-afternoon. Alexandra was a noob, so we did not ski together. I went high atop the mountain, while she stayed on the bunny hill with an attractive pro. I loathed that and kicked myself.

I wanted to turn Alexandra into putty with more than my fingers or tongue. I longed to listen to her cum dozens more times. I needed to lie in bed with her completely naked and take her in. We'd fallen in love without the benefit of first being totally in lust. Now, we had figured the latter feeling out, but there was nothing I could do.

Thinking about her tits distracted me. I went down hard on a slope and limped home. My body was less wounded than my pride at first. Unfortunately, by the time we returned for a planned dinner, I was barely able to move. Alexandra didn't play the role of the object of my desire. Instead, she played a doting wife and nursemaid—not the sexy way I wanted to end the night.

The next morning, I woke up even worse. We called for a doctor. I was stuck, my back giving me nothing but problems. I got a couple of muscle relaxers and was put to bed.

"I feel like an asshole," I said.

Alexandra handed me water and a pill. "It's not like you wanted this. You'll be good as new soon, Rick."

"I will try to be. You're an angel. I gather putting up with me isn't easy, Lex."

She blushed. "Oh, darling, it's alright."

"I am supposed to be on the slopes again—as are you."

"Stop, it's okay."

"I over-scheduled us anyhow."

"Why did you build such a mad itinerary?"

"Because I thought you would be angry with me forever and I wanted to make it as painless as possible if we had to be stuck together."

She brushed my cheek. "Well, we aren't cross. So, it's alright. I appreciate the thought, darling."

I couldn't help but love Alexandra.

"I love you. I am sorry this hasn't helped us pick up where we left off."

"It's okay," Alexandra said. "We've got forever, right? Besides, the press think we're up to no good."

"Well, to be honest, we couldn't keep our hands off one another at the wedding."

"They are sure a royal baby is right around the corner," Alexandra rolled her eyes.

Panic crossed my face.

"Don't worry. I'm on the pill."

I was relieved. "Look, I'm not ruling out kids. I agreed to this arrangement long before I was in love with you. Just... not this moment."

"God, no! I cannot even... no. Now, nap. I'm going to go watch telly or whatever. Rest."

"Watch with me," I said. "Whatever you want. Just... stay."

I didn't want to her leave. She was comfort, normalcy, and everything I needed. I wasn't sure if it was the drugs or my general love for her, but I wanted her there in my semi-broken state.

"Sure," Alexandra said. "Scoot over."

"What?"

"This is my side of the bed."

"Is it?" I said. "It's mine."

I realised now we'd never had this discussion—having never spent a night alone together in bed. Was she a cuddler? I gathered she was, but would never admit it. Alexandra loved adoration even if it flustered her.

"I'll sit over here—for now—since you're in bad shape," Alexandra said.

She crawled into bed, tucking herself under the covers. I curled up next to her. She smelled heavenly. I drifted off, now drowsy from the drugs and feeling like I was on a warm cloud. It felt safe. I hoped she felt the same—if not a bit less woozy. When I woke, she was up, and I felt a bit better. I'd slept about four hours. It was now dinner time. Alexandra brought me food in bed, and we watched French-language programming. My French was thankfully improving, but still a joke.

"*Je t'aime,*" she said.

It was the first time Alexandra said it. We barely spoke in French. I knew it meant something to her. It meant more than it did in English.

"I love you more," I said. "I still don't deserve you, but I will try to prove myself more worthy, my love."

Alexandra kissed my hand. "You are."

Thirty-Nine

Alexandra

Rick was hurting. We were a week into our honeymoon, and he was finally moving about our hotel room in Rome. He wasn't capable of much else but felt bad about leaving me hanging.

Like most things with us, everything had a false start. If my awakening on our wedding day wasn't a good omen, I wasn't sure what was. Good things came when we waited for a perfect moment.

Still, we were a third of the way into our honeymoon and hadn't managed to consummate things properly. If we were a royal couple in the dark ages, our marriage wouldn't even have been considered legal. Not that it invalidated the love I had for him. I was falling even harder by the day. It turns out that babying Rick brought out his kindest, most vulnerable side.

Rick's tough exterior was a poor facade over the man I fell in love with. Rick was kind, dutiful, and loving to his family. He chose the girls and me. I knew we were also both homesick and feeling a little awkward, but he was always sweet to me.

The mundane things we missed when separated at the palace began to make me feel differently about him, too. I had never considered what it might be like to brush my teeth next to someone or share space at the bathroom vanity.

I feared letting my guard down to let him see me completely without makeup so much that I had continually applied it for the first four days of this trip. That became unsustainable. His adoration didn't shift. He never commented on it. He said I was beautiful. If he noticed, he didn't complain.

There were other things. I lost the battle of the side of the bed, but he was insistent moving to that side hurt his back. So, I gave him that win. We cuddled like normal people. We watched television together. We ate dinner—alone like any couple. All the things we missed out on these long months before were now *ours*. It was precious.

"I still feel bad about it," Rick groaned.

We were in bed watching television.

He continued, "I promise you I will see the masseuse tomorrow again and hopefully it will help."

"It's okay, really. I am grateful we get to take a moment to be together. It feels special. I'm savouring it."

Rick looked surprised.

"What? You don't enjoy all this peace and quiet? We're finally getting to know one another like a normal couple. I relish this, Rick," I said.

He smiled and leaned to kiss me. I melted. God, it was always so good. What couldn't he manage to do to me?

"I wish I could do more than that," he said.

"Me, too," I laughed. "I want to do everything. And I still feel badly since I got off twice, you only once and... well, I feel guilty."

"Hey, don't," Rick said. "We can make up for it."

I thought about it for a moment. I wanted a lot more than this. I knew he couldn't do much at all, but I also wanted to repay him for the amazing orgasm he gave me so freely with this tongue. How could anyone *do* such a thing?

I ran my hand under the covers, down to the top of his joggers.

"Lex, don't start what you can't finish."

"Who says I can't finish?" I asked. "Why don't I repay your good deed?"

"What do you mean?"

"Why do you look so nervous?" I asked.

I put my hand inside his joggers, just over his underwear. Even though I had *seen* his cock, I'd never *felt* it. I traced my hand up and down as it stiffened.

"I... I don't... know," Rick said.

"Does it frighten you, then? Because I think I'm making you hard," I said.

"If you keep doing that, I'm going to—"

"What?" I bit my lip and stared back.

I ran my hand now into his pants. I rubbed up and down the shaft of his penis, gripping it.

"Does this feel good?" I asked.

"Yes," he said, voice tight. "Lex, you don't have to—"

"But I *want* to, Rick," I continued, my hand pumping his shaft.

Deviant in a way I wasn't before, I pressed on. I'd been afraid of everything once, but here we were—alone in this quiet moment. I longed for a bit of fun. He relished this. Protesting no more, Rick relaxed.

"Okay," Rick said. "Well, that feels good."

"Do you want me to... go down on you?" I asked.

"Well, if you're offering, yes." He ran his hand through my hair, brushing it back out of my face. "But I'm going to last all of a few minutes if you do."

"I don't care," I said.

I wasn't quite sure what he meant or what I was doing. Offering this up felt sexy and grown-up, but I was neither of those things at this moment. It was the first time I'd even touched a penis let alone done anything to one. I knew it would make him happy, though.

"You're going to have to be patient with me," I said. "And... direct me."

Rick grimaced, kicking his joggers and pants to the side. His poor back was still on the fritz. He'd not need to do much here. He sat up a bit.

"Are you alright?" I asked.

"If I lie down completely, I'll end up craning my neck watching you and—trust me—it will hurt more."

"Well, if it is bound to hurt, we don't need to—"

He played with my hair again, my hand once more on his cock.

"I want to. It would be incredibly sweet of you. If you want to, I want to."

He kissed me, sending me reeling.

"The key," he said. "Is no teeth. Pump with your hand while you go with your mouth. There isn't much to it. Because it's been so long, I am easy to please today."

I took in his directions, nodding.

"You're a good pupil. You'll figure it out, baby," Rick said.

I moved down until I was staring right at his cock. For years, I had been frightened of the idea of such things. When I first read about oral sex in the pages of my sister's intense dirty novel collection, I couldn't understand why a woman would do such a thing. Now, I realised I held all the power. He would have begged me if I'd asked him to.

I took him in my mouth, slowly figuring things out. I began to gently move my hand, trying to sync it with my mouth. Rick let out a gasp, catching me off guard. I stopped and stared.

"No. It's good. You just... you moved... it feels good."

He was at a loss for words, not unhappy.

"Oh," I blushed. "I'll go on then?"

"Please," he said.

I began once more, realising he would tense up and moan the moment I reached the head. I focused on it more. Picking up speed with my hand, I took him deeper into my mouth. His cock hit the back of my throat and elicited a gag. Feelings of power turned to fear I'd ruined it all.

"It happens," he said.

"I feel stupid," I admitted.

"No, no, don't. It's hot, okay? Don't feel stupid." His tone was sweet. He was panting. "You don't have to keep going. But I'm about to cum anyway—"

I dove back in. It was as if I was on a mission or needed to pass an exam. I stroked his balls, trying something new, and took as much of his erection in as I could. His legs quivered and he pulled my hair a bit, which I strangely liked. I heard him moan, his breath quickening.

"Lex, I'm going to fucking blow—spit or swallow I don't care."

I was trying to figure out exactly what the difference was when he jerked towards me and gripped his hands into my hair. I gagged again, realising he meant with the cum that was now in my mouth. I didn't realise one had to choose. I swallowed, gagged, and again felt embarrassed.

"Shit. I'm sorry," I pulled back.

He laughed, still breathing heavily. I was mortified.

"No, no. I'm not laughing at you. I'm overwhelmed. I... I think that is one of the first times I heard you swear, Lex."

He handed me his boxers.

"Just take care of whatever you need. I'll do the rest," Rick said.

I was still mortified, doing as he said. Rick tossed the boxers on the floor, grumbling as he settled back down in bed. He turned to look at me.

"Baby, you have nothing to be embarrassed about."

"I feel like I did a dreadful job—"

"Nah. You did well. I never would have guessed that was your first time. You aren't good at reading me yet. And I'm not good at reading you. We'll get better at it. Promise. But that was great."

"Really?"

He nodded. "Come here."

I curled up in his arms, wrapping my arm across his chest.

"You are lovely. A lot of fun, baby. Thank you."

"I promise I will get better."

"You don't need to promise me anything," Rick said. "Other than to be yourself. It wouldn't matter if you'd slept with seventy guys before me. We'd still be new to this. It would still be awkward."

"Really?" I looked at him.

"Yeah," Rick promised. "It's just part of getting to know someone. It's no different than anything else we're trying to figure out. You're good. It's not a surprise, given that you're a fabulous kisser, Lex."

"Really?"

"Yeah. That's why I just assumed... well, you're not *subtle*."

I laughed. "I don't like tiny, gentile kisses, I guess."

He kissed me, catching me off guard. It was good, but I struggled to enjoy it given where my mouth had just been, I was sure he'd be opposed.

"You don't... care?" I asked.

"About what, Lex?"

"Never mind," I said.

"You are wonderfully giving, and I will make it up to you," Rick promised.

Forty

I kissed Alexandra as we prepared for lunch at a vineyard. I was finally up and moving but struggled to do everything I wanted with Alexandra. The poor thing was so patient and gave head so freely that she deserved a trophy. "Good head" was an unexpected square on my "arranged marriage to a virgin" bingo card.

Alexandra looped her arms around my neck. Our car waited downstairs, but she paid no attention—too focused on kissing me. I was also in no hurry, pushing her back against the desk near the entryway. I heard something rattle and fall over. I was tempted to throw her up on the desk, but that didn't seem fair. She deserved her first time to be better than a quickie on a desk!

She pulled away, her gaze laser-focused. "I want you."

"Lex, we have a car waiting. I want this to be... lovely for you. I don't want it to be a wham, bam, thank you, ma'am."

"Rikard, if I do not get off, I think I might die."

I snickered. "Die? Isn't that hyperbole?"

I kissed her slowly. She responded by biting my lip.

"I want you," she whined.

The more she pleaded, the more I weakened. I wanted her, too.

There was no doubt. I was still pretty beaten up but damn if I didn't want to fuck her. Still, if I was going to have all of her and do this with her for the first time, wasn't I supposed to make it special?

"There is a car, Lex. Later? Again, I want this to be—"

"I don't care about candles and roses and such nonsense. You have already seen all of me and I know all of you. If you are good enough to walk, you're good enough to shag, yeah?"

I shrugged. "I could make do."

"Then don't you want to?"

"It's not a matter of want. I want to be good to you."

"I want you now."

Her tone got more insistent. She wasn't meek or mild. She was demanding. It did it for me.

"Bedroom and be quick about it!" I gave her ass a quick swat.

Alexandra raced to the bedroom, tossing her tights and panties aside. She lay there, her dress barely covering her thighs—happy to be on offer. I kicked off my trousers and underwear. I attempted to pull her towards the end of the bed and failed miserably. My back ached. Well, fuck!

"Sorry, baby. My back is still fucked," I winced. "I am worried I will injure it worse—"

"Can you get on your back?"

I was surprised by her suggestion. She was desperate and her need for me was sexy. Damn if I didn't want her! I flipped onto the bed, lying on my back now. She climbed astride me.

"You want this?" I confirmed.

"I do," she said.

I worried she might struggle a bit, but she didn't waste time. I was inside her within seconds. She gasped a bit.

"Just a little... pain..."

"You can stop."

"No. I don't want to, Rick."

"Take it easy. Go slow," I said. "I think that's the key."

She did take it easy... at first. Alexandra soon got the hang of it. I loved raw, impromptu sex. I lived to fuck a girl in a dress. It felt naughty. She bent down, kissing me, as she continued to grind—

soaking wet now. Her pussy tightened around me as she panted and moaned. She was loud. I loved her being noisy. Alexandra gripped my shirt as she began to climax. I grabbed her ass with both hands and assisted by thrusting—harder and harder.

Alexandra's eyes rolled back into her head, and she screamed in French. I couldn't translate, but I knew it was good. She was euphoric now, catching her breath. A wide grin spread across her face. She leaned down and kissed me slowly and sweetly.

"Good?" I asked as she pulled away.

"Fucking amazing."

She never swore, so that was high praise. I made a note that I would need to teach her to dirty talk as she had no idea what she was doing. She didn't know I'd wanted this for so long. Her face, the sounds of her enthusiastic moans, the swearing, and the enhancement of the spank bank image of her gagging on my cock was enough.

"You going to cum for me again?" I asked.

"I don't know," she said.

"I want you to try."

Alexandra moaned louder and I felt her tighten again. She was working on another orgasm. I wasn't going to last forever—not like this—so I hoped it was soon. I hadn't been inside a woman in half a year. It felt glorious. She was magnificent with her face flushed and her hair bouncing. The more her tits jiggled, the harder it was to last.

"Rick, oh God," she growled.

"Don't stop. I want you to cum," I said. "Cum for me, Alexandra."

"I'm... I'm..." she screamed out a line of unintelligible syllables.

"Good girl," I said. "Good girl, Alexandra. Was that what you needed?"

She nodded—panting and unable to speak. Her face was red, and her fists clenched—my shirt balled up into them. Alexandra came back down, but I gave her the sort of high she needed. Maybe it wasn't romantic, perfectly-planned sex, but she was right. It would do.

I came, unable to fight it a moment longer, grabbing her hips and thrusting deep inside. It was ecstasy. I was left panting, lying there, my back feeling partially functional still. Alexandra smiled from above, looking self-satisfied. She leaned to give me a long, sexy kiss.

I smacked her ass. "You're honestly far too good at that given your level of experience."

She bit her lip. "It was good?"

"Well done! We'll further adulterate you later. For now, we have a car waiting."

She rolled onto her side. I handed her the boxers I'd been wearing.

"What? Why?" She asked.

I fumbled through a drawer to find a clean pair. "You're going to want to clean up, baby. What goes in must come out."

She tested my theory, making a face.

"You might also want to run to the toilet," I said. "I think it's supposed to be a good idea."

I realised I was Alexandra's only source of sexual education, which was troubling. Yes, I was good at sex, but I had no business teaching a woman everything there was to know. Her mother should have been a source of preliminary knowledge and her friends would have supplemented it as she grew. However, she hadn't been allowed friends and her mother passed when she was very young. The poor thing was still learning.

Thankfully, what she lacked in education, she made up for in energy and willingness. We had plenty of sexual chemistry. I was relieved. I wanted her again—and soon.

"See, you didn't regret it," she returned from the bathroom. "I told you it would be fine."

"I guess we have a lot more time for drawn-out, romantic fucking."

"Is fucking the right word?"

I laughed. "For what you did to me? Yes. Lex, that was good fucking. Proper fucking."

She blushed.

"Don't be ashamed, Lex. That was good. You are fabulous in bed. You're fun and loud. Own that shit. Enjoy it. It gets me off to see you get off."

Alexandra smiled. "Okay."

"Now, we are very late for lunch," I took her hand.

We grabbed our coats, finally departing. Still giddy, we climbed into the waiting car.

"Your Majesty, Your Royal Highness," the driver said as he settled back into his seat.

"Thank you for waiting," Alexandra said. "I guess we let time get away from us."

He chuckled. "It's alright, madame. You are fine. It's a holiday, isn't it? And a honeymoon. Best not to worry about time."

She squeezed my hand. Alexandra was proud of herself. Her ascent to sexual freedom had only begun. I was part of her rise, so I felt some pride. I gave her the space she needed and intended to be a good, caring partner. The last time I fucked someone, I was the opposite. It was about using one another to get off. Meanwhile, Alexandra and I started a transactional relationship only to find love. And love her I did.

FORTY-ONE

"You like this? Do you like it when I treat you like this? Take it out on you? Get what I want and leave you wanting more? Why should I even let you cum again?"

I found myself pinned over the sofa arm, holding on for dear life as Rick took me from behind. I assumed being in such a compromising position would feel demoralising, but that wasn't Rick's intent. This was a fantasy. We were playing in this world we'd created—a cocoon of sexual debauchery.

Rick gave me nothing but pleasure since the day we wed. He was patient and loving, but I also liked him being rough. I lived for him to spank me and call me dirty names.I felt like I couldn't help but want more of it. I understood why people talked about sex so much—why the world was obsessed. It was addictive. I wanted him to have me every which way.

"Please. I've been good," I pleaded.

He picked up speed, reaching around to play with my clit. God, it felt amazing!

"You've been acting like a little slut all morning."

"How?" I gasped, feeling myself getting close. "I've been such a good girl."

"You were in that nightgown at breakfast. I couldn't stop staring at your tits. You knew what you were doing."

I had known. Of course, he'd also had me the night before and that morning. We were now supposed to go shopping in Paris, but he was distracting me like this. We'd had sex on every useful surface of both the hotel rooms we'd inhabited. My favourite, to date, was when he threw me on a kitchen island and went down on me. It was unexpected and altogether satisfying. The way he gave in and made me cum was so sexy.

I came now—screaming his name and falling limp. He pumped away harder. I heard his body slapping against mine. It was raw, dirty, and felt so good. Rick gripped my hips and thrust one last time, hard. I nearly fell over the sofa completely—hanging on by a thread.

He slapped my ass hard. "That will teach you! Go clean up the mess you made, dirty girl."

He tossed me a pair of his pants. I loathed this part. Somehow, I missed all these tidbits in dirty books. Everything couldn't fit in a novel. There was little to be said about the sexiness of post-coital cleanup. The idea of him being inside me and leaving a mark still had an appeal. I liked the feeling of him somehow being my one and only.

"Have you ever cum on someone's ass?" I asked.

He laughed. "Yes. A lot."

"Is that good?"

"Do you want me to?" Rick, asked, surprised. "Because I would."

"Would you like to mark your territory, then? Own me a bit?"

"Alexandra, you are so bad," he kissed me. "Fuck. What has happened to you?"

"I fell for the rake. Good girl gone bad," I said. "No, it could be hot. I want you to do almost everything to me."

"You like being my plaything?"

I nodded.

"I like this side of you. You're exhausting."

"You love that I'm exhausting. You love that I let you take control."

"I do."

"Now, take me shopping. I want to buy dresses that will make Celeste lose her mind."

"What about me? Will they make me lose my mind?"

"Maybe. If you want them to. What does it for you?"

"You in a dress is good, but I honestly like you dressed down. Whenever you put on those little shorts to lounge around, that does it for me."

"What? Why?"

"You have a great ass. I love staring at it. So help me!"

He pulled me close and kissed me. I never wanted this time to end. In three days, we would return to Neandia. Our beautiful three weeks of togetherness would end while the unresolved situation with my grandmother loomed large

"God, I love you," Rick sighed, pulling away. "You are spectacular. I am grateful you forgave me every day."

It was undeniably sweet of him. The more shades of Rick I saw, the more I fell for him.

"I am glad I did, too. I would miss out on this, otherwise. We're like really, really married now."

"Really, really, yes." He let out a long sigh. "I want to do this every day. I want to learn to love you properly and make you happy. I want to be dutiful."

"You are," I said. "Very dutiful. A good boy, despite what you might want to think. The girls are happy to have you around. Now, they might be prickly as they realise we're sort of building our own thing out."

"It will be an adjustment. I selfishly want you all to myself, but you need to spend time with them, baby."

He played with my hair. I held his hand on my cheek, turning to kiss his palm. He leaned in to kiss me again. It made my knees weak. I struggled to fight the urge to start over. Instead, I played with the buckle on his belt.

"Lex, you are insatiable."

"You would deny me?" I asked.

"No, not really," Rick answered. "We'll see how well I can manage this so soon."

He popped me onto the island of the kitchen in our suite again and pulled me to the edge. He was hard, thrusting inside of me. I gasped and bit his lip. I held onto the counter for dear life as he went hard and fast, wrapping my legs around him tighter. Rick sent me into orbit, hitting every spot just right. I came, screaming his name.

"You do like that don't you?" He chuckled.

"You like watching."

"Oh, I do."

I kissed him again.

"I think you finally drained me," Rick said. "I don't think I will cum again."

"Oh, boo. I feel bad."

"Are you satisfied?"

"Uh-huh," I agreed.

"Then I am, too."

I smiled again, pleased with myself. I loved him. I lusted after him. It was the best of both worlds. I was lucky that the person I was forced into this with was as good at caring for me as Rick. While I had my doubts and worried I'd never trust him again, he turned it around.

FORTY-TWO

RICK

When we arrived home, Ingrid ran headlong into Alexandra's arms. Unexpectedly, she hugged me shortly after. The girls were happy we returned. In the interim, they told school stories. I realised I missed them, too—especially little Ingrid. It was nice to be back.

Despite my threats, Celeste remained in the Queen's quarters.

"This is unacceptable," I said.

Alexandra, confused, asked, "Why did she not vacate, Lord William? She was told to do so."

"The timeline was tricky. The new apartments were unsuitable. Work must be done. The Prime Minister will need to approve the money."

"And you," Celeste said, "will need to ask him. You didn't ask."

"I didn't know," Alexandra said.

She made herself smaller.

I hated this. She balled up and disappeared into herself, frightened of Celeste's wrath.

"I am sure they are fine for now," I said.

"I cannot navigate the bath. I have a bad hip. I require a larger shower," Celeste protested.

"Why was none of this brought to our attention, Lord William?"

"Sir, you were not around long. And, either way, these are decisions which must be made by Her Majesty."

"We speak united on this issue—"

"It is nice you think that, Rick," Celeste said. "But it's not your place."

Alexandra squeezed my hand. "We do. Rick has my best interest in mind, and we do need space and privacy. We will get none with the adjoining room that I share with Asti. We're married. We live in a bloody palace, but have no space."

"Well, I was set to move into a bank of rooms in the other wing. You see how *you* like it."

"Put us there then," Alexandra said. "Until the Dowager Queen can remedy her current situation. Moving back into my old quarters is unacceptable."

"It will take time, ma'am," Lord William sighed.

"Fine, then let's find a way to make a move to more suitable accommodations," I insisted.

"I think it will be fine down there. You have the second-best bank of rooms," Celeste said. "But all you do is whinge."

"Grand-Mama, I share a bathroom and a sitting room with Astrid. Rick and I need personal space. We're a married couple. And his clothes won't even fit in my wardrobe."

"Perhaps you all can stick to your current arrangement?"

"That is unsuitable!" Alexandra livened.

"Why's that?"

"You know why! We won't be sleeping in separate rooms like teenagers."

I nodded in agreement. "Do you want grandchildren, Celeste?"

"Very much, yes. But given that the two of you were so cold as of late, I didn't think that would phase her."

"Do not make assumptions about what we do or don't do," Alexandra said. "I can assure you we need the space and Astrid doesn't want to be aware of our goings-on. We're newlyweds, after all."

She might have well said we were fucking like rabbits—which we were—but it was in the politest way possible. I rubbed Alexandra's back. She found her voice. I tried not to talk over her. Undermining her was the worst thing I could do.

"I am retiring to our ridiculous, unacceptable quarters!" Alexandra grabbed my hand and led me down the hall towards her room.

We made it there, weary from a delayed flight from Paris. Fortunately, neither of us was particularly daunted.

"I want you right now," she said. "This is a ridiculous arrangement, and I am sorry, but we haven't gotten up to no good yet today."

"You can say we haven't fucked, baby. It's okay to be direct."

"You adore my euphemisms. You think they are inventive."

I chuckled. "I adore everything about you right now, but I want you to tell me what you want."

She blushed.

"Tell me or I won't do anything," I said.

She kissed me, whispering, "I want you to go down on me."

"You want me to eat you out?"

She nodded.

"I'd like that, too, Lex."

We got naked like it was second nature. By now, I knew every inch of her. I knew how to make her cum fast and hard. She loved it and I yearned to break her walls down. She'd turn into jelly, unable to speak.

She was already wet as I kissed her. My fingers toyed with her clit. She shivered and grabbed my hand, pushing my fingers inside.

"You're greedy, Alexandra." I pulled back.

"Please."

"Please what?"

"Lick my…"

"What?"

She wouldn't say it. I ran my finger up and down her inner thighs, teasing.

"My pussy," she finally said. "Get down there and lick my pussy."

"Yes, ma'am," I obliged, disappearing between her legs.

The thing I loved about eating her out was how fast she went from zero to sixty. And, working with my fingers and tongue, I could make her cum even faster.

"*Mer, mer, mer*," she groaned, gently thrusting her hip towards my face.

More, more, more. Alexandra spoke some of her mother's native Dansk, but the fact that she invoked a phrase I understood well at this moment made me want to lose it. I did oblige her.

"Oh, fuck, yes, yes!"

She came with an aggressive growl. Her fingers gripped my hair hard. Her legs quaked. She lay there still. I loved this version of her—the woman who came undone with a simple stroke of my tongue. This woman would now do whatever I asked of her. However, I didn't get to bask in it long because I realised we had an audience.

There was a knock on the bathroom door. Alexandra and her sister shared a bathroom—each with their own door.

"Alex, can you *please* keep it down? I'm in here with the little girls," Astrid said.

"God! Sorry!" Alexandra said. "I will... we will... keep it down."

I kissed my way back up, towering over her now.

"We must be good," Alexandra whispered.

I kissed her. "Yes, we must."

There was then a second knock.

"Ma'am it's—" a maid entered.

I turned to see her there. I didn't dare move and expose Alexandra's entire naked body to the woman. I couldn't believe she walked in without an invitation. True to form, she turned away from us, allowing us to duck under the covers.

"I apologise, Your Majesty, Your Highness. The Dowager Queen told me you would like to begin your evening with dinner in your room. I brought you some drinks—"

"We did not order such things," Alexandra said, annoyed. "We shall take our dinner in the dining room—alone, thank you."

"Of course, ma'am. It will be ready shortly."

She left. Alexandra looked at me. We burst into a fit of laughter.

"She saw your entire bum," Alexandra giggled.

"She did, yeah. Oh well."

"She should thank you. It's rather nice." Alexandra kissed me. "Well, so much for privacy. I will miss our time abroad."

"Let's go to Lundhavn," I said. "We have no plans for the weekend. Visit my parents. And we can bring the girls."

"Really?" Alexandra asked.

"Yeah. Let's get away from here. Make the old bag angry."

"You would take all four of us to Blavenberg?"

"Ja," I laughed. "It's good for them to travel. I consider it an essential experience. They should get out more. I promised to help with that."

"Mmm," she sighed. "I love you. You are a good person in the end."

"I love that you think that. Can you please tell my father? Might improve things with him?"

"I think seeing us happy has improved things with him already. This is a mutually beneficial arrangement."

"Right about now it is," I agreed. "Baby, we should get dressed for dinner."

"It will hold," Alexandra said. "I am happy to have time with you right now."

"Oh?"

"Yeah," she bit her lip. "I think I'm going to blow you before dinner as a thank you."

"Who am I to refuse you then?" I laughed.

I was pretty sure I deserved nothing but was glad to be indebted to her and the girls. It made me feel useful and drove me to do better. I loved her more than she comprehended. She made me happy.

FORTY-THREE

ALEXANDRA

The girls, Rick, and I arrived in Lundhavn only to be escorted to the family's house on the edge of Blavenberg. It was a fairy-tale castle with a grand dining hall and cosy sitting rooms in its various wings—a lovely escape for a long weekend away. The girls were preoccupied with Rick's wonderful mother. She was quick to adopt them as her own.

Rick grew up in this place. He said it was their home nearly every weekend and all summer. After taking us to the stables and introducing me to his old horses, we walked the grounds. It felt like heaven. Then, it all came crashing down.

Saturday, I felt exhausted. I went to bed early. For the first time in about three weeks, Rick and I hadn't had sex because I was too tired to function. I worried I was coming down with something. Then, I woke Sunday morning feeling seasick. I didn't want to leave for breakfast and couldn't keep anything down. Rick called for his mother. He was worried.

"What do you feel like? A fever? Anything?" Karolina asked.

"No," I answered. "Just... tired. Seasick. No other symptoms. But I'm not on a boat."

"Maybe it's stomach flu," Rick said.

"Or, maybe it's something else," Karolina said in Rick's mother tongue.

"Like what?" I asked.

"When was the last time you had your period?" Karolina asked.

"I don't get them. I'm on the pill. I just started a new pack."

"You don't get periods on the pill?" Karolina cocked her head. "You should. Do you have your pills?"

I directed Rick to the location of my pills and he brought them to his mother.

"These white pills are the ones where you should have a period," Karolina said. "You didn't have one?"

I shook my head, my blood running cold.

"No one told you that?"

I shook my head again.

"She was sheltered," Rick said, sweetly. "Not allowed to ask questions."

"Astrid and I arranged for these prescriptions to come. It was touch and go. We're not trying to have a baby right now," I said.

"I can understand that, but, sweetheart, I worry you might be pregnant. Does your back ache? Do your breasts hurt?"

"Mamma!"

"What? It's an important question!"

I looked down. "Yeah?"

"We need to get you a test," Karolina said.

Rick appeared ready to faint. This wasn't the news either one of us wanted. If it was true, it would be awful for him. If positive, I was about to carry a baby to term worried I'd fall victim to my mother's sad fate.

Karolina was magical because a test arrived within the hour. By then, I'd been in and out of the toilet more times than I could count. Karolina explained what I needed to do with the test. I followed the directions, placing it on the bathroom vanity.

"I can leave if you would like space," Karolina said. "I don't mean to intrude."

"Please stay," I asked. "Because I'd want my mamma right about now and... just stay."

Karolina rubbed my back. "Alright, sweetheart. I can do that. It must be hard sometimes."

"Sometimes, I miss her more than others, but I always do," I admitted. "God, I feel so stupid! I did something wrong."

I couldn't bear to look at the test, but Karolina refused to read it for us. So, Rick went in. My fate hung in the balance as I sat on the bed in his childhood bedroom, wondering what would happen next. To his credit, Rick was supportive. He hadn't squawked at me, but I was frightened. It was as if we'd discovered a secret magical retreat within ourselves every time we had sex, but was it worth it? I wasn't ready to have a baby.

"You two will be fine. No matter what, *min skat*." Karolina squeezed my hand. "They never come when you want them to, anyway."

I burst into tears.

"Oh, sweetheart, do not cry. I am sorry—"

"No... you sound like my mother. She used to call us that. It's... a real comfort."

Karolina hugged me tight. "I am so sorry she isn't here. Your mother was a delight. A beautiful person. She would be proud of you."

"Is it good? One line or two?" Rick's voice echoed from the bathroom. It gave nothing away.

"Two is pregnant. One is not," Karolina said.

"What if it's like one and a half?" Rick asked.

He walked over and showed the test to his mother.

"If there is any second line, pregnant," Karolina said. "So, here."

She handed me the test. I nearly fainted.

"I would say congratulations," Karolina said. "We are elated to have another grandchild, but I am aware there are a lot of emotions here. I love you both. Ask if you need something."

She patted Rick on the cheek lovingly and disappeared out the door.

I sat, holding the test. The light pink line glared at me. I was infuriated, upset, violated, and frightened. Rick stared at me, similarly surprised. I assumed this was how it ended. His love and attraction for me was gone. I felt him pulling away. Of course, he didn't want a baby! Neither did I! He had a choice, but I did not.

Then, a strange thing happened.

Rick wrapped me up in his arms and held me tight. I released my sobs into his shoulder. Normally, I would hide these from him, but I felt like I both needed to let it out and was safe. I sobbed and sobbed until finally, we pulled apart. He hopped up to bring me a tissue and then sweetly dabbed my eyes as I tried to pull myself together.

"I'm so sorry," I finally said.

"Why, Lex? You did nothing wrong."

"You don't want a baby. You're frightened!"

"I didn't say I didn't want a baby. I mean, I didn't want a baby, but does that mean I don't *now* want a baby? I think those are different things."

"I don't want a baby. My mother died in childbirth. I'm not ready to die."

"I am not about to let you die. I am sorry that happened. It must be scary, baby, but... it is so unlikely."

"It doesn't matter. God, I have no choice."

"Not as a royal woman, no," Rick said. "I feel awful right now. It took this long for me to knock someone up. It's a wonder it took so long."

"Rikard!"

"What? It's true!"

"Not helping."

He cupped my face in his hands. "Lex, I love you—all of you. If that means we must bump up the timeline a bit, I'll manage. I love you too much to tell you no."

Rick kissed me. Despite my runny tears and puffiness, he kissed me.

"Don't worry about me," Rick said. "Let's keep you healthy, okay? Focus on you."

I nodded. "Thank you for not hating me."

"I couldn't anymore. You are too good a person. You are the best person, Alexandra."

Forty-Four

Rick

"How could it happen?" Alexandra asked.

"It's not a hundred per cent," I said.

Alexandra wailed, "I had sex for the first time. I waited all this time and was such a good girl. I waited and waited. And then, boom! I have married, sanctioned sex and got pregnant while trying to prevent it. I swear to God, this is unbearable!"

She was emotional. We had both been on edge trying to hide a pregnancy from everyone and living in close quarters. I suspected Astrid was aware of what was going on. She was the most street-smart one of the four of them.

"Baby, I am sorry," I said.

"Don't tell me you are sorry one more time, Rikard or so help me! You don't have to do anything. Your life is made!"

I wanted to shout back that I was in the same boat as she was, I hadn't abandoned her, and I was doing my best. However, I liked having my head and balls attached to my body and I feared her retribution. Moreover, I knew this came from a hormonal place. She was a mess and felt unsettled. It wasn't what either of us wanted. And, tomorrow, we had to go see if this unknown being had a heartbeat. I tried not to feel anything about it.

I wanted to talk about the pregnancy. I wanted to tell her sisters. They would be an important support for her more than ever, but we were limited.

"I love you, okay? I am sorry this is so scary and so sudden. I am sorry your body has made you feel like this. But, Alexandra, I'm not going anywhere."

She sobbed. There was a knock.

"Alex, are you okay?"

Great, now Astrid was involved.

"I'm fine," Alexandra sobbed.

"I don't trust you are."

Astrid's assumption I would hurt her sister offended me, but I understood her protective inclination.

"What is going on?" Astrid opened the door before glaring at me. "Rick, what are you doing to her?"

"He's not doing anything," Alexandra sobbed. "My life is over. Everything is over and—"

"Why, sweetheart?" Astrid asked.

She practically pushed me out of the way, sitting on the bed. I was no longer wanted or needed here. In a fit of rage, I knew what I had to do.

"I'm going to go take a walk, leave you ladies to talk," I said.

No one spoke to me as I left. That was alright. I was on a mission. Alexandra would loathe what I was about to do at first, but she was already upset with me. In the long term, she would get what she wanted and needed. I stormed down the hall and demanded to speak to the Dowager Queen.

"Rikard, I do not see the point of chatting," Celeste said as I was escorted into her cat-centric sitting room yet again.

We'd have to work hard to get the smell of cats out, I thought.

"I don't much care," I said. "Celeste, you must vacate these rooms. We will buy you a house for you to live with your twenty-seven cats and enjoy your golden years, but you cannot stay here."

"We have discussed—"

"Would you like great-grandchildren?" I asked.

"Yes," Celeste answered. "But I hear nothing about them from Alexandra. She seems resistant. I was aware she was on medication. Staff told me. The cardinal would be very upset if he knew."

She was oblivious to Alexandra's struggles.

"Ah, well, about that... I am working on it."

Celeste perked up.

"Yes. I think I have converted her to the idea."

Celeste raised an eyebrow. "Oh?"

"The main issue is that she is very..." I looked for the words as the gears spun in my mind. "She is almost prudish. She worries about anyone *knowing* and seems to fear letting on to anything to her young, impressionable sisters. Neither of us put a foot wrong before we wed. You can stop demonising Alexandra for that. She was the picture of pious behaviour."

"Well, it is good if you have talked her out of it. We're in a bit of a succession crisis if she cannot produce an heir. Can you imagine Astrid taking over? Nonsense!"

"She wouldn't much like it, no," I said.

"I was thinking we wouldn't much like it. Alexandra is very... malleable. Meek. Astrid is a hell-raiser."

The idea that Alexandra was prudish, weak, or pious was ridiculous. Her assessment of Astrid was accurate. I knew that was why Astrid would hate the yoke of being a monarch. But Alexandra was her own person. She was growing into her shoes and far from prudish these days.

"So she understands how it works? Did you explain all of that to her?"

I cringed, appalled anyone would neglect to tell a young woman about her body. I was *far* from the appropriate sex educator. Lots of sex did not a teacher make. Thankfully, Alexandra hadn't come into this with no knowledge—clearly with no thanks to her grandmother.

"She is aware... yes."

"Well, is she... acceptable?"

"I'd rather we *not* discuss this about my wife," I said. "She would be mortified by your question. If you are asking if we are happy, the answer is yes."

"I will assume that is a yes, then. Well, good. At least she's not a cold fish. That's an issue with new brides."

I wanted to lash out and say I could understand why if no one taught them about sex or ever gave them space to discuss it or learn about it. Waiting until twenty-two to have one's first orgasm was too painful to endure in my eyes. Now, the woman was insatiable. I was suddenly grateful for the awkward sex talk my father had with me when I was about ten.

"She's a sweetheart," I said. "I love her. Now, this is why we need rooms of our own—properly away from children. She will not even consider the idea until we have space and aren't at risk of bothering the girls."

"Can you not simply be... quiet?"

"That is not within my power alone. She is very prudish. As I said. She worries."

She was also loud. I loved it.

"Fine. If this will allow you to move forward and produce an heir, I will move out—temporarily. It has been a long while since I went back to our country home for the winter holidays. It might suit me. If you do not conceive an heir in the next three months, I will blame Alexandra and move back."

"Please don't blame her," I said. "These things take time."

"I conceived her dear father on our honeymoon. It is the least she can do. She is good for little else."

Celeste's words stung. Good for little else? My heart broke for Alexandra. Then, I was enraged. I kept a lid on it and played along. It pained me. Alexandra was good for many things. She was kind, patient, and loving. She saw people for who they were deep down and was willing to forgive even though I didn't deserve her love. The idea that she was now reduced to the contents of her uterus offended me.

"So, I shall give it a few days and then move to my country house. Please don't destroy the place in the meantime."

"Of course not," I said. "Wouldn't dream of it."

Forty-Five

Alexandra

The blub-blub of a heartbeat and its telltale flicker on the screen suited Rikard and me. Our baby had a heart. It was healthy for now, even if *I* wasn't. I felt as if I had been smashed by a trash compactor and still upset about my circumstances. It was difficult to accept that my wonderful, newlywed existence had been upended by my stupid body's betrayal. Yet, I struggle to ignore the sheer happiness on Rikard's face upon seeing our future child.

I didn't expect him to accept it—let alone be excited about this news. Maybe it was because he was older? He was happiest when he got to take home the photos from our scan—a look at our beautiful little bean—face *proud*. He was blissfully in love.

While Rick could be happy and only happy, I worried about my health above all else. The doctor explained what happened to my mother was rare and was due to a delivery at home. While that was still the protocol for royal births in Neandia when I was born, it was not the tack we'd take. He explained how they would have intervened with a modern approach. I was less reassured and more traumatised.

We settled back at home. I climbed into bed to take a well-deserved nap. I tried to block off my afternoons now so I could get some shut-eye. Being pregnant was exhausting and I did a poor job hiding it. I didn't mind giving it a few more days. I wasn't in a hurry to make everyone ask me how the baby was and touch my stomach as people often do.

"Maybe we could start thinking about names," Rick rattled on.

"Rikard, please," I said, annoyed.

"What?" He hopped into bed next to me. "Too much?"

I nodded. "It's wonderful to see you happy. I am relieved all is well. I remain very frightened."

"The doctor told me—"

"That my mother's death was preventable, Rick," I said. Tears welled in my eyes. "That it could have been stopped."

Rick's smile disappeared. He looked serious.

"I'm sorry, Lex. I didn't think about it like that. Why did she give birth here? In Lundhavn—"

"Your mother gave birth to you in a hospital room like everyone else?"

Rick nodded. "A public hospital. Lex, that place we went to was fucking fancy. But it is the scientific way."

"It wasn't done. Celeste will fight me on this. She always preferred us to have everything done at home. She would not accept my feelings on the matter."

"She doesn't have a say." Rick touched my face lovingly. "She cannot have an opinion. And she won't find out. That's why I wanted to hide it."

"I thought it was because I wanted to?"

"Nah. I did something. You may hate me for it."

"Rick!" I groaned.

"Hold on. Hold on. I got the old bat to leave us."

"What? How?"

"I implied you were a prude who was afraid to have sex if anyone impressionable could hear. I played into the fact that she was sure you'd never get pregnant."

"What?"

"She knew about your pills. I told her I convinced you to have a child. I implied you were a frightened virgin who I was taking advantage of, more or less. It made me feel like I needed a shower. I hated it. I do not think that about you. You're my wife, we're doing this together, and I would never pressure you or call you a prude."

"Of course not."

His face softened. "So she is leaving for the countryside."

"She used to go with Grand-Papa every year," I said. "Maybe she is getting nostalgic?"

"She only cares about the line of succession. Really. If we can stick with this plan and hide it a few more days, we can get by."

"What's the catch?"

"She claims the move is temporary, but we've essentially evicted her. She agreed to stay away if you fell pregnant. You did, but I worry if she finds out, she'll never leave. She's sure we'll never make it happen. She wasn't certain you knew how to have sex. She asked if I taught you."

I giggled.

"Why are you laughing? That is abhorrent!"

"Your face. You are pulling an adorable face. And it's because you loathe the idea. You were kind to me. I love you, Rick. And also, I love that this kills you."

"Why? You love to torture me?"

"No, because it shows how much you do love me. So much."

"You're my wife. Of course, I do."

He kissed me. It made me so happy every time he called me his wife. If one good thing was to come of this, at least he had gotten her to move out. I'd believe it when I saw it, but I crossed my fingers. If she was willing to sign over the regency, she'd be willing to do the same. Overall, Rick had done this for us—mostly me. It was sweet. I didn't mind him doing this. He knew it traumatised me to get into a screaming match with her. I shut down. With Rick there, I was safer.

"You know I'm going to be okay, right?" I asked.

"Yes. We will get through this, baby."

I suddenly had an idea.

"I think we can best her, too!"

"How?"

"We should wait until she is settled there and then again use the media to our advantage," I said.

"Go on."

"Let's plant a leak. We will be forced to announce it. We will beat her at her own game. There will be no moving back in."

"You're a genius!" Rick said.

"I am using one of the few things at my disposal to fuck her over, darling. That is all."

"I love it when we scheme to blow shit up."

"Me, too."

His glance didn't leave me. I realised maybe I wasn't so tired at all. I leaned over and kissed him. A cascading scene of events led to us going at it furiously and loudly. Astrid returned from class about this time, probably hearing it. For once, I didn't much care. We were a team, and we were about to burn it down together.

Epilogue

ALEXANDRA

The day I held Linnea for the first time was undoubtedly the best day of my young life. I was terrified, stuck with a horrifying labour that lasted nearly two days. I hadn't eaten and was worn ragged. At one point, I asked Rick to put me out of my misery. He looked frightened then and begged a nurse to do something. She assured him this happened all the time. I loved my husband, but being cool under pressure in times like those was not his strong suit.

Linnea, despite her long progression into this world, came quickly once she finally put her mind to it. I pushed for all of ten minutes. Then, we heard her little screams. I was grateful to have her, but still feared my fate. I tried to preoccupy myself with her perfect face—and Rick's chin—to boot while trying also not to panic that I was about to die from blood loss.

It wasn't until they gave us a moment alone as a family that I calmed. Then, I could lie there with her sweet face pressed against my chest. She was the only thing in the world either one of us cared about. Rick was in love. I never saw him stare at anyone or anything with as much adoration as he did our little bundle of joy.

A year before if you told me the scoundrel who wandered into our home out of obligation would sit in a hospital room with me stroking our newborn's little bald head so sweetly, I would have laughed. We weren't perfect. Sometimes, he wanted to run for the hills. Sometimes, I wished he would. Mostly, we were happy.

In contrast, Linnea was pure perfection, borne of the strangest love imaginable, and free of any blame. We named her Linnea Karolina after my late mother and my angelic mother-in-law. Settling back home for the first night with her, we relied on the care of our staff. Karolina also pitched in, arriving in the final weeks leading up to the birth to hold my nervous hand.

"I am glad she is a girl." Rick burped the baby.

"Why is that?" I asked.

"I have become accustomed to being overrun by women and I find it less unnerving and more character-building," Rick admitted.

The baby let out a loud belch.

"She's powerful!" Karolina giggled.

"Why is she so gross?" Ingrid grumbled.

"Ingy! Don't be mean!" Odette said.

"I am not. She made an inconceivably loud rude noise! All she's done since arriving home is pass gas out both ends, vomit on Rick's shoulder, and shit herself!"

I laughed. "Ingy, language. But you are correct. Babies are a bit grotesque. They cannot help it. They're only babies."

"She's good to go. Who wants her?" Rick asked.

There were open arms all around. Everyone but Astrid fought to hold her. She was a bit nervy. Things with her had been hard lately. She'd been holding something back.

"Asti, I insist," Rick said. "I will be personally offended if you do not hold my amazing child. She's perfect. You cannot dispute it."

The little girls giggled. Astrid rolled her eyes.

"No one needs me to hold this baby. You have a staff—"

"She needs you, Asti," I said. "She must know her aunt is there for her. Trust me, when she grows up, she will lean on you. At least, that is my hope. And I need you, too."

Astrid looked at me, almost tearful. "Okay. Come here."

Rick showed her how to support the baby's head like he had been doing this his entire life. My heart swelled. Part of me already wanted another. The logical side of me said to wait a couple of years. Still, he was so lovely with her. My ovaries were working overtime now.

"Why don't we go make some cocoa?" Karolina asked. "That would be nice, right, girls?"

"Yes, please!" Odette declared.

Ingrid hopped up to follow.

"I'm going to go make sure everything is ready for her in the nursery if we ever get her to bed." Rick sensed Astrid and I could use some time.

Rick had become good at reading the room. He never wanted to insert himself or make things harder on Astrid and me, but things were forever changed. He was mine; I was his. No matter what Astrid and I had said to one another the day before my wedding, everything changed. The closer Rick and I grew, the more we relied on one another. The emotional support I needed from Astrid was now granted by Rick. In that, Astrid had probably lost my support. I felt guilty sometimes.

"She's a nice baby," Astrid said. "Well, as far as babies go. I am not sure what a not-nice baby is. The problem is she looks like Rick."

I snickered. "Yeah, but he is devilishly handsome, so hopefully she will be a more feminine version of him. Oh, she's so sweet, though. Isn't she?"

"She is," Astrid said.

"Asti, I don't want you to think about this like it's us versus you. I know you feel that way, but... it's not. Rick and I love you. Rick cares for you very much. We both feel strongly that this baby will have a wonderful aunt in you. I've been waiting to see this."

Astrid teared. "I don't want to make you feel bad for choosing him. He's your husband. And I don't want you to think I don't like him. I do. He may have begun as Prickard. You're still too clever for him, but he has several redeeming qualities. He has been good to all of us."

"He has been, yes."

"And he's doing a bang-up job here. He seems to know what he's on about."

"I think he does."

"I thought he was making up all that stuff he was reading. Then, I found the stack of books in the sitting room."

I giggled. "He put so much effort in."

"What a fucking nerd!"

We laughed together. The baby startled and fell back to sleep. I reached over and put my finger in her hand. She grabbed it instinctively.

"You must do this," I said. "It's the sweetest reflex."

Astrid tried, giggling. "That's amazing."

"Babies are wonderful creatures."

"Not for me," Astrid shook her head.

I cocked my head. "Not ever?"

"Maybe. I dunno. I must find a guy first. Or, at least, I must give one a chance."

"Oh? Am I missing something?"

Astrid looked at Linnea and back at me. "Um, I've been talking to that Tim guy. I went to see Riot Elephant again."

"Oh, did you?"

"I am thinking about moving to the UK—not for him. For school. I have a lead on a place to stay. Some other nepobabies like us have a house in Shalestone and... well, I'd be closer to London. It sounds amazing by all rights."

"So I learned when I was there," I admitted. "London is a lovely city."

"I only feel bad leaving because... the baby."

"Well, you wouldn't be leaving immediately—"

"In a couple months. I applied and got into Shalebrook," Astrid said. "To their politics MSc. I... I don't know. I'd be leaving you and the baby."

Her words wounded me. I tried not to show it. Deep down, this is what I always suspected. She could leave. She *should* leave. I'd always said I wanted that for the girls. Now, it stared me in the face. As she held Linny, emotions rushed over me. Tears welled, then rolled, and I couldn't hold back.

"Oh, Alex, no," Astrid said. "Well, that sorts it. I won't go—"

I shook my head. "You must go! I didn't do all of this for us for you to suffer here. I mean, don't go chasing after the frontman of a mediocre band."

She laughed. "Okay, they aren't the best, but they're alright."

"Don't do it. But go, get an education. You are the clever one. You should go to Shalebrook and debate and live your dreams, sister. Astrid, I love you. Yes, it hurts to think of a day when I won't have you right here. Yes, I am sure we will miss you like mad. And yes you will miss some things with Linnea, but... she is going to need an aunt who is ready to take over the world someday. And without Celeste around, the sky's the limit!"

Astrid was in tears. "I can't promise that, Alex."

"Well, you stand a better chance if you go, right?"

She shrugged and put her finger back in Linnea's hand.

"She's beautiful, Alex."

"She is. You'll have to soak up as much time with her as you can now. I will allow you to be the most selfish of all of them. But I want you to go."

"Really?"

"Rick and I wouldn't have it any other way."

"Okay. But... you are sure—"

"I insist. It's complicated, but you must!"

"It's hard to remind myself I can go and do things. Impossible sometimes!"

I related. Celeste was gone for many months now. Things were better. Even her courtiers changed their tune to keep their jobs. They turned on her in the end. She hadn't yet met the baby. I was still prickly about that. Even without her here, the shadow loomed large, but we had freedom.

"I get it," I agreed. "Asti, you are the future. I am here. I must stay and be a mother. I must be queen and lead from here. But you? You were always meant to be brave and spread your wings. If you stay here, you'll be bored and miserable. Go! I want you to be wild and set an example for the little girls. I want them to know they can be anything."

"You sound like a mother," Asti said.

I looked adoringly at Linnea. "I am."

Rick returned. "Ah, she's fine now."

"I got the hang of it," Astrid admitted. "Your spawn looks just like you."

"Obviously," Rick said. "Strong genes."

"Well, here, strong man. Take her back. I'm going to go help them with whatever it is they are doing."

Astrid handed the baby to Rick. He sat next to me. I lay my head on his shoulder, staring down at Linnea as she dreamt of whatever it was babies dreamt of. Probably comfy blankets and boobs? What else did they enjoy?

"Astrid is moving to the UK," I murmured.

"What?"

"To go to Shalebrook," I elaborated. "An MSc in politics."

"Damn. Good for her!" Then, his tone changed. "How do you feel about that, Lex?"

"It's bittersweet. I'm a ball of hormones, so I cried. I will miss her to bits, Rick."

"I know, baby."

"She must go. That's what she needs, and I will adjust."

"You always wanted them to be happy, my love."

"I did," I agreed. "I did. She needs this. If I keep her here, she will resent me—and you. She feels out of place. It's time for her to make her own happiness as I did mine."

"I thought we were forced into a loveless marriage?" Rick joked.

"Well, initially, but... that's not what I feel today."

"What do you feel?" Rick asked, wrapping his arm around me.

"Like I want half a dozen of these," I said. "And that I never want her to grow up."

Rick kissed my forehead. "I can promise you that neither one of those things will come to fruition, but I love you all the same, Alexandra."

"At least two more?"

"One," Rick laughed.

"Two," I said. "Three is good. Could be four. Four girls?"

"I had four girls in a house. I don't need eight."

"Well, with Astrid gone, it will only be seven," I pointed out.

Rick chuckled. "Three—eventually. Three is fine. No more. She is addictive."

I sighed. "Yes. She's the product of a well-matched pair of parents who are the most surprised of all."

"Well, mission accomplished?" Rick asked.

"Mission to be continued," I said. "Again, I'm not anywhere near done with my plotting. There is much more to be said about things here."

Rick rubbed my arm. "Okay, well, as your henchman—your desperately tired henchman—I am begging for you to have mercy on me before we start on our next scheme, Alexandra. I am the old one."

"Well, keep up," I said. "If you know me, it will be a wild ride."

LOVED IT?

Leave a review on Amazon!

Want a free preview of the next book - *Royally Rivalled*? Click here or scan the code below!

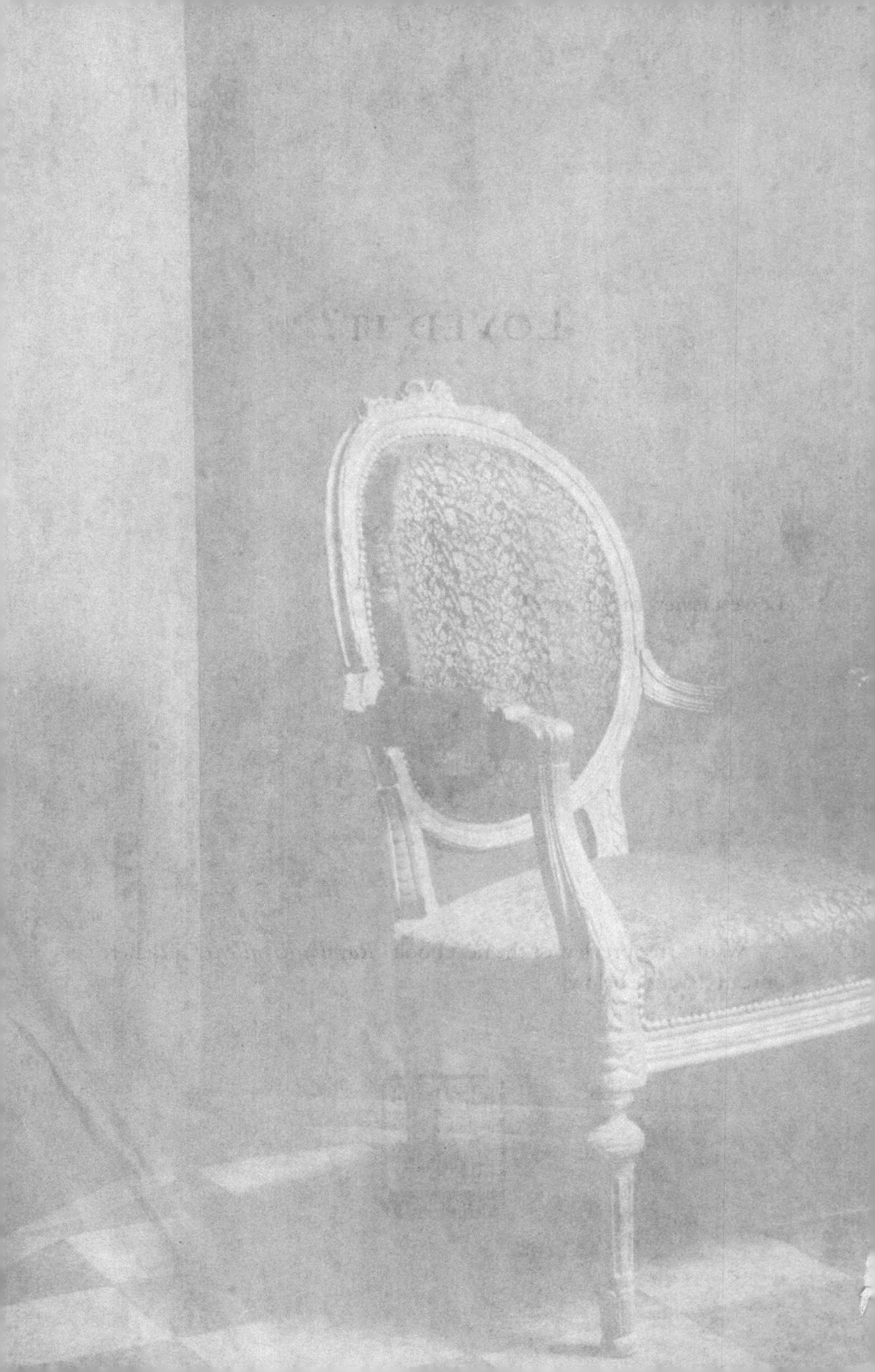

Acknowledgments

I have several alpha and beta readers to thank for their review and support of this manuscript. To Becky, thanks for alpha reading, encouragement, and assistance in brainstorming this text. This book never would have looked this good and the burn wouldn't have been so precious without your comments on pacing and banter. To Leah, Dani, and Elizabeth, thanks for you beta reads and developmental feedback. To my husband, thank you for reading my spice as always and keeping your feedback light-hearted when you could.

About the Author

Maude Winters writes cozy, spicy fiction. She's a horse girl through-and-through and lives in Michigan with her husband, horse girl daughter, and three dogs.

Maude loves to write strong female characters who challenge institutions and find strength in relationships with their sisters in the world as well as heroes who are always there to support the women in their lives.

Maude has lived throughout the world but attributes her interest in writing about the intersection of modern politics, feminism, and royalty with her time spent in the UK as a twenty-something.